Lai was overcome with joy and relief—and some amazement.

But, how did I end up here? The last thing I remember was, the ship was close to crossing the black hole's event horizon.

"Uh, Doctor... I'm having trouble with my memory. I don't recall how I got here—to the hospital, I mean."

"I'm not surprised you don't remember, Lai. You were unconscious when the rescue ship found you. You've drifted in and out of consciousness since then. I'm glad to see you alert and talking—that's a good sign!"

"Rescue ship? How did..." Lai started to ask before she realized: *They knew I was coming!*

"NASA was expecting you," Dr. Kapoor confirmed as she made some notes on her pad, then stopped writing on the pad and looked up at Lai. "It's not every day we get visitors from 100 years ago. You're the first, in fact."

MATURE (18+) FOR STRONG LANGUAGE & MATURE THEMES

The Lightning in the

Collied Night

8/19/24
DAVID BACKMAN
DB
"Love never fails"

db

Copyright © 2024 by David Backman
All rights reserved. No part of this book may be reproduced in any manner whatsoever without written permission except in the case of brief quotations embodied in critical articles and reviews.
First Printing, 2024

Publisher's Cataloging-in-Publication Data
Names: Backman, David.
Title: The lightning in the collied night / David Backman.
Description: Apple Valley, MN : David Backman, 2024.
Identifiers: ISBN 9798991189705 (pbk.) | ISBN 9798991189712 (ebook)
Subjects: LCSH: Space travelers – Fiction. | Wormholes (Physics) – Fiction. | Climatic changes – Fiction. | Time travel – Fiction. | Physicists – Fiction. | Women physicists – Fiction. | BISAC: FICTION / Science Fiction / Action & Adventure. | FICTION / Science Fiction / Space Exploration. | FICTION / Science Fiction / Time Travel.
Classification: LCC PS3602.A25 L54 2024 | DDC 813 B--dc22

For Joanna,

with love

THE LIGHTNING IN THE COLLIED NIGHT

Or, if there were a sympathy in choice,
War, death, or sickness, did lay siege to it,
Making it momentary as a sound,
Swift as a shadow, short as any dream;
Brief as the lightning in the collied night
That, in a spleen, unfolds both heaven and earth,
And ere a man hath power to say, Behold!
The jaws of darkness do devour it up:
So quick bright things come to confusion.

William Shakespeare, *A Midsummer Night's Dream*,
Act 1 Scene 1

PROLOGUE

February 7, 2035

For immediate release – **2:35 p.m. EST** – **Tetyana Diduch, Public Affairs Specialist, NASA**

The following is an excerpt from NASA Director Mire Bashir Siad's remarks earlier today at the Space Telescope Science Institute (STScI) in Baltimore, Maryland:

"I am excited to share with you two important announcements regarding the Large Ultraviolet Optical Infrared Surveyor space telescope. LUVOIR was conceived almost 20 years ago as the successor to the Hubble space telescope. With LUVOIR's multi-wavelength capability—including infrared, optical, and ultraviolet—and dual mirrors as large as 15 meters, it will enable transformative advances across a broad range of astrophysics, including the search for habitable planets.

"The lifespan of Hubble was extended to as late as 2045 by a robot repair mission five years ago by our partners at the European Space Agency. It is essential that LUVOIR stays on schedule, to avoid a lengthy gap between Hubble and its replacement. To that end, I am pleased to announce that LUVOIR's development will enter Phase C—Final Design and Fabrication—next Monday, February 12. With the accomplishment of that critical milestone, LUVOIR should be ready to launch into space by mid-2045. I offer my congratulations on this tremendous achievement to the entire LUVOIR team.

"And now, I am delighted to share with you the second announcement concerning LUVOIR. Henceforth, LUVOIR will be known as the Neil deGrasse Tyson Space Telescope, in honor of one of the greatest astronomers of our age. Dr. Tyson recently retired as the long-time director of the Hayden Planetarium. Throughout his illustrious career, he has made astronomy and astrophysics more accessible to billions of people around the world. Given LUVOIR's mission to make the wonders of space more accessible to the people of Earth, I and everyone at NASA believe it is fitting that this revolutionary telescope bears the name of my friend and colleague, Neil deGrasse Tyson."

December 21, 2035

Although it was nearly midnight, the White House was ablaze with light, as if the entire mansion were still celebrating the joyous event that had occurred earlier that day. The few remaining White House staff members were making their way out of the West Wing. Their smiles and laughter—and unsteady gaits in a few cases—carried over from the evening's festivities. As they stepped out into the balmy December night, the staffers shared their plans for the upcoming Christmas, Hanukkah, and Kwanzaa holidays. Because of what had transpired that day, the words from an old song of the season were especially meaningful that night: *Your heart will feel the message real, Of peace on earth, good will to men.*

"They're in a happy mood," Daniel remarked as he peered out through a large arched window at the West Wing below. *And by*

God, they should be, he thought. *They've worked so hard to make this day happen.*

"Do you want to go down and join them?" Aida kidded him.

Daniel turned away from the window and stepped over to the large eggshell chenille sofa, returning Aida's smile. "No… let them enjoy themselves. They've earned it." He sat down next to Aida, who was reclined in the deep sofa cushions. He set his whiskey tumbler on the coffee table in front of him and looked at the president's face. *She looks utterly exhausted. No wonder, given the strain she's been under these past few months.*

They were in the West Sitting Room, celebrating and also recovering from a very long, momentous day at Camp David—and many long days before it. The First Gentleman had retired to the White House master suite half an hour ago. The president had asked her vice president to remain for a while, to enjoy the peace and quiet and share a toast of William Heavenhill 15 Year Kentucky Straight Bourbon, which Aida had been saving for just such an occasion.

"It still doesn't seem real," Daniel said. "There were many people—most everyone, really—who said it was *impossible*."

Aida looked at Daniel with a tired smile. "Hell, I was one of them… 10 years, even five years ago."

"But, you got it done, Aida—as you promised you would." The president had pledged during their 2032 re-election campaign to get final agreement on the Camp David Covenant by the end of her second term. She'd accomplished that goal with over a year to spare. There was still much work to do with Israeli and Palestinian leaders, among others, to finalize details. But the first giant step toward peace and security for that region had been made.

"Daniel, you know I couldn't have done it without you—and many other people."

"Okay, be humble," Daniel kidded. "But it's a wonderful legacy for your presidency. The only question is, what do you do for an encore next year? The Toronto Climate Agreement, yes?"

"Yeah... I hope so," Aida said quietly. She picked up her whiskey tumbler, took a generous sip, set it back down and looked up with a somber expression at the bald man sitting beside her. "Daniel, there's something you need to know. My cancer has relapsed. It was confirmed last week when I had my checkup at Walter Reed."

Daniel's mouth fell partially open from shock and dismay. "Aida! I'm so sorry to hear that. What did the doctors say?"

"They're not hopeful. It's pretty advanced. I thought I'd beaten it, but..." The president's doctors had told her that the long hours and strain of her job, especially in the past year as she'd fought for agreement on the Camp David Covenant, were key factors in the relapse. "I'm sorry I didn't tell you sooner. I didn't want anything to threaten our work at Camp David. I'm going to tell the nation tomorrow night."

"I understand." *I hope the American people, and the press, are as understanding about her waiting to break the news.* "Did your doctors discuss a treatment plan?"

Aida shook her head slowly. "There won't be any treatment plan." She looked at Daniel's distraught face. "You'll need to take over for me soon... probably *very* soon."

Daniel was devastated, but he tried not to let his grief show on his face, for her sake. "Aida, I'll do whatever I need to do, for you, and for the country. But, you've fought this before—you can beat it again!"

"No... not this time, my friend. What's that quote I've heard you say? 'I have fought the good fight, I have finished the race, I have kept the faith.' I think I've finished the race—my part of it, anyway. And it's time to hand the baton off to you for the final lap." She mustered as much of a smile as she could. "You'll be a great president."

Daniel looked at the woman sitting next to him on the sofa. Her short brunette hair had turned mostly gray and her face had aged markedly during her nearly seven years as president. The deep lines etched into her face were reminders of the immense stress of one of the most difficult jobs on Earth. "I appreciate your confidence in me, but you know, you've set the bar very high."

Aida smiled slightly and sat up on the sofa. "With all your experience in the Senate and as veep, I can't think of anyone better prepared to be president. You've been leading our efforts on the Toronto Agreement, and I know we're in sync about the American Security Act—that must *not* see the light of day."

"Don't worry. I'll get the Toronto Agreement ratified, no matter what. And I'll do everything I can to ensure the ASA is squashed." Daniel had misgivings about being able to accomplish both critical objectives, but he didn't think it was the right moment to raise his concerns.

"I know you will. And while you're at it, maybe you could resurrect that 'conspiracy of love' you emphasized in your Senate days and your '28 campaign. I haven't heard you say much about that in recent years. The country, and the world, could use more love right now, don't you think?"

Daniel smiled and nodded, "Indeed. We *could* use more of that." *But I'm going to need a lot more than a conspiracy of love to pull off that balancing act on the ASA and the Toronto Agreement.* Daniel leaned back on the sofa and looked at Aida. "You know… maybe you should have stepped down last year, as we discussed."

Daniel knew her doctors had strongly advised her to resign, as the continued strain of the presidency would greatly increase the odds of a relapse.

Aida gazed toward the large arched window for a few seconds, then turned back to Daniel. "I have no regrets. I wouldn't trade the last year, and the breakthrough at Camp David, for anything. But," she continued, "how about you? Will you have any regrets if you leave the Oval Office in a year?" Daniel had announced several months earlier that he wouldn't be a candidate for president in 2036. He wanted to focus on the Camp David Covenant and other initiatives of Aida's administration. Also, he believed it was time to let a younger generation, one with new ideas and fresh perspectives, lead the country. "There's a lot you could accomplish as president—for example, working to mitigate climate change under the Toronto Agreement, and improving our relations with China."

"Yes, I suppose." He looked at Aida. *She gave the job everything she had... she literally gave her life for her country—for the whole world.* "All right. . I'll think about it."

Aida reached out, grasped Daniel's hands, and gave him her warmest smile. "Thank you, Daniel. I hope you know how much I truly appreciate all your help and support these past seven years." She released his hands and glanced at the antique clock on the side table. "What do you say we call it a night? We have another big day tomorrow."

"On that, we are in complete agreement," Daniel replied wearily.

Aida took one last sip from her drink before getting up from the sofa. "That was pretty damn good bourbon, wasn't it?"

"It was amazing. Thanks for breaking it out for the occasion, Madam President," Daniel replied as he stood up and buttoned the coat of his dark gray suit.

Aida smiled. "My pleasure, Mr. Vice President." *I have another bottle ready for the Toronto Agreement ratification... I hope I'm here to open it.*

"Cardinal to Chickadee One, I'm ready to head for home. I'll meet you at the north exit in 10 minutes," Daniel spoke into his watch.

"Roger, Cardinal—north exit in 10 minutes," came the reply—a deep male voice with a hint of a Kenyan accent.

"How's the new agent working out?" Aida asked.

"Benjamin? He's great. Not that new anymore, though—he's been on my detail for a little over a year. Very thorough; very careful." He smiled, "Maybe a little too careful for my taste, sometimes."

"The Secret Service can never be *too* careful," Aida replied. "I think you'll appreciate that more when you're president." Aida unconsciously brushed out the wrinkles in her blue elbow-sleeve square neck dress. "Good night, Daniel."

"Good night, Aida. I'll see you at eight for the Cabinet meeting."

As Daniel walked out of the West Sitting Room, he thought, *What a day... what a wonderful, horrible day.*

March 12, 2038

It's not like him to be this late, Kapono thought as he checked his phone and saw it was 4:17. *He's always so punctual and considerate.* The Cal Berkeley sophomore was sitting on a bench in the hallway adjacent to his professor's office in Oppenheimer Hall, one of the largest physics buildings in the world when it had opened over 100 years ago under a different name. He didn't mind the wait; it gave him more time to mull what he was going to say to the man who was not only his favorite professor but also a mentor who'd made him feel welcome at the huge university that was 2,400 miles from home.

Kapono heard quick footsteps echoing in the distance and turned to see the professor—a short, middle-aged man with black hair, wearing a dark brown suit—walking briskly down the long hall toward him. "Good afternoon, Dr. Shen," Kapono said as he stood up from the bench.

"Good afternoon, Mr. Ailana," Shen replied as he caught his breath. "I'm so sorry to be late. Please, come in." He opened the office door and motioned toward it with his right hand. Kapono stepped into the office and stood before one of the two wood and leather chairs in front of the professor's old oak desk. Shen followed Kapono into the office and closed the door.

"May I get you anything? Some tea, perhaps, or water?"

"No, thank you, Professor."

Shen sat down at his desk, then Kapono sat down also. The professor shuffled some papers off to one side, folded his hands on the desktop, and gave Kapono his full attention. "It's good to see you again, Mr. Ailana. How may I help you?"

Kapono shifted uneasily in his chair. *This is going to be difficult.* "Well, Professor, you'll recall that we've talked about my major, and that I need to make a decision soon."

Shen nodded. "Yes, I remember our conversations." He'd encouraged Kapono to study quantum physics, followed by graduate work at MIT or Berkeley. The professor had been impressed by Kapono's aptitude for the subject and inquisitive nature during his *Introduction to Quantum Physics* class the previous semester. He thought the young man would make a fine physicist.

"And I appreciate your guidance, Professor." Kapono had enjoyed his physics classes at Berkeley, particularly Dr. Shen's class in quantum physics, and had seriously considered majoring in that discipline. "But, I've decided to major in marine biology."

Shen's expression changed to one that Kapono had seen several times in the professor's class: a blend of surprise and curiosity, with raised eyebrows and a wrinkled forehead. "I see," Shen said quietly, with a tinge of disappointment. "May I ask why you've decided to pursue that path, Mr. Ailana?"

"As you know, Professor, I've lived in Maui my entire life before coming to Berkeley. I love the ocean and marine life—all animals, really. I like physics, also. But, I believe marine biology is a better fit for me."

Shen had clasped his hands under his chin as he'd listened to Kapono's response. He placed his folded hands back on the desktop. "Thank you, Mr. Ailana. I understand. Your choice is well-reasoned. But, this is an important decision—one of the most important you will ever make." He glanced at the framed photo on the desk of himself, his wife, and his daughter and smiled slightly. "Almost as important as with whom you'll choose to share your life. Thus,

I urge you to take your time and consider not only the present, but where your decision may take you in the future."

Shen reminded Kapono that quantum physicists are responsible for explaining how *everything* in the universe works by uncovering the properties and behaviors of the very building blocks of nature. He explained that quantum physicists study the smallest objects in the universe and how those objects relate to the world and space around us, using the principles of quantum mechanics to explain the behavior of matter—for example, the behavior of black holes and wormholes.

"It's an exciting time to be a quantum physicist, Mr. Ailana. With existing and planned space-based telescopes, we'll soon be able to discover and study phenomena such as wormholes that have only been theorized. Quantum physics has no boundaries on Earth and in space… and perhaps even across time. The possibilities, and opportunities, are literally *endless*." Shen paused, and he smiled as if embarrassed. "I apologize. I sometimes get carried away."

Kapono returned Shen's smile. "No need to apologize, Professor. I always appreciate your perspective and insight." One of the reasons Kapono had developed a liking for physics was because of Dr. Shen's obvious love for his life's work and his ability to infuse his students with that passion.

"But, of course, you must do what you believe is best for *you*, in your mind—and in your heart." Shen paused, and his expression turned somber. "I regret to tell you, this will be our last meeting. I've been dismissed from the university, effective immediately. That's why I was late; I was meeting with Dean Pereira."

Kapono couldn't believe what he'd just heard. "*Dismissed?* Why, Professor? That is, if you don't mind telling me."

"Not at all—you deserve to know." Shen collected his thoughts. "It's because of the scrutiny that Chinese nationals like my wife and me, and even many Chinese Americans, have faced since the American Security Act became law." Shen shook his head and looked at Kapono with a pained expression. "The FBI suspects I'm an agent—a *spy*—for the Chinese Communist Party! I've been teaching here for over twenty years. My wife and I love America. It's... unbelievable."

Kapono was devastated—and angry. "It *is* unbelievable, Dr. Shen, that anyone would think you're a spy for the CCP! Isn't there some way you can appeal?"

"Yes, and I intend to pursue it. But, I'm not hopeful. The dean was under a great deal of pressure to act. I don't blame her. It's that despicable law... it's hurt so many people. Perhaps when the FBI investigation is completed and my wife and I have been exonerated, I'll be allowed to return." He stood up. "But soon I'll be escorted from the building. Therefore, I regret that I have no choice but to say goodbye, Mr. Ailana. It's been my great pleasure to know you."

Kapono stood, saddened by the thought that he may never see the man standing before him again. "The pleasure, and honor, has been mine, Professor. I'm sorry I wasn't always as prepared as I should have been for your class. I hope you can forgive me."

Shen looked at Kapono with a puzzled expression. "There is nothing to forgive, Mr. Ailana. I enjoyed your creative approach to problem solving. But, if it's important to you... I forgive you."

"Mahalo—thank you, Professor." Kapono said something else so quietly that Shen couldn't make it out. "And, thank you for *everything* you've done for me. I'll carefully consider what you said about quantum physics before making a final decision on my major. I hope someday I can repay you in some way for all of your help."

The professor smiled at his former student. "All I can ask is that you strive to be the best student, the best scientist—the best *person*—you can be. No one knows what the future holds. There's an old saying: 'When the old man from the frontier lost his horse, how could he have known it would be a blessing in disguise?' Perhaps this adversity will be a blessing for me—for both of us—in some way."

Kapono wanted to hug his teacher and mentor, or at least shake his hand, but Shen bowed slightly to the young man. Kapono returned the bow, with respect and gratitude. *A hui hou, Dr. Shen.*

September 29, 2039

Ru and Jun waited anxiously outside the front entrance to the federal prison in California's East Bay. They strained to see any sign of movement in the vestibule beyond the glass door of the nondescript gray building. Ru checked his watch. *What's taking so long?* he thought. *She should've been out of there 10 minutes ago.*

Jun looked at her husband with a concerned expression. "You don't suppose…"

Ru took his wife's hand in his and squeezed it gently. "Don't worry. It should be only a few more minutes."

Then the door opened, and a petite young woman with long, tied-back black hair, wearing blue jeans and a black t-shirt, stepped slowly onto the concrete sidewalk. She blinked as her eyes adjusted to the bright mid-morning sunlight.

"Lai!" Jun called out excitedly. When Lai saw her parents, a smile spread across her gaunt face and she ran up to them, embracing her father first, then her mother, who held her tightly. "My baby, my treasure… it's over, it's finally over."

With her mother's hug and greeting, Lai could no longer hold back her tears, and they streamed down her cheeks. "Mom, Dad… I'm so happy to see you!" *And glad to be out of that fucking hellhole!*

Lai broke the embrace with her mother, but Jun continued cradling her daughter's arms. "How are you, sweetheart?" *She looks thin*, Jun thought. She also noticed a few faint marks on Lai's arms; the marks resembled bruises that had mostly healed.

"I'm… I'm okay, Mom. But I'm really tired. I just want to go home." *I can never tell them what really happened in there and what it did to me. One thing's for sure—I'm sure as hell not my father's Little Angel anymore.* It was true that Lai *was* very tired. She hadn't gotten a good night's sleep her entire time in prison. One of her cellmates had snored, loudly and constantly. And, there were other reasons Lai hadn't been able to sleep more than a few hours each night. She decided to keep those details to herself.

"Let's get you home," Ru said gently to his daughter as he put his left arm around her shoulders. They started walking toward the visitor parking lot.

"I'm going to make a nice dinner for you—all of your favorites," Jun said cheerfully. She enjoyed cooking traditional dishes for her family when she had time. And she'd had plenty of time since being dismissed from her job as a public defender with Santa Clara County 18 months earlier due to suspicions of spying.

"That sounds great, Mom."

"Lai," Ru began, "I've been asking around at some top universities about your restarting your physics studies, perhaps as soon as this semester."

Lai was only half-listening to her father. She was thinking about dinner, then burying herself under the covers of her bed for a very long time. "Uh-huh... okay, Dad..."

"I've checked into transferring your credits from Stanford," Ru continued. "And yesterday, I spoke with an old friend who's the dean of the Physics department at the University of—"

Fuck! Lai stopped walking and looked at her father. "Dad... please... not now. I appreciate your trying to help me, but I... I just can't think about that right now. Okay?"

"I'm sorry," Ru said softly. "That was inconsiderate of me. I understand. Of course, that can wait—whenever you're ready."

Jun looked at her husband. "It's fine if she wants to take some time for herself." She turned to her daughter, "If that's what you want, sweetheart."

"Thanks, Mom. I do need a little time." *Hell, I'm gonna need a shitload of time to get over this.*

They reached the parking lot, climbed into a red hatchback, and started off toward home.

August 18, 2042

Katherine and Paige walked through the main entrance to the Congressional Ballroom of the Fairmont Hotel in downtown Austin. The evening reception for the astroscience conference had started nearly an hour ago, and there were already a few hundred people milling about the expansive room, talking and enjoying the free food and libations. Both women wore business casual attire: black slacks and an emerald green blouse for Katherine, and a blue and white mid-length fit and flare dress for Paige.

"I hope they left some food for us," Paige joked as they weaved through the crowd toward one of the large buffet tables. "Oh my gosh—do you see what I see?" she said excitedly. "Jumbo shrimp! I haven't seen shrimp like that since—I don't remember when!"

Katherine stared at the large mound of boiled, peeled shrimp on the table in front of her and smiled. Shrimp of *any* kind were extremely difficult to find in recent years, and prohibitively expensive when they were available. *Our conference fees at work*, Katherine thought wryly. They grabbed plates, scooped shrimp and cocktail sauce onto them, added bruschette topped with tomato and basil from the other end of the table, and looked around for a good place to stand. Katherine turned toward the western wall of the ballroom and was awestruck by what she saw through the floor-to-ceiling windows.

"Paige, check this out," Katherine whispered to her colleague as she motioned with her free hand toward the window wall. Paige turned around and saw the stunning sunset. The entire sky was ablaze with vibrant hues of pink, orange, and purple. The women looked at each other and smiled, then they headed toward the windows as if drawn there by some giant magnet.

"I don't know if anything at the conference will top this," Katherine remarked as she watched the fading sunset and took another bite of shrimp.

"A tough act to follow," Paige agreed. "What are you going to see tomorrow?"

"After the main tent session, I'm going to a Quantum Drive update."

Paige finished a bruschetta. "That's still experimental, isn't it?" Quantum Drive was a revolutionary spacecraft propulsion technology that had been in testing for almost 20 years, without success.

"Yes," Katherine replied, "but recent tests have been promising. It would be great if we could use it on our ships—it would be a game-changer." Katherine was a project director for Boeing Launch Services; Paige was the company's associate director of engineering.

"It sure would be," Paige agreed. "What else is on your schedule for tomorrow?"

"There's an update on the Tyson telescope in the afternoon. Then, I have to jump on a call with my project team. How about you?"

Paige pulled out her phone and clicked on the conference's app. "Main tent, of course. Then there's a session on SpaceX's next-gen Starship, followed by a preview of the latest spacecraft design from InfiniTrek—the Voyageur IV." SpaceX and InfiniTrek were two of Boeing Launch Services' main rivals for reusable spacecraft.

Katherine smiled slyly at Paige. "Checking out the competition, eh?"

"Nah—scientific curiosity," Paige winked.

Katherine eyed Paige's phone. "Is that one of those new hPhones?" Paige nodded. "How do you like it?"

Paige shrugged, "It's fine as a smart phone—the AI is really good. But the holography needs a *lot* of work. That's what I get for buying Version 1.0, I guess. The holograms on my holopad are a lot better."

"You've got one of those, too?"

"Of course!" Paige laughed.

"From what you've told me, I think I'll hang onto my old phone for a while." Katherine picked up another shrimp from her plate, turned away from the window wall and looked around the ballroom. She saw two familiar faces: NASA Deputy Director José de la Cruz and Senator Irene Wilkes.

"Look who's here," Katherine said to Paige as she motioned with her head toward the two people conversing about 20 feet away from them.

"Deputy Director de la Cruz! I've been working with him on our latest bid for NASA. Really nice guy… charming, even."

Katherine leaned her head toward Paige and spoke quietly to avoid being overheard. "Paige, José *is* quite charming. But, be careful… I've found he can't always be trusted."

Paige's eyes opened wide in surprise. "Oh! That's good to know. Thanks, Katherine. I'll watch my back with him." Paige looked at the woman speaking with de la Cruz. "That's Senator Wilkes talking with José, isn't it?"

"Yes. I think both of them are speaking in the main tent session tomorrow."

Paige noticed the frown on Katherine's face. "I take it you and Senator Wilkes aren't the best of friends?"

Katherine chuckled, "You could say that." She'd interacted with Wilkes a few times and couldn't escape the feeling that the senator held some sort of grudge against her—and she had no idea why. She'd always been respectful and professional with Wilkes… except for on one occasion, five years earlier. The senator had conspired with José de la Cruz to back out of a NASA deal with Boeing Launch Services that they'd sworn to Katherine was "done," and she'd staked her professional reputation on it. It had taken her several years to recover from their treachery, but she had done so with a lot of hard work.

"Hellooo?" Paige asked with a smile. Katherine snapped out of her unpleasant memory.

"I'm sorry, Paige. What were you saying?"

"Just that I promised Bob I'd go with him down to Sixth Street tonight to listen to some country music." Paige's husband had accompanied her to Austin.

"Oh, right—you mentioned that earlier. I didn't know you like country music."

Paige laughed. "Oh I don't! I like jazz. But Bob's a native Texan and a *huge* country music fan. And he goes with me to listen to jazz sometimes. I read once that a great marriage is when an imperfect couple learns to enjoy their differences. So I guess that means Bob and I have a great marriage."

Katherine smiled and pointed toward the main entrance. "Get out of here! Have fun."

"We will, thanks. See you tomorrow at breakfast—8:00?"

"Eight it is—see you then, Paige."

Katherine watched as Paige made her way through the crowd and exited the ballroom. *I envy her, how she manages to balance her family life with her career. I wish I were better at that.* Katherine hadn't been in a serious relationship since grad school, over 10 years ago. She'd had many opportunities since then for casual hookups and friends-with-benefits arrangements, but those didn't interest her. She wanted a long-term, committed relationship, but was unsure if she'd be able to devote the time that such a relationship required—and deserved. *I'm only 34... there's still time for love...*

"Katherine!" José de la Cruz called out as he walked toward the red-haired woman, smiling broadly. "It is good to see you again!"

Crap. Katherine managed what she hoped looked like a pleasant smile. "Hello, José," Katherine replied as he gave her a quick embrace. *Eeewww.* "How are you?"

"I am very well, thank you. And you? How is your project at BLS coming along?"

Katherine wanted to say, *Do you mean the project I had to fight tooth-and-nail for after you and Irene nearly ruined my career?* But instead she replied, "It's going well, thanks. Almost ready for Phase B Review."

"Excellent, I am glad to hear that. And, I am glad you are here," de la Cruz continued. "There is someone I would like you to meet. Do you have time now?"

Katherine tried to think of some excuse for a quick exit, but nothing came to mind. *What the heck, this is boring anyway—and it looks like the shrimp are all gone. Who knows, this could be interesting.* "Sure," she replied as she set her empty plate on a service tray.

"Please, follow me."

Katherine trailed behind de la Cruz as he walked across the ballroom. They were headed toward three people who were standing and talking in a pocket of relative calm in the noisy, crowded room. Katherine thought she recognized one of them: a tall, slim man with a prominent nose, sharp chin, widely-spaced gray eyes, and black hair with gray temples. He was wearing a black suit coat, black slacks, black Oxfords, and a dark gray banded-collar linen shirt. As they got closer, Katherine realized that the man was familiar... *very* familiar, in fact.

XXX - PROLOGUE

Oh God, not HIM!

October 16, 2048

I think I've seen more than enough for one day, Minwaadizi thought glumly as she sat on the living room sofa, watching and listening to the TV. "TV off," she said as Anong came out of his bedroom into the living room.

"Nothing good on TV, Mom?" Anong asked as the flat screen went dark.

"I thought I'd watch the news until your uncle arrives." Minwaadizi looked up at her son with a sorrowful expression. "It was very depressing."

Anong sat down on the sofa next to his mother. "How so?"

"There was a story about Phoenix," Minwaadizi began in a somber tone. "The situation there is getting desperate. They're running short of water in Maricopa County. Homes and buildings are collapsing because the ground is sinking from taking all the water from it. There's talk about relocating six million people to a new city to be built in northern Arizona. But, that will take years."

"Wow," Anong whispered. He'd known about the water shortage in Phoenix, but not that it had become so dire. He thought of an old Native American saying: *Man belongs to the Earth, Earth does not belong to man.* "That *is* depressing. What else is going on?"

Minwaadizi shook her head, "Tensions are rising with North Korea and China. The Navy is sending another task force into the South China Sea. Here, both Red Lakes are down to only 36 percent of capacity. And we hit a new record high today, 98. We could see 100 tomorrow." She looked at her son. "You're careful out there, aren't you? Drinking lots of water?"

Anong thought about reminding his mother that he wasn't seven years old anymore, but he realized sarcasm wasn't any way to thank his mother for her concern and love. "Yes, Mom. I'm keeping hydrated."

Minwaadizi smiled. "Good. So, how is your project coming along?"

"I just submitted my application to use the space telescope. I hope to get an answer in a few days—maybe a week."

"Do you think they'll approve it?"

"I honestly don't know, Mom. We'll see." Anong knew his request for time on one of NASA's space telescopes was a long shot. *I may have to come up with a different project. Maybe I should work on something that could help with our problems here on Earth, instead of searching for life on other planets.* His thoughts were interrupted by a knock on the front door, and he popped up from the sofa. "I'll get it, Mom." He opened the door to a familiar, smiling face.

"*Boozhoo!*" the visitor exclaimed as he hugged Anong. "How's my favorite nephew?"

"I'm your *only* nephew, Uncle Bizaan."

"Yeah, okay—you're still the best." Bizaan walked over to the sofa, and Minwaadizi stood up to greet him. He embraced his younger sister, "*Boozhoo, nishiime.*"

"*Boozhoo, nisayenh.*" Minwaadizi stepped back from her brother's hug and started heading for the kitchen. "Supper's almost ready. Why don't you men get ready?"

"Okay, Mom," Anong replied. He and his uncle followed Minwaadizi into the kitchen to wash their hands at the sink.

"What are we having?" Bizaan asked as he waited for Anong to finish at the sink.

"Food. And you'll like it. You always do," Minwaadizi joked as she worked at the stove.

Bizaan laughed, "Yes, I do, because you made it. And I'm always grateful."

"I know—as Anong and I are when you cook for us."

After Anong and Bizaan finished at the sink, they joined Minwaadizi at the kitchen table, standing behind their chairs. She was thinking about what she'd heard and seen on the evening news.

"Would you mind if, instead of our usual prayer before eating, we say the *Anishinaabe Kagiizhiitaagoziwin*?" she asked.

Anong smiled. "That's perfect, Mom." His uncle nodded his agreement. They joined hands around the table and said an Ojibwe prayer of thanks:

Boozhoo Manidō, Gaa-kii-zhay-wat-ti-zi-yen! / Hello Creator who is so kind!

Ki-ka-gii-zōmigō Kina-naa-komigō. / In a humble way I thank you.

Mide Aki, Gaa-kii-zhay-wat-ti-zi-yen! / Mother Earth who is so kind!

Ki-ka-gii-zōmigō Kina-naa-komigō. / In a humble way I thank you.

Kii-na-waa Min-na-waa / You also

Ni-mishōmis-si-tok En-dis-son-daan-i-mak / The Grandfathers of the Four Directions

Ki-ka-gii-zōmigō Ki-naa-na-ko-mi-ni-nim. / In a humble way I thank you.

Ka-miin-nii-yang Ishkotay... / I thank you for giving us the gift of Fire...
Nibi... / the gift of Water...
Pa-git-ta-naa-mo-win... / the gift of the Breath of Life...
Min-na-waa Mii-jii-win. / and also the gift of Food.
Sha-way-na-mish-naam Manidō! / Have pity on us Creator!
Sha-way-na-mish-naam Manidō! / Have pity on us Creator!
Sha-way-na-mish-naam Manidō! / Have pity on us Creator!
Sha-way-na-mish-naam Manidō! / Have pity on us Creator!

| 1 |

November 12, 2048

By most measures, Proxima Centauri is an unexceptional star. It's a small red dwarf, only one-seventh the size of the Sun—too faint to be seen with unaided eyes from its position in the constellation Centaurus. It has only three known planets, with the unimaginative names Proxima Centauri b, c, and d. But it does have a few characteristics that made it worthy of interest by astronomers in the decades following its discovery in 1915. Notably, it's the closest known star to Earth—just over four light-years away. Also, Proxima Centauri is a *flare star* that randomly increases dramatically in brightness. And most importantly, Proxima Centauri b lies in the star's Habitable Zone, within which water could exist in liquid form on a planet's surface. And with water comes the chance, however slight, for extraterrestrial life.

Despite the possibility of life beyond Earth and Proxima Centauri's other noteworthy features, it is but one small, dim star in a galaxy of 100 billion stars. And thus, after decades of interest and study, astronomers turned their Earth- and space-based telescopes away from Proxima Centauri toward more intriguing stellar phenomena.

Fortunately, one person was still interested in Proxima Centauri.

Am I seeing things? Anong blinked twice in the dim light. Then he rubbed his eyes before staring again at the two monochrome images displayed side-by-side on the screen of his old Windows 15 computer. One image had been taken by an orbital telescope one week earlier. The other image was from that morning. As Anong studied them, he saw—or *thought* he saw—something on the newer image that was absent from the older one.

Anong zoomed into the latest image as much as his computer's freeware would allow. He saw a tiny, bright speck that touched a dimmer dot that was Proxima Centauri, at about 10 o'clock relative to the star. At least, it *appeared* to touch the star. In reality, the speck—whatever it was—could be millions of miles, even millions of light-years, from the red dwarf. *What the heck IS that?*

Anong had no idea. *But,* he decided, *I'm going to find out... try to find out, anyway.* It was a lot more interesting to him than the original purpose of his study of Proxima Centauri. He wondered if anyone else was taking high-resolution photos of the star just then. *Maybe no one else has noticed this tiny blip of light yet.*

He clicked into his computer's web browser, jumped onto the Space Telescope Science Institute site, and entered his credentials. Then he typed the targeting coordinates for the telescope orbiting Earth, for the next 15-minute window when the powerful scope was his to command.

He logged off the STScI site, locked the computer screen, grabbed his gym bag off his bed, and dashed off to football practice at his high school.

| 2 |

February 10, 2049

Hubble was dying.

The orbiting telescope's demise had been predicted for over two decades. Hubble's support team at the Goddard Space Telescope Operations Control Center originally thought the end might come in the 2020s due to component failure or orbit decay. But when Hubble stubbornly refused to die, the European Space Agency launched a repair mission in 2030 using a robot spacecraft. It was hoped those repairs and updates would extend Hubble's life to as far out as 2045. That would mean little, if any, interruption of service before Hubble's replacement, the Tyson space telescope, launched in mid-2045. But when the huge, complex Tyson scope was delayed by three years, Hubble soldiered on, dutifully performing the mission it had begun nearly 60 years earlier.

It won't be long now, Christa thought sadly as she sat at her console at the Goddard STOCC. The lead engineer for Hubble's support team had helped keep the telescope functioning for over 35 years. She liked to tell her colleagues, "We've grown old together—but not out!" But now, as Christa reviewed the status of Hubble's many components, she realized time *was* running out. Among other issues, the telescope was down to its last backup transmitter—and that was operating at less than 30 percent efficiency. When that failed—*It could be within days... perhaps hours,* Christa thought—the telescope would be silenced forever. There would be no more repair missions; they were deemed unnecessary following the Tyson scope's deployment several months earlier.

Christa had applied to join the Tyson support team once she'd wrapped up the Hubble mission. But she'd also considered another possibility: *Maybe I'll walk with you out the door, old friend.*

Anong gripped the arms of his metal desk chair with white knuckles and rocked back and forth as he stared at the small computer screen in front of him. "C'mon, c'mon, *c'mon!*" he nearly shouted into his dimly lit bedroom. But the pixels forming the image on the screen of the old, slow machine refused to be hurried. *5 percent... 6... 7...*

"I can hear you all the way in the kitchen," Minwaadizi said as she popped her head through the bedroom door. "What's got you so *onza-amenimo?*"

Anong swiveled in his chair to face his mother. "You know my science fair project—using the Hubble telescope to search for signs of life on the planets around Proxima Centauri?"

"Of course I know about it," she replied, smiling at her only son. "It's all you've been talking about for months."

"Yeah, okay, Mom, I *am* pretty excited about it, like you said." Anong glanced back at the screen—*12 percent... 13...*—then turned back to his mother. "I'm waiting for the latest image from Hubble. If it shows what I hope it will, it's going to be *huge*... I think."

Minwaadizi stepped all the way into the room, sat down close to her son on the edge of his unmade bed, and looked at the image slowly taking shape on the screen. "'Huge' as in ... little gray men with big eyes?" she smiled mischievously.

"No, Mom. That's not what I'm looking for. I mean, even if I were, there's no way I'd be able to find it." Anong shot another glance at the screen: *19 percent... 20...* After his months of work, this wait seemed intolerable despite his knowing the long, circuitous route that the monochrome images from Hubble had to take before they could be resolved in full color on his computer.

There had already been a few miracles during Anong's project. That Hubble was still functioning, several years after its expected end of life, was a minor miracle. But a bigger miracle was the Space Telescope Science Institute approving his application for time on Hubble, spread over four months, for his high school science project. No doubt the fact that Hubble was less used ever since the more powerful Tyson telescope deployed a few months earlier helped considerably. *If the Tyson scope hadn't launched when it did, I would've probably needed to find a different project*, Anong thought. And then, the latest miracle: his accidental discovery three months ago. *Now all I need is one more miracle...*

Anong and Minwaadizi stared at the screen as the image build crept along: *51 percent... 52..* She silently urged the computer to hurry up, for her son's sake. She knew how important this project was to him and how many days and nights he'd labored on it, sometimes to the exclusion of eating—and, she noted with a smile as she looked down at the bed, keeping his room picked up. But she didn't mind. Those things could wait.

"Look, Mom! *There!*" Anong nearly jumped out of his chair as he thrust his forefinger at the center of the evolving image on the screen.

Minwaadizi leaned forward and squinted at the screen; she regretted leaving her bifocals in the kitchen. "What... what is *that?*" she asked in wonder. She saw a round white and yellow swirl with a black center and a bright disk across the center—*Like Saturn's rings, but brighter*, she thought. And it also had what looked like a long tail of milky white filaments extending from its center—*Almost like a tornado.* "It's *miikawaadad!*"

Anong turned toward his mother. "That, Mom, is a wormhole. Well, actually, it's the black hole at the entrance to the wormhole. And it *is* beautiful, isn't it?" Anong's most difficult task during his project had been to apply the latest wormhole detection methods to determine with high probability that what he and his mother were looking at was in fact the entrance to a wormhole.

"I've heard you talking about those. Isn't it like… some kind of tunnel in space?"

"That's not far off, Mom," Anong smiled, proud of his mother who had only a high school education but was a voracious reader. She had encouraged her son's pursuits in astronomy and physics. "But, this isn't just *any* wormhole."

"What's special about it—other than you discovered it?" Her eyes smiled with love for her son.

"Lots. First, it's the only known wormhole that's anywhere close to Earth—only about 12 AUs—uh, a billion miles—away."

"That's *close?*"

"In astronomical terms, oh yeah—really close." *Almost too close for comfort.* "But that's not the biggest thing about this wormhole. The images I've captured from Hubble over the past three months show that it could be a *stable* wormhole—the only one known to exist in the universe! Well, in the Milky Way at least."

Minwaadizi thought for a moment. "What does 'stable' wormhole mean? Does that mean it stays around in the same place?"

"That's right!"

"Okay. So… why is that important?"

Anong reached out and held his mother's hands in his. "That's a long story, Mom. But I'll tell you this… I think it could change *everything*."

But explaining the ramifications of a stable wormhole to his mother could wait. First, he had to finish his project report and stream it to his physics teacher… and, Anong mused, maybe also to NASA.

| 3 |

October 22, 2052

Fuck, this is long! Lai felt exasperated as she scrolled and scrolled through the seemingly endless non-disclosure agreement on the holopad. *Whatever I'm here for, I bet it's something big.*

She looked up from the pad as the conference room door opened. A middle-aged, red-haired woman dressed in a tailored navy skirt suit and white blouse entered, smiled at Lai, and extended her right hand. "Good morning, Dr. Shen. Katherine Etter." Lai stood up quickly and shook hands. *Dr. Katherine Etter!* Lai thought with surprise and excitement. *Wow, this IS something big!*

"I'm honored to meet you, Dr. Etter. You're a legend in the astroscience community." Because Lai had spent her childhood and much of her adult life in Northern California, her speech lacked a discernible accent but did exhibit the idiosyncrasies of people from that region.

"Thank you, Dr. Shen, you're too kind. Your reputation in the astrophysics community, and more recently with fusion research, certainly precedes you. But, of course, that's why you were asked to come here today." Katherine's voice had a hint of Midwestern nasality. "Please have a seat. And please, call me Katherine." They sat down across from each other at the tired, government-issue conference table in the drab, gray-walled, windowless room typical of second-tier Department of Defense facilities. "Did you have a chance to review and sign the NDA?"

"I was just finishing it—it's pretty long! Oh, and please call me Lai."

"Certainly, Lai. What I'm about to discuss with you is critical to national security." *Actually, way beyond national security.* "I'm able to discuss it with you at a high level only because of your Secret clearance. But even then, we require the non-disclosure agreement. If you could please finish reading it and sign it, we can proceed."

Lai skimmed over the last two pages of the NDA, scribbled with her forefinger on the pad at the *X*, and handed the pad to Katherine. "Here you are."

"Thank you, Lai." Katherine glanced at the signature on the pad, touched the *Submit* button on the screen, and set the pad aside. She considered the petite, black-haired woman in a dark gray skirt suit in front of her while gathering her thoughts. "First, thank you for coming here today on such short notice. I hope it wasn't too disruptive of your work at Lawrence Livermore."

"No, not at all, ma'am. After all, it's not every day I get an urgent meeting request from Director de la Cruz," Lai replied. She recalled her surprise and excitement when she'd received the email a few days earlier. "In fact, I thought it was a joke at first—the head of NASA asking me to come to Kansas City for a hush-hush meeting."

"Sorry we had to keep you in the dark. I think you'll understand once we've talked." Katherine paused. "I assume you've heard of the Wagamese Wormhole?"

"Oh, yes!" Lai remembered the thrilling announcement in early 2049 of what was perhaps the greatest scientific discovery of the century: the wormhole discovered by Anong Wagamese, a high school student from the Red Lake Band of Chippewa Indians in northern Minnesota. "I really wanted to join the NASA project studying it, but I was recruited for the fusion project at Livermore." Lai had worked on the fusion research project at Lawrence Livermore National Laboratory in California for nearly three years. While she was proud of her accomplishments there and understood the importance of the project to the country and the world, she longed to return to her first love: astrophysics, especially research into black holes and wormholes.

"What do you know about the wormhole, Lai?"

"I've read several papers on it. But, much of the research is Top Secret..." Katherine noticed the puzzled expression on Lai's face as she continued, "... which seems odd for purely scientific research, and I don't have that clearance. But then, this is no ordinary wormhole, is it?" *No shit, it's the only known stable wormhole in the galaxy!*

"What I'm about to tell you is classified Top Secret—which is the reason for the NDA. Going forward, I'll arrange for you to get Top Secret clearance."

Forward HOW? Lai wondered. *And getting me that clearance might not be as easy as she thinks.* But she replied simply, "I understand, ma'am."

Katherine leaned forward, her hands folded on the table, and looked directly at Lai. "As you know, NASA has been studying the Wagamese Wormhole for over three years. What has not been publicly revealed is that NASA sent a probe to the wormhole nearly two years ago." Katherine saw the look of shock on Lai's face.

"But, the wormhole is over one and a half *billion* kilometers from Earth! How could NASA get a probe there so quickly?"

"Something else that hasn't been publicly revealed... NASA and DARPA successfully tested a prototype Quantum Drive engine three years ago. It was used for the probe. It took only a few hours to reach the wormhole."

Lai was stunned. She knew that Quantum Drive was supposed to be able to propel a spacecraft at up to 20 percent of the speed of light, using no fuel other than electricity. "I thought Quantum Drive was only experimental! It's *real?*"

"Very real. At least, the prototype worked for the probe. But the reason you're here today is because of what the probe discovered. That, too, is Top Secret." *If she was that shocked about the Quantum Drive, she'll love this.* "The probe found that the wormhole is a time portal—specifically, a portal to the future."

Lai's eyes opened wide, and she swallowed. "How *far* into the future?"

"We don't know, precisely. Based on the probe's telemetry, we think about 100 years."

Lai pondered what she'd heard. "Okay, 100 years into the future. What do we do with…" *Shit, they're going to try to send someone through the wormhole!*

Katherine could tell from Lai's expression that she already knew the answer to the question she'd started to ask. "Yes, we're going to attempt to send someone into the future. Your next question is probably, why are we taking that risk?"

"Yes, ma'am, that's exactly what I was thinking."

Katherine paused. "You've heard of the RAND Corporation, haven't you?"

"Certainly—the global think tank and research institute. I've worked with them on some of my projects."

"Yes," Katherine replied as she continued more quietly. "What almost no one on the planet knows about is a Top Secret research project that RAND conducted for the DoD, by order of the president. The objective was to study the impact of climate change, pollution, and global political instability on the world and create a long-range forecast with some degree of accuracy."

Lai nodded. "I see. Quite a study! What did it find?"

Katherine looked at the brilliant, eager young scientist sitting in front of her. *How do I tell her this?* "It's not good," Katherine said softly. "The RAND study concluded with 95 percent probability that the world faces almost total devastation of the human race by war or ecological collapse, or both, within 60 years." Katherine looked sympathetically at Lai as she absorbed the news.

"But, they could be *wrong*! It's just one study!" Katherine saw that Lai was trying to control herself despite being shaken to her core.

"Unfortunately, it's not just that one study. Two similar studies were conducted independently of the RAND study: one by the UN Commission on Science and Technology for Development, and the other by the European Science Foundation. They came up with almost exactly the same conclusions as the RAND study."

A wave of disbelief and sorrow gutted Lai. The ending of the classic movie *Planet of the Apes* flashed in her mind—maybe because she was feeling the way Taylor felt in the movie when he realized that humanity had nearly destroyed itself due to senseless hatred and intolerance. But then Lai realized, *Director de la Cruz and Dr. Etter asked me to come here for a reason—maybe they think I can help turn this around!* And that thought calmed her.

"Dr. Etter—sorry, Katherine... why haven't the results of these studies been released? Maybe they would help ensure support for the Toronto Agreement, and other efforts to fight climate change and the other forces ravaging the world?"

"That's a good question, Lai. The hard answer is, these studies have been kept under wraps because they all concluded that even with best efforts from now on, the effects of climate change, pollution, water shortages, and political instability will result in global collapse. It was felt that releasing the results to the public would cause more harm than good—mass panic, riots, insurrections and so forth."

Lai nodded slowly. "I see. Then, how does attempting to send someone 100 years into the future help?"

Katherine felt sorry for Lai, but also was proud of her for handling it as well as she was. "Have you ever wished you could see yourself far into your future—know how everything worked out for yourself? And based on that, you might act differently—make different choices in the present?"

Lai tilted her head thoughtfully. "Yes! I *did* do that, when I was young, into my teens and early twenties." *Mostly I wondered if I'd still be alive,* Lai thought as she remembered her painful past.

"I think most people do at one time or another—I know I did," Katherine confided. "This wormhole is our chance to do that for the entire world: to see how things turn out about 100 years from now." Katherine could see the wheels start to turn in Lai's brain, her energy level rising. "Do these dire predictions come to pass? Or, does the human race find some way to 'beat the odds'?"

"Okay, okay, interesting," Lai pondered aloud. "Suppose we're successful and someone gets a peek at what Earth is like 100 years from now. How does that help us? Unless we can—"

Katherine started to respond, but Lai burst out, "Holy shit!" Her cheeks flamed. "I'm sorry, Dr. Etter. We—there's a way to bring this person back from the future, isn't there? The wormhole is bi-directional!"

Katherine smiled inwardly at Lai's excitement and her quick grasp of the situation. "We *think* so. But we're not sure yet if we can return someone to the present, from the future. This is the first wormhole we've been able to study. We have a lot to learn." Katherine paused. "And that's why you're here today." Lai listened intently, literally sitting on the edge of her threadbare swivel chair.

"I'm the director for Project Prometheus—the time-jump effort. I want you to join my team as chief scientist. We need your expertise in quantum mechanics, particularly black holes and wormholes, to help us send someone into the future *and* bring them back home. And we need to move quickly—time is, as they say, of the essence."

Lai nodded. *It's a stable wormhole, but stable for how long?* "I understand. I'm honored that you want me to join your team, Katherine. I can't think of anything I'd rather do."

Katherine exhaled with relief. "Wonderful! But, we haven't discussed any details yet. I think you should know what you're getting yourself into. For example, because this is an under-the-radar project, known only to a few people in NASA, the DoD, and the federal government, we have a tight budget. So, I can't pay you anything close to what you're making at Livermore."

Lai grinned, "Maybe I shouldn't tell you this, but I'd work on Prometheus for free."

"You're right—you shouldn't have told me that," Katherine said, half-kidding. "Also, for security you'll need to live with the rest of the

| 6 |

November 5, 2052

Lai's head jerked up from the pillow as she heard what sounded like a chime coming from the comm panel on the wall of her dark quarters.

"Dr. Shen?" a female voice asked from the comm panel.

"Yes," Lai replied as she sat up on the bed, wincing from a kink in her lower back. *Katherine wasn't kidding about the low budget, either.*

"G'day, Dr. Shen. As you may recall from our conversation the other day, I'm Dr. Etter's assistant. Dr. Etter would like to meet with you this morning at 0730 hours. She apologizes for the early start, but she'd like to check in with you before her call at 0830."

"Uh, sure, yes." Lai looked around for her phone to check the time. *Damn!* She remembered saying goodbye to her phone yesterday. "What time is it?"

"It's 0701 hours, Dr. Shen," Sirai replied. "Dr. Etter will meet you at your quarters at 0730 to escort you to her office."

"Great, okay. Thanks." *Uggh... feels more like five a.m. to me... oh crap!* "Hey, can you do something for me?"

"No worries, Dr. Shen. How may I help you?"

"Can you let Kapono know that I can't meet him for breakfast today? Tell him I'll meet him for lunch instead, and I'll get back to him with the time. Okay?" Lai hoped there was only one person named Kapono on the project team.

"No dramas! Message sent. Anything else, Dr. Shen?"

"Just one thing—please call me Lai."

"Certainly, Lai. I'll remember that. I hope you have a pleasant day. Cheers."

Lai jumped out of bed, found the switch on the wall for the overhead light, put on her robe and slippers, grabbed her toiletries bag, and headed off to the women's communal latrine down the hall.

***

"How was your trip, Lai?" Katherine asked after they'd sat down at a small round table in her office. "Any problems?"

"No, ma'am. Well, just one little thing. My phone was confiscated yesterday. I feel kind of naked without it."

Katherine smiled, "I know what you mean. We get attached to our phones, don't we? After we're done here, I'll take you over to Ops to get your hardened phone and holopad."

"Great, thanks."

"Oh, and on the way to Ops I'll show you where the food service is. I apologize for the early meeting. I wanted to touch base with you before a call I have in a little while."

"No problem. Your assistant explained the situation to me."

"Good. And how are your quarters? I know they're pretty spartan. If it makes you feel any better, everyone on the project has the same setup."

"They're fine, ma'am. Reminds me of my room at Cambridge."

Katherine laughed. "I've been there! Is there anything else you need?"

"Well, you mentioned something about uniforms? Although it looks like they're not required," Lai said as she thought of Kapono's casual attire.

"Oh yes, you can pick those up at Ops, too. That is, if you want to wear a uniform. They *are* optional. Most team members wear them—makes things simpler, I suppose. That's why I wear them. But some choose not to—Kapono, for example. You met him last night, correct?"

"Yes, he showed me to my quarters." Lai paused. "Interesting guy."

Katherine smiled, "Yes, Kapono is a very interesting man. I think you'll enjoy working with him." Katherine noticed that Lai seemed taken aback by that.

"Oh. So... he's one of the scientists on the project?"

Katherine studied Lai's face. *I wonder what's going on here? Well, whatever it is, time to nip it in the bud.* "Yes. *Doctor* Kapono Ailana is one of the world's foremost theoretical quantum physicists. Dr. Ailana *was* the chief scientist on Prometheus. But when he heard you might be able to join the team, he voluntarily stepped aside because he felt your exceptional background and experience in quantum mechanics would be critical to the project's success."

Ailana... oh yeah, I've heard of him. He's done lots of work on black holes, I think. "Oh, I see," Lai said as she processed what Katherine had just told her. As someone always driven to succeed, to be the best and be recognized as the best in whatever she set out to do professionally, she had trouble understanding how someone could voluntarily step back from a lead role in a project as important as Prometheus so that someone else could be at the forefront. She was sure she wouldn't have done the same in Kapono's place. *Maybe he wasn't sure he could handle the pressure*, Lai mused. She turned her thoughts back to the meeting. "Looks like I owe Dr. Ailana a big 'thank you' when I meet him for lunch today." *And probably an apology...*

"Good, I'm glad you're going to get to know each other better." Katherine smiled. "By the way, he'll give you what-for if you call him anything other than Kapono, or just K. You may have noticed he's not big on formality."

Lai returned Katherine's smile, thinking of Kapono's Hawaiian shirt, shorts, and flip-flops. "I noticed!"

"I know you must have a million questions about the project." Katherine glanced at the clock on her holopad. "I have a call shortly with the Prometheus Oversight Committee. How about I take you to Ops so you can get provisioned, then after your lunch with Kapono he and I will brief you on the project. Let's meet back here at 1300 hours, all right?"

Lai looked over the lunch menu at the commissary and shrugged. *Not exactly haute cuisine. And it sure doesn't compare to Livermore's cafeteria. Well, at least it's free.* She ordered a veggie pizza and black coffee. *The pizza doesn't look that great, but this is the best damn coffee I've had in years!* Lai had been pleasantly surprised—amazed, actually—by the coffee when she'd grabbed some on the way to Ops that morning. It almost made up for her cramped quarters and thin mattress.

"Good choice!" Kapono remarked. "The best pizza within a 20-mile radius. Also the *only* pizza within a 20-mile radius," he joked. Lai heard him order a burger, side salad, and iced tea. They collected their food and found an open table in the small seating area.

"Did Katherine get you all set up? I see you found the uniforms," Kapono said as he nodded toward Lai's crisp, new ultramarine blue coverall-style uniform with gold piping and a Project Prometheus badge on the right shoulder. The dark blue circular badge with gold and white stitching depicted Prometheus, the Greek titan who could see the future, holding a stylized black hole as a spaceship sped toward its event horizon.

"Yup, uniforms and holopad and—a phone!" Lai grinned, holding up her new hPhone.

"I'm not a uniform kind of guy, but it looks good on you," Kapono offered as he attacked his burger. "Goes well with your green eyes... which are rare in someone with Chinese ancestry, aren't they?"

"Thanks, and, uh, yes, I guess green eyes are pretty rare for Asians. Some people tell me I must have some Roman ancestors," Lai said with a wink, then she looked at Kapono as if seeing his face for the first time. *Oh my god, his brown eyes are gorgeous!* "How's the burger? I wouldn't think a place like this could afford to serve beef, even if they could find any."

Kapono laughed, "Oh, they can't! Not at $250 a pound." He held up the sandwich. "No, *this* is the best imitation of beef that science can engineer." Lai noticed his face assuming a far-off gaze. "When I was growing up on Maui, we had all kinds of fresh fish, and *real* beef from the island's ranches. I didn't realize then how lucky I was." He set his burger down. "How's your pizza?"

"Not bad," Lai opined as she finished a bite. "Not like what I could get in California, of course. But even there, speaking of fresh fish, it's hard to get good seafood anymore. I won't touch that test-tube meat, though," she said with a scrunched face. "But then, I don't care for meat—I'm pescatarian."

"Where in California?"

"I was at Livermore before coming here, but I studied physics at Stanford."

"Go Cardinal! I got my bachelor's at Berkeley."

"Great school. My father taught physics there."

Kapono started. "Dr. *Ru* Shen?"

"Yes, that's him! Were you in some of his classes?"

"I was! What a wonderful teacher and mentor. I owe a lot to him. He encouraged me to pursue quantum physics when I wasn't sure which direction to take, and to apply to MIT for grad school. And… here I am!" Kapono's smile disappeared. "I was upset when he lost his professorship. That whole business seemed very unfair."

"Yes… it *was* unfair." *And it destroyed him*, Lai thought bitterly.

"I lost track of him. How is he doing?"

Lai looked up at Kapono, her face an expressionless mask. "My father and mother died a few years ago."

"I'm so sorry," Kapono said softly. "That's hard, to lose a parent—both parents, for you."

"How about your parents? Are they well?"

"My dad still lives in Maui. He's doing fine, but I think he misses having me around to tend the garden." Kapono's wistful expression vanished. "My mom died in the Maui fire of '23."

Lai's mouth fell open. "Oh my god, that's terrible! You were so young!"

"Almost five," Kapono nodded, his eyes closed. "It was hard, for my dad, and for me. I miss her a lot. She nurtured my interest in science." He smiled, as if thinking of a fond memory. "She used to tell her friends that she'd like to be able to say someday, 'My son, the doctor.' She's probably saying that now to anyone who'll listen."

Lai looked at Kapono with sympathy and empathy. "I'm sure she is," she said softly. *What a small world, with how paths cross and lives intertwine, and how experiences are shared, like both of us losing parents through tragic events.* Then she remembered something. "Kapono... I want to apologize for how I treated you last night. You tried to be helpful and I acted like—like a bitch."

Kapono looked surprised. "Oh, not at all, Lai! You were probably dead tired, and you'd been bounced around this way and that. Then this weird guy shows up in flip-flops. I'm sorry about that. Would you please forgive me?"

Is he serious? Forgive HIM? "Well, really, I don't think—" But he seemed sincere. "Sure, yeah. If you'll forgive me?"

"Mahalo. And yes, of course, I forgive you." He said something else under his breath, which Lai couldn't make out. Then her phone buzzed, and she glanced down at it.

"Hey, we have that meeting with Katherine in 10 minutes."

"Right! Let's get you up to speed so you can solve all the problems I left for you," Kapono joked as he got up from the table.

"Okay, but what will we do next week?" Lai got up and followed Kapono to dispose of their trays.

"Good one! Brilliant, *and* a sense of humor. I think I'm going to like having you as my boss."

Boss? Oh, right, I guess I am his boss. This WILL be interesting! They headed out of the commissary toward Katherine's office.

"Well, Lai, what do you think?" Katherine asked after she and Kapono had briefed her on the project objectives and status during the past 90 minutes.

"Uh, wow—it's a lot to take in," Lai answered honestly. "Thanks for your patience with me, getting me ramped up."

Kapono chuckled. "Three months ago, I was sitting where you are now. I think I understand what you're feeling."

"Right, thanks." Lai straightened up in her chair. "Let me try to summarize what I heard, to make sure I didn't miss anything."

Katherine nodded. "Good idea, please do."

Lai took a deep breath. "Equipment-wise, the two spacecraft—primary and backup—are here in their silos, and we're working on adding Quantum Drive to them," she began. "Once that's completed for at least one of them, we'll do static tests and then a non-piloted, short-range flight, to Mars and back. Right?"

"Correct," Katherine confirmed.

"And we're working to get that done no later than the end of next year, yes?" Kapono and Katherine nodded. "Okay. Meanwhile, my primary responsibility is to work with Kapono and the other physicists to finalize the calculations for wormhole injection and help program the spacecraft's AI—what's that called, again?"

"Aileen," Kapono replied. "And yes," he added with a smile, "she has a bit of an Irish accent."

Lai returned his smile. "At least it won't sound like HAL, huh? And maybe Aileen will bring a four-leaf clover along for the trip." Kapono and Katherine laughed. *She does have a sense of humor*, Katherine thought. *Good—she'll need it.*

"And you also want me to work on confirming whether a return trip from the future is possible—otherwise, what's the point, right?"

"Exactly," Katherine agreed. "And if everything looks good, we hope to send someone through the wormhole by early '54."

"Okay, got it. And who will be the lucky pilot?" Lai noticed Katherine shooting a glance at Kapono before she answered.

"Well, Aileen will be the pilot. But, of course, a scientist will be on board to, hopefully, find out if and how Earth overcame its many challenges and bring that knowledge back to the present."

"Sure, okay. But, who will that person be?" Katherine shot Kapono another subtle glance, and Kapono looked at his phone and stood up from the table.

"I'm sorry, I just realized I'm late for a meeting with the Engineering team. Lai, I'll catch up with you later—at dinner, or tomorrow morning for sure. Aloha!" He opened the door.

"Uh, sure, see you later," Lai said, taken aback by his quick exit. Kapono left the room and shut the door. Lai turned back to Katherine, who folded her hands on the tabletop and looked directly into Lai's eyes.

"Lai, one of the responsibilities of the chief scientist is to make the historic leap into the future." She stopped to let that sink in.

Holy shit, that's ME! "Oh—wow! I'm, uh, I don't know what to say..."

"I should have told you up front," Katherine apologized. "We both know how risky this mission is. But, frankly, the fact you have no family was one of the reasons you were recruited for this role—and your exceptional experience in quantum mechanics, of course."

"Oh, no, Katherine! What I meant was, I don't know what to say to tell you how excited and honored I am to be the one chosen for this mission! I'm a little overwhelmed by it right now, that's all. To be the first human to travel through time, it's... well, it just blows my mind, you know?"

Katherine smiled and nodded. "Yes, I think I know. Kapono had a similar reaction when I told him about it when he was chief scientist. He understood the risks, but he was as excited as you are."

Fuck! Kapono gave this up when he volunteered to step down as chief scientist so I could join the team! How could he have done that? I don't think I could've given that up, for anything or anyone.

| 7 |

December 10, 2053

"Five... four... three... two... one... *ignition!*" Flight Director Haruto Hirano called out in his Texas Hill Country drawl. The Prometheus team members who were gathered in the cramped Flight Control room—repurposed from the ICBM control room from when the base belonged to the Air Force—were riveted to the main monitor. The booster rockets on the primary Prometheus spacecraft roared to life, pushing the sleek white spaceship out of Silo 1. It rose slowly at first, then with increasing speed as it cleared the silo and jumped into the clear blue winter sky above the Kansas prairie to the cheers of the observers in Flight Control.

"One thousand meters... 3,000... 5,000..." Haruto called out the craft's progress as it sped past three miles and accelerated. The ship tracked straight up from the Prometheus base to avoid sightings from nearby cities, and to avoid provoking concerns from non-friendly nations. The launch window had been carefully planned to steer clear of commercial flights in the area.

"C'mon, baby!" Kapono hollered, urging the spaceship onwards.

"Flight Control, status board is Green," Aileen's calm voice reported from the CapCom loudspeaker. "All systems are nominal. I recommend proceeding with Trans-Martian Injection. Please advise."

Haruto turned to Katherine and Lai. "Everything looks good for TMI, y'all. Current altitude is 85 kilometers. TMI is planned for

40,000 kilometers, to get past all those satellites in geosynchronous orbit and all that other space junk."

"Excellent," Katherine replied. "I don't see any reason to not proceed. Lai, Kapono?"

"Let's go!" Lai exclaimed. Kapono gave a two-thumbs-up gesture.

"All right, then. Haruto, 'second star to the right and straight on 'til morning'," Katherine ordered with a smile.

"Yes, ma'am!" Haruto returned Katherine's smile. "*Chronos 1*, this is CapCom. You are Go for Trans-Martian Injection at 40,000 kilometers—please confirm."

"Confirmed, Flight Control. Booster shutdown, Quantum Drive activation, and breakaway for Trans-Martian Injection in, mark, 36,424 kilometers," Aileen replied.

Peter Pan? Lai wondered, thinking of Katherine's reference to the book she'd read to her father at bedtime several times as a little girl, as he lay half-asleep on her bed. *Well, who knows—maybe there is a bit of magic in all of this.* As she waited for TMI, she closed her eyes and thought about everything that had happened in the past 13 months to get to this critical milestone of testing a spacecraft with Quantum Drive. In addition to augmenting both spaceships with Quantum Drive engines and other necessary equipment, they'd made considerable progress on the wormhole injection calculations and the quantum mechanics around returning from the future. Lai was convinced it would be possible, theoretically at least, to not only travel to the future, but return to the present. However, theory was much different from actually doing it. There was much work to do yet. Then Lai opened her eyes and sat up when she heard Aileen's voice on the CapCom speaker.

"Flight Control, T-minus 10 seconds to TMI... nine... eight... booster shutdown, mark... six... five... four... three... Quantum Drive activation, mar—" Suddenly, the CapCom loudspeaker fell silent.

"*Chronos 1*, come in. Aileen, please confirm TMI!" Haruto nearly shouted.

"What happened, Haruto? What's wrong?" Katherine asked.

"I don't know yet, Katherine. I'm tryin' to re-establish the audio link with the spacecraft. Aileen's not responding."

"I'll check with Flagstaff," Katherine said as she pulled her phone out of a pocket in her uniform. "Sirai, please contact the US Naval Observatory Flagstaff Station on a secure channel—ask for Commander McDowell, and put the call on speaker."

"Calling," Sirai replied. Then, after a few seconds, "Katherine, I have Commander McDowell on secure channel. Please go ahead."

"Hello, Commander, this is Katherine Etter with Prometheus. We just lost contact with our test flight. What do your telemetry and visual tracking show?"

"Hello, Dr. Etter. Yes, we were tracking the spacecraft until a few moments ago, then we lost telemetry. And—*what was that?*" McDowell asked someone who was in the room with him. "Please say again!" Katherine and everyone else in Flight Control waited with tense anticipation as they heard someone talk to McDowell. Finally he returned to the call. "Dr. Etter, I've just been informed that visual tracking observed a large flash at the same instant we lost telemetry. Then we lost visual entirely." He paused. "It appears that there was a catastrophic event with the spacecraft. It's gone."

Everyone in Flight Control sat immobilized, in stunned silence. Then Katherine said quietly, "Understood, Commander. Can you please send us your telemetry and visual record as soon as possible?"

"Of course, Dr. Etter. It's a big upload, but you'll have it within the hour. And, I'm sorry about the loss of the spacecraft. I know you and your team have worked long and hard to get this far."

"Thank you, Commander. It's a big loss for us, but we're grateful there was no one on board."

"Amen to that, Dr. Etter. We'll get going on the upload now. Goodbye."

"Goodbye, Commander." Katherine tucked her phone back into her uniform and looked around the room at the solemn faces of her core team.

"Aileen, we hardly knew ye," Kapono whispered.

Katherine stood up. "Haruto, let me know as soon as we have the telemetry and visual record from Flagstaff."

"Of course, Katherine. I'll get right on it with Meira and her Engineerin' team."

"Thank you." She turned toward Lai and Kapono. "I'd like both of you to assist Haruto and the engineers in analyzing the data and finding the root cause, then working on remediation, as your top priority."

"Absolutely," Lai replied for both of them. Then she turned to Haruto, "I'm thinking the best place to begin is with the Quantum Drive start-up components and code. The accident seemed to happen at the exact moment Aileen engaged the new engines. What's your take?"

"I agree, Lai—I think that's the logical place to start, unless the telemetry points elsewhere. But, we tested and re-tested those engines. I wonder what happened?"

"We could have missed something," Kapono suggested. "This was the first flight with Quantum Drive and this type of spacecraft. Real world can be much different from the lab." Haruto and Lai nodded.

Or, it wasn't an accident, Katherine thought as a cold chill ran down her spine. *Maybe it was sabotage.*

| 8 |

December 12, 2053

I am NOT looking forward to this conversation, Katherine thought glumly as she sat at her office desk and waited for Sirai to connect the call. In a few seconds, NASA Director de la Cruz's hologram materialized on her holopad. It looked like he was sitting at his desk in his Washington office.

"Buenos días, José. Thank you for taking my call."

"Buenos días, Katherine. It is always good to talk with you... although we have unpleasant matters to discuss, yes?"

Katherine sighed. "That's true, José. As we discussed two days ago, my team is investigating the cause of the explosion that destroyed our primary ship. They haven't reached a definitive conclusion yet, but they believe the root cause is most likely a flaw in the Quantum Drive's activation module. They hope to have it pinned down in the next few days."

"I see. Thank you for the update. I and the rest of the Prometheus Oversight Committee look forward to their findings." De la Cruz paused. "Have you thought more about what we discussed on Wednesday—the possibility of sabotage?"

"Yes, I have. Our chief of security, Major Goebel, is reviewing recordings from security monitors in and around the spacecraft, and also call logs for the past three months. So far nothing out of the ordinary has shown up."

"Good. What about interviewing team members who had any access to the spacecraft or its programming?"

You mean interrogating team members, don't you? "Not yet. We thought we'd check the security tapes and call logs first. Major Goebel and I agreed we should keep his investigation under wraps for now, to not interfere with the team's work—especially their investigation of the explosion—and also to not tip our hand if there *is* a saboteur."

"I see. And who is involved in the investigation of the explosion?"

"Flight Director Hirano is leading it, assisted by the Engineering team and Drs. Shen and Ailana." Katherine noticed the scowl on de la Cruz's face.

"Katherine, may I remind you that I advised you of the risks of bringing someone onto the project against the strong recommendation of the FBI?"

Katherine felt the cheeks on her fair face redden. "José, you can't think Lai had anything to do with this! She's been nothing but an asset to this project since arriving here. Her work, and her behavior, have been exemplary!"

"Yes, well, I would not expect a foreign agent to advertise that fact." De la Cruz's eyes from his holographic image bored into Katherine's. "I and the rest of the Oversight Committee believe it would be prudent to have Major Goebel interview Dr. Shen at least, and perhaps also her close associates—Dr. Ailana, for instance."

Stand down, Katie Rose—you're not going to win this one. "All right, José. I'll arrange for those interviews at the first opportunity after Major Goebel's preliminary investigation is completed." *And that opportunity won't come any time soon, if I have anything to do about it.*

"Excellent, thank you, Katherine. Now, let me update you on your request for a replacement spacecraft. I am afraid I have bad news on that subject."

Damn! "How bad?"

"I took your request to the Oversight Committee, and to the president himself. After careful consideration, they have decided that a replacement cannot be funded at this time. I am sorry, Katherine. I did my best to persuade them."

"Careful consideration" my ass—it's been less than two days! "What does that mean, José—'at this time'? How soon can we get another spacecraft? You realize, we *must* have a backup ship available for rescue, should something happen during the trip to the wormhole. No other craft on Earth can fill that role!"

"Yes, I understand. But Project Prometheus is competing for funds with many critical projects. For example, construction of the sea walls to protect New York, Miami, Baltimore and other cities on the East Coast, and completing the core infrastructure for New Phoenix in time. And the DoD priorities, of course. Repairing *Enterprise* so she can return to the South China Sea will cost nearly $8 billion by itself. Then there is the vital modernization of our ICBMs with the latest hardware and AI to counter the rising threats from China, North Korea, and Russia."

Katherine was surprised that the president, who was almost one year into his second term and thus a lame duck, wasn't more supportive of expediting the replacement ship. He'd enthusiastically approved the Prometheus Project after RAND's devastating study *The Future of Humanity* had been released in early 2049, just two months into his first term and a few weeks after the Wagamese Wormhole had been discovered. However, Katherine had worked with NASA and the Department of Defense for many years, and she was painfully aware of the harsh realities of federal funding. She decided to take a conciliatory tone with de la Cruz.

"José, I know there are many priorities and finite funds, which lead to difficult decisions. But please remember the purpose of Project Prometheus: *to ensure the survival of the human race*. I ask you, what is more important than *that*? And remember, José—time is not our ally. We have no idea how long the Wagamese Wormhole will be there."

De la Cruz nodded and looked directly at Katherine. "Yes... yes, Katherine, Prometheus is very important, there is no question. But the president has decided to focus on solving problems in the here-

and-now rather than investing the nation's limited funds on projects that, quite frankly, have a low probability of success."

De la Cruz's last words cut through Katherine like a jagged knife, but she forced herself to respond calmly. "What should we do while we wait for a replacement ship? We certainly can't risk sending someone to the wormhole without a rescue craft available."

"In the short term, find the root cause of the explosion and fix the problem. Of course, if the cause was sabotage... that will be a bigger problem, yes?" Katherine nodded her agreement. *It sure will be.* "I know this is disappointing to you and your team. I promise I will do everything I can to procure the replacement ship for you as quickly as possible. But I think, realistically, we are looking at the end of next year at the earliest. Let us talk again next week. Goodbye, Katherine, be well."

"Goodbye, José, and thank you for your efforts on our behalf. I do appreciate them." De la Cruz's hologram vanished.

The end of next year?! It might as well be the next century! As Lai would say—"Fuck!"

| 9 |
December 15, 2053

Major Albert Goebel sat down in the chair opposite Katherine at the small round table in her office. Goebel was a security expert on loan to Project Prometheus from the Air Force. Unlike the project's civilian team members, Goebel wore the standard Air Force OCP uniform with its tan and green camouflage pattern.

"How are you, Major?" Katherine asked the tall officer with short, jet-black hair and wire-rimmed glasses. "Except for our brief conversation the other day, I haven't spent much time with you in the past few weeks. How are Susan and your children doing?"

"Everyone is doing well, thanks for asking." *Good memory!* Goebel appreciated Katherine's inquiry about his family, whom he'd mentioned to her only once, many months ago when he'd joined the project. "I think my kids would like to see their dad more than just on weekends, and Sue would like to know where the heck I go when I disappear Monday through Friday every week. But they're doing okay."

"I'm glad to hear that. I know this type of assignment can be tough on spouses and families. As I've told you before, I'm grateful to have someone with your credentials in charge of security here. It allows me to focus on our scientific mission."

"I'm glad to be here, Dr. Etter. You have a great team. Until recently, I haven't had much to do!"

Katherine smiled, "That's good to hear. Now, let's talk about your investigation. Where does it stand?"

"I've completed my review of the security monitor recordings and call logs. Nothing out of the ordinary showed up. I also checked the main entrance logs, and there's no concern there. In fact, there's been very little traffic in and out of the base in the past few months."

"The team is very dedicated to their work." *But maybe they should get out more. They're under a great deal of stress and work long hours.* In fact, Katherine had never seen another group of people work so well together for so long, with so little conflict, under such conditions. It was gratifying, but also mystifying.

"One more thing I could do is to interview the team members—maybe only selected team members, those who have access to the silos and the ship's programming. What do you think, Dr. Etter?"

I wonder if José has been talking with Major Goebel? "Thank you, Major, but that won't be necessary right now."

"Dr. Etter, I think it would be a good precaution. You do have some team members with interesting backgrounds."

Like Lai, you mean. "That's true, Major. But the entire team has been vetted, and I trust them implicitly. Besides, I need them focused on finding and fixing the cause of the explosion on *Chronos 1* so the project can move forward."

Goebel's face flashed disappointment, but that look quickly vanished. "Understood, Doctor. You're in charge. Please let me know if you change your mind. I promise to be respectful and unobtrusive."

"I know you will, Major." Katherine stood up and extended her hand. "Thank you for your diligence."

"Glad to help, Dr. Etter," Goebel said as he stood and shook hands with Katherine. "Good day." He opened the door and saw Lai leaning back against the far wall in the corridor; she appeared to be out of breath. "Good morning, Dr. Shen," he said cordially.

"Hi, Major Goebel!" Lai peered through the office door and signaled with her facial expression to Katherine, *Can I see you right now?*

"Lai, come in," Katherine called toward the corridor. Lai slipped past Goebel into the office, a big smile on her face.

"We found the root cause!" Lai exclaimed happily. She closed the door and sat down in the chair vacated by Goebel.

"Wonderful!" Katherine felt what seemed like a load of bricks slide off her back. "Tell me about it."

"Okay," Lai gasped as she caught her breath—she'd sprinted to Katherine's office from the Engineering lab. *I gotta hit the treadmill more!* "It *was* the Quantum Drive activation module, just as we suspected. One of the circuits was faulty—a manufacturing defect, most likely. But it was a microscopic defect—that's why it never showed up during static tests. We believe the stresses of the launch were just enough to cause it to short-circuit when the Quantum Drive started up. And with all the electrical energy in the Quantum Drive plus the fuel left in the boosters—*BOOM!*"

"That makes sense. Congratulations to you and the team for finding the cause so quickly. How long do you think it will take to remediate?"

"Hmm, let's see," Lai said thoughtfully. "I need to confirm with Haruto and the engineers, but it'll take a while to check the circuitry of the remaining ship—and I mean check *all* of it, starting with the Quantum Drive, with a microscopic scanner. I estimate a couple of months at least, if we put everyone on it—maybe a little longer. We'll want to run the same checks on the replacement spacecraft, too, when it arrives." Lai looked at Katherine expectantly. "Do you know when that will be?"

"Lai... I have some good news, and some bad news on that."

"Good news first!"

"All right. The good news is, we have plenty of time to fix this problem."

Lai's face fell. "Because...?"

"I've talked with Director de la Cruz about the replacement ship. He believes we won't be getting one before the end of next year, at the earliest." Lai's face twisted into her signature *WTF?* expression, and

Katherine anticipated Lai's next question. "Budget issues—too many needs that take priority over Prometheus. I'm sorry, Lai."

"But, Katherine, the director and the rest of the Oversight Committee and, I hope, the president know how important this project is to the future of the country, and the entire world! I can't believe they're that short-sighted!"

"I know how you feel. I feel the same way. It appears they're prioritizing projects that will bring concrete benefits today, rather than spending more money on a project that they view as a risky venture with no guarantee of success." Katherine noticed Lai looking more determined than she'd ever seen her.

"Well, I think this project has an *excellent* chance of success. It's risky, yes—but we always knew that."

"I agree, Lai. But those who control appropriations do not."

"All right. But…" Lai leaned forward and spoke in a conspiratorial tone, "… we still have a ship. In a couple of months, it'll be ready to fly. So—let's fly!"

Katherine sat back in her chair. "Lai, you *know* we have to have a second ship, for rescue in case of a problem with the mission."

"I'll be flying that ship—okay, Aileen will be flying it, but I'll be in it—and I'm willing to do it without the backup. It's going to work this time—I know it will!"

At that moment, Katherine wanted to hug Lai, but decided it wouldn't be appropriate to hug someone who reported to her. "Lai, no. *No.* It's too big a risk. I couldn't live with myself if something happened to you."

Lai reached out and grabbed Katherine's hands across the table. "Katherine—listen to me! I've *got* to do this!" she pleaded. "Please, let me do it! We're talking about the future of the world here! Isn't that worth a little risk?"

It's not a LITTLE risk. But there's something she's not telling me… "Lai," Katherine asked quietly, "is there some other reason you're willing to risk your life for what could very well be a one-way trip?"

Lai looked directly into Katherine's eyes and released her hands from Katherine's. "Yes. This... this is *personal*."

"How do you mean?"

Lai stared at the wall for a couple of seconds, then turned her head to look at Katherine again. "I think you know that my parents died several years ago."

"Yes, I know. I found out during your background check. I'm sorry, Lai."

"Thanks. But, you don't know *how* they died, right?"

"Only that they died in an accident. The report didn't have details about it."

Lai took a deep breath, as if to steady herself. "Many years ago, my parents bought a cabin on a small lake in northern Minnesota. It was their retreat from this 'crazy world,' as they called it. They'd spend time up there every summer, in the quiet and peace of the north woods, with only the calls of the loons to disturb the solitude. It was their little slice of heaven on Earth."

"That sounds wonderful."

"It was." Happy memories from Lai's childhood—summertime visits to the cabin with her parents—flashed through her mind. She loved swimming in the lake on hot summer days; nighttime campfires, back when open fires were still permitted; and going fishing with her father in his rowboat. "I suppose you also found out in my background check about my father being dismissed from his professorship at Berkeley, over some ridiculous accusations of spying." Lai's voice sounded bitter to Katherine.

"Yes, I did learn about that. And for what it's worth, I think it was a travesty of justice." Lai looked at Katherine. *And she hired me in spite of that, and in spite of the felony charges and the jail time, too. She's quite a lady.*

"Thank you. That means a lot to me." Lai licked her lips. "After that, my father couldn't get another teaching job, so he and my mother spent lots of time at their cabin, pretty much year-round." She paused and took another deep breath. "Nine years ago, they were driving up to the cabin, in the dead of winter. There was a sudden outbreak of severe storms, with a swarm of tornadoes. Two EF5s touched down in the Chippewa National Forest as they were driving through it. They had no warning." She paused again, her voice growing quieter. "Their car was tossed into the air like a toy and smashed into some pine trees about 700 meters away." Lai shut her eyes as she remembered that awful day—January 13, 2045—when the director of the Harvard Center for Astrophysics had called her to his office. There, the director, a plain-clothes lieutenant from the Cambridge Police, and Harvard's Buddhist chaplain had given her the news. It was devastating.

Katherine reached out to place her hands on top of Lai's. "Oh Lai—I'm so sorry..."

"*There aren't supposed to be EF5 tornadoes in northern Minnesota in January!*" Lai cried. "This world is *fucked up*! Those studies you told me about say we're *screwed* within 60 years! If there's something—ANYTHING—we can do to prevent that, we have to do it—*I have to do it!*" Lai stopped, wiped her eyes, and looked at Katherine. "Do you understand?"

"I do. And... I agree. We've got to do what we can." "*All I ask is a tall ship and a star to steer her by*"—*and one very brave woman*, Katherine thought, remembering an ancient poem she'd learned many years ago. *Maybe I should have my head examined, but...* "Let's do it."

"That is very good news, Katherine, about finding the root cause," José de la Cruz's voice said from the speaker in Katherine's phone. As he was in a car headed for the airport, there was no hologram. "And, what about the possible sabotage? What did Major Goebel find in his investigation?"

You just won't let that go, will you? Katherine bristled. "I spoke with Major Goebel less than an hour ago. He found absolutely nothing that concerned him—no evidence of sabotage—during his thorough investigation." *I just hope José doesn't ask about the interviews.* "And our flight director, the Engineering team, and our top scientists are certain the manufacturing defect in the Quantum Drive circuit is the root cause."

"I see. Uh, excuse me for a moment, Katherine." Katherine heard de la Cruz tell his driver, "Delta, please," before he returned to the call. "Do you know how long it will take to correct the problem?"

"Yes—the team estimates it will take two months. Plus, they'll need time to inspect the circuits on the replacement spacecraft, when it arrives."

"Very well. But, you know, Katherine, there has been no change in priorities. I still believe the earliest we can procure another spacecraft for Prometheus is the end of next year, and that is optimistic."

"I understand, José. But, I have good news on that subject: Lai Shen has volunteered to command the mission to the wormhole using our remaining ship."

"Wait, Katherine—what is that you are saying? You are proceeding with the mission *without* a rescue ship? And Dr. Shen will be the mission specialist?" De la Cruz's concern was evident in his voice, even over the phone's speaker.

"That's correct, José. In fact, Lai not only volunteered, she insisted."

"Katherine," de la Cruz said in a harsh voice, "first of all, the risk is too extreme to proceed with only one spacecraft. There will be no chance of rescue should something go wrong. Also," he continued, "I and the rest of the Oversight Committee believe it is ill-advised to have this mission depend on Dr. Shen. You are aware of our reservations about her."

"Yes, Director, I am well aware of your reservations!" Katherine said sharply into her phone. "And, respectfully, sir, I have had more than enough of them. Not only is Lai Shen the most qualified person for this mission, she willingly accepts the risk, because she knows what this project means to the future of humanity. I am very proud of her, and I completely support her commanding this mission." Katherine paused for emphasis. "If you do not support my decision, you'll need to find a new director for this project."

"Katherine, wait. You are irreplaceable. If you feel this strongly about Dr. Shen leading the mission, without a rescue craft... I will allow you to proceed. I will need to persuade the other committee members, but I should be able to do that. *However...* be aware that if there is any problem with the remaining spaceship, there will be no others available to the project for a very long time."

"I understand, José," Katherine said in a now-composed voice. "And, thank you for supporting my decision. We won't let you—and Earth—down."

"I know you will do your best, Katherine. You always do. Please send my thanks and those of the Oversight Committee and the president to Dr. Shen for her brave action. And please extend my wishes for good luck to the entire Prometheus team."

"Thank you, José—I'll do that." *And we're going to need every bit of that luck.*

| 10 |

February 26, 2054

"Boosters?" Lai called out from the checklist on her holopad.

"Green," Kapono replied as he checked the booster rocket status readouts on the main control panel of *Chronos 2*. He was perched in the co-pilot's chair in the cramped cockpit of the spaceship sunk into Silo 2 at the Prometheus base. Lai was sitting to his left in the custom, ergonomic command couch she'd use during her upcoming flight.

"Starboard maneuvering thrusters?"

"Green. And, since I know you'll ask... port, dorsal, ventral, forward, and aft thrusters are also Green."

"Thanks!" Lai recorded the status on her pad. "And, last but certainly not least... Quantum Drive?"

Kapono carefully studied the gauges and multicolored readouts on the main control panel. "All indicators show Green!"

Lai exhaled a sigh of relief—that was the big one. The entire Prometheus team had worked long hours over the past 10 weeks to ensure the problem that destroyed *Chronos 1* would not reoccur.

"I think this ship is ready to fly—everything checks out mechanically," Kapono said as he sat back in the co-pilot's seat, which would be empty for Lai's flight. He looked at Lai and smiled, "And I think the mission specialist is ready to fly."

"I hope so!" She felt well-prepared from the nearly 250 hours of training she'd completed for the mission. Aileen would perform navigation and piloting, but Lai had to be ready to take over in the unlikely event that both the primary and secondary guidance computers failed.

"I *know* so. You've aced all the prep. You're as ready as anyone could be."

"Thanks. I hope you know, I couldn't have done it without you." Kapono had been at Lai's side during almost all of her flight prep, helping her make sure no detail was overlooked. She'd gained a tremendous appreciation for his scientific knowledge, but also his patience and kindness. For some reason, she always felt calmer when she was with him.

"Lai," Kapono said quietly, "I know you don't have any family. I don't mean to pry, but I was wondering if there's anyone back home?"

I wonder why he's asking? In case something happens to me during the flight? But she quickly put that thought aside and looked at Kapono. "No, there isn't. I just didn't seem to have time for that at Livermore." *Which is only half-true...*

"Well, I'm surprised. I'd think you'd have to beat suitors off with a stick with your green eyes and that blurry face."

Blurry face? "What the hell is *that*—what's a blurry face?"

Kapono chuckled. "Oh, you've never heard of that? It's, uh, a face with good symmetry, oval-shaped for a woman, and no prominent features. Like, for example, Mei Yao."

Lai raised her eyebrows. *Is he kidding—Mei Yao?* Mei Yao was China's lead ambassador to the United Nations—and was also generally considered to be one of the most beautiful women on the planet. Lai was taken aback, and her cheeks flushed. She wondered if it was just a come-on line—she'd heard a few of those. *No, I don't think so,* she decided. *Not Kapono... he's not that kind of guy. He's probably just being kind.*

"Gee, thanks," Lai finally replied. "But, no—I didn't need a stick. I haven't dated anyone for a hella long time. I'm probably too rough around the edges to attract someone, anyway." She paused and looked at Kapono, and despite wondering if she should keep going... she did. "But, I wasn't always like this."

Kapono cocked his head a bit, and he wore a slight smile. "Really?"

"Yeah. It might be hard to believe, but I was the Perfect Child—my father's Little Angel. I could do no wrong in his eyes. Always got straight A's..."

"*That* I believe!" Kapono said with a grin.

Lai shot him a *Ha ha, you're so funny!* look. "I never got into any trouble. I even had some friends, back in grade school and high school. Then..." Lai paused and looked straight ahead at the main control panel, her voice growing quieter, "... I learned I couldn't trust so-called friends."

"What happened?" Kapono asked, matching Lai's quietness.

I don't know if I want to go into all this with him right now. But he seems genuinely interested, and he's acting as if he actually cares. What the hell, I've gone this far. Lai took a deep breath. "I had a close friend my senior year in high school. Really nice guy—or so I thought. He found out no one had invited me to the senior prom, so he offered to go with me—'just two friends hanging out,' he said. I really wanted to go, so I said yes." Lai paused. "I had a great time... until he stopped his car on the way back to my house... and raped me."

"Oh my God!" Kapono gasped.

Although the flashbacks and nightmares from that gruesome night had subsided over the years, the horrid details were still etched in Lai's memory. *He doesn't need to hear about those*, she decided. "I shut down after that, for a long time. Then during my sophomore year at Stanford, I got involved in student protests against the American Security Act. There was a senior named Jared, a poli-sci major, who was a leader of the protests. I admired him and trusted him. I considered him a friend." She looked up at Kapono. "We planned a big protest on the campus on the third anniversary of the ASA being signed into law. Jared promised me—he *swore*—there'd be no violence." Lai bit her lower lip. "Hoover Tower was fire-bombed." She closed her eyes as she remembered the deafening blast and the fireball that had burst from the historic building's main entrance. "Luckily, no one was seriously injured. I learned afterward—after I'd been arrested for domestic terrorism and 31 counts of attempted murder—that Jared and others had planned the bombing all along."

"Oh Lai, how terrible! What happened then?"

"I was lucky. The attorney my parents hired was able to prove I wasn't involved in the bombing, and my felony charges were reduced to a class A misdemeanor. I paid a fine—well, my parents paid the fine—and I went to jail for 60 days. Jared got 18 years."

Her thoughts flashed back to her two months at FCI Dublin. Being a new inmate, only 20 and physically slight, she'd been the target of abuse by other inmates. She'd tried to fend them off using self-defense skills she'd learned after the rape in high school, but she was no match for her abusers. Then the toughest, most-feared woman in the prison, who was known only as "Queen," had taken a liking to Lai and offered to protect her. Lai was desperate, and she agreed. The abuse by other inmates stopped. There'd been a price to pay for Queen's protection, of course. And although paying that price was debasing to Lai, she figured it was preferable to living every minute of every day and night in fear. Those experiences, along with the rape in high school, had caused Lai to become detached and withdrawn, and had also hardened her.

"I learned a lot of choice cuss words in there... and got used to saying them," she shared with Kapono. *No need to share ALL the details*, Lai thought. "After that, I decided I didn't need friends. I focused on school, then my career... which almost didn't happen."

"How do you mean?"

"When I was working on my PhD at Cambridge, the professor who'd be grading my thesis hinted strongly that the chances of getting my PhD would improve a *lot* if I'd go to bed with him."

"Oh, Lai...!"

"I brushed him off and thought that was that. Then one night he invited me to his office to, he said, discuss my progress on my thesis. Like a damn idiot, I went. Then, he tried to rape me." She looked at

Kapono with a wicked smile. "The Wing Chun lessons I took after the date rape in high school came in handy—he never knew what hit him." She remembered the satisfaction she'd felt then when she'd given the professor a swift, hard kick between his legs, plus a few other well-placed blows.

"Oh that's great!" Kapono grinned.

"I told him to leave me the fuck alone and that I'd report him to the dean if he didn't give me a fair score on my thesis."

"And?"

Lai smiled. "Ninety-nine."

Kapono absorbed and considered what Lai had just told him. "Wow... you've been through a lot."

"Yeah, I guess I have." She looked into Kapono's eyes. "I... I've never told *anyone* about this—the date rape, the attempted rape at Cambridge—not even my mother. Honestly, I'm not really sure why I'm telling you now. I guess... I feel I can trust you. I *can* trust you, right?"

Kapono looked into Lai's eyes. "Absolutely you can. This is just between us." He paused. "I'd think this was very hard for you to bear by yourself, all these years. Do you feel any better?"

"Yeah.... yeah, I do." *Like a 1,000 kilos weight's been lifted off my shoulders.* "Thanks for listening, K. I guess... you're the closest thing I have to a friend right now."

"Lai, I'm honored to be your friend." He noticed the chronometer on the main control panel. "Hey, it's getting late. How about some dinner? I don't know about you, but I'm starving."

"Okay, but under one condition—it's on me"!"

Kapono laughed at her joke. "You got it! But be forewarned, I'm going to order the most expensive thing on the menu!"

| 11 |

March 6, 2054

I should've brought an e-book, Lai realized as her sleek white ship sped through space. It was completely silent except for a faint hum from the Quantum Drive and periodic progress updates from Aileen. Since the flawless launch and Trans-Wormhole Injection just over eight hours ago, there hadn't been much for Lai to do. She gazed out of the spacecraft's small windows at the stark beauty of deep space and occasionally checked the readouts and flat screen displays on the control panels that surrounded her in the cockpit. Aileen monitored those, of course, but it gave Lai something to do.

"Aileen, how're we doing?"

"All systems are nominal, Lai. Maintaining speed at 0.21 c, which is 62,956.3 kilometers per second. ETA to the wormhole is 10 minutes 12 seconds. Would you like any other information?"

"No, thanks. Let me know when we get within visual range of the black hole, okay?"

"Certainly. Is there anything else I can do for you?"

"Not right now. You're doing great—carry on!" Despite having used AI for almost her entire life, it still seemed a little weird to Lai to treat Aileen as if she—*it*—were a person. But Aileen's responses were the most human-like that Lai had ever experienced from an AI—plus there was the Irish accent. *I have to compliment the AI team when I get back,* she thought.

Lai settled back in her ergonomic command couch and became mesmerized by the light show in the ship's forward windows. The spacecraft's deflector laser array—an upgrade made necessary by the Quantum Drive and the properties of traversable Randall-Sundrum II model wormholes in five-dimension spacetime—swept the path ahead of the ship, destroying any particles that might strike it. At the ship's speed, impact with even a tiny particle could be catastrophic. Lai wore a G-suit with a helmet, but those offered only a modicum of protection. The deflector array would also be critical to ensure no particles entered the wormhole at the same time as the spacecraft. If they did, the wormhole could collapse back into a black hole.

If only they could see me now! Lai smiled as she thought of her parents and remembered their disappointment, but also their support and love, when they'd visited her in prison almost 15 years ago.

"Lai," Aileen's voice announced, "you should be able to see the black hole now, although it will be faint."

Lai sat up in the couch and peered out the forward windows. She saw a small, pale-yellow dot straight ahead. *It isn't very large, for a black hole—and that's a good thing,* she thought as she considered how close the black hole was to Earth. She watched intently as it slowly grew larger and larger.

"Lai, Dr. Ailana asked me to play a musical selection for you at this time. Is that all right with you?"

"Sure." Lai was curious as to what Kapono had in mind for her. "Go ahead." She heard a deep, sustained bass tone followed by three long notes from trumpets through her headset. Then her helmet filled with a crescendo of strings and brass replete with thunderous drums: *BOOM-boom, BOOM-boom, BOOM-boom, BOOM-boom, BOOM-boom, BOOM-boom, BOOM!* She couldn't help but laugh out loud. *That crazy Hawaiian!* She smiled and shook her head as the soaring music continued. *Leave it to him to come up with something like Also sprach Zarathustra from 2001: A Space Odyssey.* But, she had to admit that it seemed a perfect fit for the occasion.

As the black hole that fronted the wormhole loomed closer and larger in the forward windows, it began to look like the images from Hubble that Lai had first seen five years ago, when Anong Wagamese had discovered the wormhole subsequently named after him: a swirling white and yellow corona surrounding the dark event horizon shadow, with what resembled a ring—the accretion disk—across its center and a milky-white jet of plasma gas spinning out from the corona. She'd met the young man and his mother a few summers ago, when she'd made the short drive from her family's cabin to the Red Lake Nation reservation where he lived when not studying astrophysics at Harvard. In recognition of his achievement, NASA and the university had awarded him a full scholarship. *I wish he could see this. He may never know how important his discovery turned out to be for the world.* But then she thought, *Given the risk, it's just as well he's not here.*

"Lai, ETA to the wormhole is two minutes; reversing Quantum Drive now," Aileen reported. "I think you should prepare for insertion. The G forces will be extreme."

"Understood." Lai turned her full attention to the serious business at hand. She knew that, theoretically, the gravitational forces from a wormhole could approach 20 Gs, perhaps more. The question was, for how long? Lai also knew the human body could withstand over 10 Gs for only a few seconds without blacking out or injury, and anything over 30 Gs would likely cause severe injury—or death. Her G-suit would mitigate the G forces a bit, but if they exceeded 20 Gs, the suit wouldn't protect her from injury.

Lai strapped herself into the command couch and lay face up—the optimal position for high G forces. "Aileen, how does our approach vector look?"

"Approach vector is exactly as programmed, Lai. Thirty seconds to the event horizon. Shutting down Quantum Drive and switching to maneuvering thrusters. Would you like a countdown?"

Lai considered it. "No. Report instead on G force, please."

"Grand. Current G force is 1.27. I'll report G force in integer values from now on, all right?"

"Perfect, thanks." Lai braced herself, although she wasn't sure if it were possible to adequately prepare for the G forces she'd experience. She'd done some high-G training in a NASA centrifuge a few weeks ago, but that hadn't come close to 10 Gs, let alone 20 Gs. And, Lai winced from the memory, it had left her violently nauseated.

"2 Gs... 3 Gs... 4 Gs... 15,000 kilometers to event horizon... 5 Gs..."

This is it! Lai strained to keep looking out the forward windows while her cheeks flattened and the rest of her body was pushed harder and harder into the command couch. She didn't expect to see much of anything; the wormhole itself would likely be invisible as she traversed it, not a psychedelic light show as was often depicted in science-fiction movies. But her curiosity made her strain to keep her eyelids open.

"6 Gs ... 8 Gs... 10 Gs—G force approaching danger level, Lai!" At that instant, the master alarm blared and bathed the cockpit in flashes of red. "Should I abort?"

"N—n—no!" Lai struggled to shout as the ship shook around her. *I sure as hell am not quitting now!* She also realized that the spaceship was already caught in the gravitational well of the black hole "front door" of the wormhole, and attempting to abort now would either burn out the ship's engines, leaving her marooned in space, or tear the ship apart. The words *"To infinity and beyond!"* popped into her mind. She couldn't remember where she'd heard that—it was probably many years ago, when she was a child.

"Acknowledged. 13 Gs... 15 Gs... 20 Gs—G force at a critical level! Are you all right, Lai?"

Lai tried to respond, but she couldn't make her mouth and tongue move against the crushing gravitational force. Then Aileen's voice started to fade. Lai barely heard Aileen say "twenty-five," then for Lai there was only silence, and darkness.

| 12 |

Date: Unknown

Lai awoke to a faint beeping sound that repeated every second or so. She slowly opened her eyes and realized she was lying on a bed, looking up at a sage-colored ceiling that was softly illuminated. No lights were visible—the entire ceiling seemed to glow. She looked to her left and saw a large flat panel screen. The screen displayed the outline of a person—*Me?* Lai wondered. All of the bones, muscles, organs, veins, and arteries were shown, along with some text and numbers that changed occasionally. Lai noticed the display of the brain showed some areas in green and some in red. There were also a few red splotches in the figure's neck, back, arms, and legs. Lai tried raising her head—and immediately regretted it as she winced from the pain. *Must be why the neck on the screen is red.* She looked at her left arm and saw it had an IV attached to it. *Where the hell am I?* It seemed to be a hospital room, except it was unlike any hospital she'd ever seen.

Then Lai heard someone enter the room and walk up to the side of her bed. Except it wasn't a *someone*—it was clearly a robot, but a very advanced robot with a reasonable facsimile of a male human face and blue "eyes," dressed in what looked like nurse's scrubs.

"Good morning, Dr. Shen," the robot said in a pleasant male voice with no discernible accent. "Can you hear me?" Lai nodded once. "Good! I'm William, your duty nurse. I'm glad to see you're awake. Dr. Kapoor will be here shortly. I'm going to check your IV. Is there anything I can do for you before the doctor gets here?"

This robot is amazing—I've never seen anything like it! She started to respond, but only a croak emerged. "My... I could really use some water," Lai rasped. "And... can you tell me where I am, and *when?*"

"You're at Walter Reed Medical Center. As for when," William smiled, "I'm going to leave that to Dr. Kapoor. Let me get you some water." William reached for a pitcher on the bedside table to the right of the bed and poured some water into a small cup, then capped the cup and inserted a straw. Lai marveled at how lifelike the robot's movements were, and how natural its speech was. William lifted the straw to Lai's lips; she sucked down the water gratefully. "Go slow with that, okay?" Lai took a few more sips, and William set the cup on the table. Then as the robot checked the IV, a middle-aged woman in a doctor's coat strode briskly through the door, which slid open silently. She carried what resembled a small holopad. As she approached the bed, William nodded to her and left the room, the door gliding shut behind him.

"Hello, Dr. Shen! You're looking much better today! I'm Dr. Kapoor, your attending physician. How are you feeling?"

"Like... like I've been hit by a truck," Lai said weakly.

"That's not far off!" Kapoor said, smiling. "You had quite a rough ride getting here—you experienced at least 25 Gs during your voyage. But," the doctor reviewed the bedside display, "your vitals are looking much better. I think you'll be up and about in a day or two."

"Doctor... *what's the date?*"

Kapoor looked surprised. "William didn't tell you?" She grinned. "It's July 20, 2153. Welcome to the 22nd century, Dr. Shen!"

Holy shit, I made it!! Lai was overcome with joy and relief—and some amazement. *But, how did I end up here? The last thing I remember was, the ship was close to crossing the black hole's event horizon.*

"Uh, Doctor... I'm having trouble with my memory. I don't recall how I got here—to the hospital, I mean. Oh, and you can call me Lai."

"I'm not surprised you don't remember, Lai. You were unconscious when the rescue ship found you. You've drifted in and out of consciousness since then. I'm glad to see you alert and talking—that's a good sign!"

"Rescue ship? How did..." Lai started to ask before she realized: *They knew I was coming!*

"NASA was expecting you," Kapoor confirmed as she made some notes on her pad, then stopped writing on the pad and looked up at Lai. "It's not every day we get visitors from 100 years ago. You're the first, in fact. Congratulations on your tremendous achievement!"

"Thanks. It's hard to believe I actually made it to the future." Lai's head was bursting with questions. "Can you tell me, Doctor..."

Kapoor held up her hand. "Okay, I know you're excited and probably have a million questions. But, I'm not the best person to answer them. Director Lovell—sorry, that's NASA Director James Lovell—will be calling shortly; I let his assistant know you're awake. I'm sure he can do a much better job on your questions than I can."

James Lovell... why is that name familiar? "Oh sure, I understand. And I *do* have a million questions."

"It's great to see you smile! Director Lovell should be beaming in here in a few minutes." The doctor put her hand gently on Lai's shoulder. "I'll let you relax for a bit and check back with you in an hour or so."

"Thanks, Doctor." Kapoor left the room through the sliding door. Lai reached for the cup of water on the table, but before she could take a sip, a male voice came from the comm panel on the wall next to the bed.

"Hello, Dr. Shen. This is NASA Director Lovell's assistant. Is this a good time for the director to talk with you?"

"Uh, yes, absolutely!"

"Excellent. He's calling now. Goodbye, Dr. Shen."

In a few seconds, a three-dimensional image materialized a few feet from Lai's bed: a standing middle-aged man about six feet tall, his brown hair tinged with gray, dressed in what Lai guessed served as business attire in the 22nd century—dark blue jacket and slacks, and a white mock turtleneck shirt. There was a NASA insignia on the jacket's breast pocket. And, Lai noticed with awe, the holography was nearly *perfect*—it was almost as if the director were actually in the room with her. Only a tiny flicker on the outer edges of the projection every so often betrayed it.

"Hello, Dr. Shen! I'm NASA Director Jim Lovell. It's my honor to officially welcome you to the 22nd century. I can't tell you how excited I, and everyone else who has clearance to know about your historic voyage, are to have you here." Lovell paused. "How are you doing? I heard you had quite a ride."

"Hello, Director." Lai tried to sit up a bit in her bed, but she still felt woozy. "Yeah, it was pretty bumpy. But, I don't remember much of it—I must have blacked out right before entering the wormhole, then I woke up here."

"It appears your ship's AI pilot was able to navigate successfully through the wormhole, and the Starship *Armstrong* was standing by to ensure you got back to Earth safely." Lovell smiled. "Yes, we knew exactly when you'd show up on our side of the wormhole. We've been looking forward to your arrival for a long time."

"*Starship?* Does that mean—"

Lovell nodded. "Hyperdrive was invented around the turn of the century. The round trip to the wormhole took less than an hour, and that wasn't even close to pedal to the metal! I'm sure you have many other questions." Lai nodded. "Fire away! I'll do my best to answer them."

"Thanks, Director—I really appreciate it. Do you mind if I ask you a personal question first?"

"Not at all. And please call me Jim."

"If you'll call me Lai."

"That's a deal!"

"I was wondering… are you related to a James Lovell who was with NASA a long time ago—I think in the late 20th century?"

Lovell smiled and nodded. "Indeed I am. That Jim Lovell was my great-great—well, *lots* of greats—grandfather. Two of my other ancestors were in NASA also; one of them was an astronaut. I guess space must be in our blood."

"How about you, Jim—have you been into space?"

"A few times, yes. My last trip was a mission to Europa." His expression changed and looked wistful to Lai. "I really wanted to be part of the first mission to Proxima Centauri, but I couldn't get medical clearance. So now I fly a desk," Lovell chuckled.

"Hey, that's important, too!" Lai thought about how she'd never have made it to the future without Katherine's leadership.

"Yes, I suppose so. What else is on your mind, Lai?"

"Well, the most important question—the reason I'm here, actually—is... how is Earth doing? When I left it almost 100 years ago, it wasn't doing really great. There were lots of smart people who thought the human race might not make it to 2153."

"Right! The 21st century was besieged by one crisis after another, wasn't it? Well, the answer to your question is a long story—and a good one—but I'll net it out for you: we still have some of the same problems Earth faced 100 years ago. For instance, we're still dealing with the effects of global climate change. And, sadly, some people just can't seem to get along with each other, so there's a civil or international conflict occasionally. But, on the whole, I'd say Earth is doing really well. Most of the issues of the 21st century have been resolved, or we're close to resolving them. I think you'll like what you'll see, once you feel well enough to get up and explore this strange new world of the future."

Lai wasn't sure if she wanted to laugh, or cry. She ended up doing both at the same time as a torrent of pent-up emotions poured out of her. "Oh my god! I don't—that sounds almost unbelievable! We were so fu—messed up, in so many ways!" *Earth beat the odds! Fuck you, RAND Corp!*

"Well, believe it, it's true. Soon you'll see it all for yourself."

"I can't wait!" Lai said as she wiped the tears from her eyes with her right hand. "What—tell me, Jim: what was the cause, or the causes, for the big turnaround?" She watched him as he appeared to ponder her question.

"I suppose one of the biggest drivers was the transformation to nearly carbon-free energy worldwide about 40 or 50 years ago."

"Really! How did that happen?"

"Practical fusion power was perfected at Lawrence Livermore in the 2060s. It took a while to commercialize it around the world, but now almost everything is powered by electricity from fusion energy. That's allowed the damage to the air, oceans and climate to be largely reversed, but we still have a ways to go. And once cheap, pollution-free energy became widely available to everyone, in almost every nation, it made people less desperate for resources and less prone to get into fights over them."

Lai was overjoyed about the tremendous accomplishment of the scientists—perhaps some of them her former teammates—at Livermore, and she felt pride and satisfaction. *Maybe the work I did there played some small part in it.* "That's wonderful! I worked on that project for a few years before joining Prometheus. We always hoped that fusion power would bring benefits to the world like those you described."

"And it did! But, you know, there were other factors in Earth's turnaround."

"Such as…?"

"Well, probably the biggest besides fusion power was the LOA movement." Lai stared blankly at Lovell. "Sorry… Love One Another—making love for others the cornerstone of the law. In lots of countries, including the USA, 'love one another' *is* the law."

Lai thought she'd misheard Lovell. "Uh… *what* was that? Did you just say something about loving others being the *law*?"

"Yes, that's the gist of it. If you want I can—"

"Director—Jim—look, I risked my *life* to get here! And I don't think your little joke is hella damn funny!"

Lovell shook his head. "It's no joke, Lai. But I understand how it could be difficult for someone who hasn't lived through it to believe it. Maybe if I took you through how..."

Lai?

Lai heard someone call her name—probably from the comm panel by the bed. "What is it?" she replied.

Lovell kept talking, but now he sounded to Lai as if he were inside a tunnel, and his hologram—and the entire room—began to blur. "...LOA evolved over several decades, you wouldn't think..."

Lai, can you hear me?

Lai started to reply to the voice but realized her eyes were closed. She opened them and saw Kapono's smiling face beside her.

"Time to wake up, sleepyhead," he said gently.

| 13 |

May 21, 2054

Lai felt dazed and confused. "Ka... Kapono? How... uhh..." She could hardly speak. She felt as if her brain had short-circuited and her mouth had been numbed with Lidocaine. "How did you get... uhm... where's... where's Jim Lovell? Where's..." Her eyes darted frantically around the room. She was still in a hospital room. But this room was much different from the room she'd been in, or *thought* she'd been in, a few moments earlier. And it was much more familiar: pale green walls, overhead light fixtures, an assortment of beeping medical monitors, and the typical smells of a hospital.

"Try to lie still—you've been through a lot," Kapono said as cradled Lai's right hand. "The doctor will be here shortly."

"But how... how did I get back here? I was in... I made it, K! I was... I was in the 22nd century!" She looked at Kapono's face; his expression blended concern and sympathy. "I... I didn't make it to the future... did I?" Lai said sadly as she realized the truth.

"No. I'm sorry, Lai. You got really close, though." He turned toward the curtain screening the room from the hallway as a woman in a white lab coat, tortoise-shell browline glasses, and black hair tied in a bun brushed the curtain aside and entered the room. "Doctor, your patient is awake again."

"Excellent!" the woman said as she walked over to the left side of Lai's bed. "Hello, Dr. Shen. I'm Dr. Cheong, your attending physician. How are you feeling?"

"I'm really groggy… like my head is full of fuzz," Lai replied slowly. "What happened? *Where am I?*"

"You're in ICU at the University of Kansas Hospital in Kansas City," Cheong replied. "The reason you're feeling groggy is, three days ago you awoke from an induced coma. We had to place you in a coma due to severe trauma from your flight. You've been sleeping almost continually since then." She checked the monitors. "But the coma and rest seem to have done wonders for you—your vital signs are looking much better now. We were able to remove your breathing tube two days ago."

"I… I don't remember that. I don't remember being, uh, awake at all before this."

"I'm not surprised. Your cognitive functions, including memory and speech, should improve fairly rapidly now. But it'll be several weeks before you're feeling close to 100 percent."

"How… how long was I out?"

The doctor glanced at Kapono, then turned back to Lai. "I should look in on some other patients; I'll stop back in a little while." She touched Lai on her shoulder and said with a slight smile, "Try to stay on the ground for a while, okay?"

"I'll second that!" Kapono said as the doctor left the room through the curtain.

"Shit… I sure as hell don't feel like… like getting close to any wormholes for a while," Lai groaned.

"That wish will be pretty easy to grant—we're out of spaceships."

"*What?* K… tell me what happened! I was headed for the, uh, the event horizon when I blacked out."

"Okay, sure. But to answer your earlier question: it's May 21st. You were in that coma for nearly 11 weeks."

"Geez," Lai whispered. "So… what happened after I blacked out?"

"Best we can tell from telemetry and the black box recording, the ship entered the event horizon at too shallow an angle. So, it bounced off instead of going into the wormhole. That's why you experienced such high G forces—up to 28 Gs. Had the ship entered the wormhole, the G forces would've been a lot less—no more than 20, we think."

Fuck, my insertion calculations were wrong! "Damn... I checked and rechecked those calculations! I... I messed up someplace. The mission failed, and it's my fault." Lai was despondent; tears pooled in her eyes.

Kapono put his hand gently on her right forearm. "No, it *wasn't* your fault. We discovered something about the wormhole from your ship's telemetry: its position is stable, but the wormhole itself isn't *static*."

"Meaning...?"

"It's been *shrinking*—about seven percent since the probe visited it three and a half years ago. Not a lot, but enough to throw off the insertion calculations." Kapono looked straight into Lai's eyes. "You couldn't have known. We only found out about the shrinkage by comparing your ship's telemetry to the probe's data."

Lai appreciated Kapono's efforts to console her, but she wasn't in a mood to be consoled. "I should've known," she muttered, her head bowed. "Wormhole contraction over time is... is theoretically possible. I knew that... or *should* have known that." *At least the fuzz starting to clear out of my brain.*

"Okay, so it's theoretically possible. But even if you'd wanted to, you couldn't have taken it into account because you had no current point of reference to compare to the data from the probe."

"Well... yeah, okay... I see what you mean," Lai admitted. *Time to stop with the self-flagellation.* "What about the ship? How did I get back to Earth?"

Kapono smiled. "You have Aileen to thank for that. The ship was in bad shape—the boosters were damaged and over half of the maneuvering thrusters were out. Luckily, the Quantum Drive still worked. Aileen was able to steer the ship back to Earth orbit and land it—crash-land it, actually—in a secluded area not far from the base. And what's weird..." Kapono added, with a puzzled look on his face, "... she wasn't programmed to be able to do that—not with a crippled ship, anyway. Her developers still aren't sure how she managed it."

"She must have brought that four-leaf clover with her," Lai offered with a slight smile.

"Sure and begorrah, 'tis the truth!" Kapono said in his best imitation of an Irish accent—which Lai noted with amusement, wasn't very convincing. "Anyway, the important thing is you made it back in one piece—well, *almost* one piece."

"Fuckin' A!" Then, turning serious, Lai asked, "What about the ship?"

"It's beyond repair, sorry to say. Aileen did a great job just getting it back to Earth at all. As I said, it was a crash landing—and more crash than landing. Anyway, Katherine's working on getting replacements." He leaned back in his chair. "But now I want to hear more about what you were saying when you woke up—something about making it to the 22nd century, and... Jim Lovell?"

"Oh my god, K... I had the *weirdest* dream! And it seemed so *real*—or most of it did, anyway. I dreamed I *did* make it through the wormhole, and I was in the future... 2153, I think it was. I was in a hospital... but *what* a hospital! There was this robot nurse named William—"

Kapono laughed. "*William?*"

"Yes! And a doctor—Dr. Kapoor." *Weird... I had a professor named Kapoor at Stanford.* "And then the NASA director, Jim Lovell—a descendant of NASA's Jim Lovell from the last century—came to talk with me... a hologram of him, that is. And what a hologram!"

"What did you talk about with him?"

"Lots of stuff... how I got there, for example. They sent a rescue ship for me—a starship! They'd invented hyperdrive!"

"'Warp Factor Two, Mr. Sulu!'" Kapono joked. Lai smiled; she knew Kapono was a fan of old sci-fi shows like *Star Trek*. She'd seen some episodes of the original *Star Trek* as a frosh at Stanford. Her roommate loved the show and talked Lai into watching a few of the videos with her. Lai thought they were terribly corny, although she related to the "Mr. Spock" character—his intelligence and logic... and his vulnerability, which he did his best to conceal.

"Yeah, hella funny! But then I asked about how Earth was doing. Turns out, it was doing great! And then it *really* got weird."

"How so?" Kapono asked as his eyebrows went up.

"I asked the Jim Lovell hologram what had happened to turn things around. First, he talked about the adoption of fusion power starting around 2060, and how that helped reverse the effects of climate change and reduce conflicts over resources. And, you know, that all made some sense."

"Sure. That's why many people around the world are working to perfect fusion energy. So, what was the weird part?"

"Okay, so then Lovell starts talking about something called LOA—which stands for Love One Another."

Kapono leaned forward. "Really? What was that all about?"

"Lovell said that many nations of the world had changed their laws to just 'love one another.' I thought he was kidding, but he insisted it was true and started explaining how it all happened. Then I woke up." She frowned. "Isn't that the most ridiculous shit you've ever heard?"

Kapono's expression changed to a far-off look, as if he were lost in thought. "Well... maybe. A really fascinating idea, though."

"'*Fascinating*'? Oh come *on*, K! How could just changing the law to 'love one another' make everything hunky-dory? And how could that even *happen* in this *real*, fucked-up world? It's *bullshit!*" Lai paused her rant to catch her breath; the crash landing and induced coma had taken a lot out of her. "And you know what's even *more* weird about it?"

"What's that?"

"Why would I ever dream about something like that? I mean, what little corner of my brain did *that* idea come from?"

Kapono leaned back again in his chair. "I'm not a psychologist, and I've never been good at trying to explain dreams. But I know the subconscious is a mysterious animal. I read once, 'Deep within, there is something profoundly known, not consciously, but subconsciously.' The question is, how do we know what's profound and what's bullshit?"

Lai shrugged her shoulders—then wished she hadn't as she winced from the pain. "How the hell do I know? I'm just a quantum physicist."

Kapono grinned. "So am I! And I don't know the answer, either. It's just… something to think about."

| 14 |

June 8, 2054

"Welcome back!" Katherine exclaimed with a big smile. She motioned to the chairs at her small round meeting table as Lai stepped into her office, with Kapono right behind her.

"Thanks, it's good to finally be back!" Lai replied as she and Kapono sat down.

"You look a lot better than you did two weeks ago in the hospital. How are you feeling?"

"Pretty good, thanks. I'm not going to run a 5K any time soon, but the headaches are almost gone, and my back doesn't hurt much at all now." *Except it still takes a few minutes to crawl out of bed in the morning.* She'd almost cried when, earlier that day, she opened the door to her quarters and saw the thick orthopedic mattress Katherine and Kapono had purchased for her in Lawrence.

"I'm glad to hear that. We really missed you here the past three months. Let's bring you up to date. Kapono, what's the latest on the problem with the insertion formula and the shrinking wormhole?"

"Good news, there. We think we have a solution that'll take care of that problem." He turned his head slightly to his left and looked at Lai. "Right, Lai?" He'd kept her updated during his frequent visits with her in the hospital.

"Right! But the credit goes to Kapono and the rest of the Science team. They figured it out while I was laid up in the hospital. All I had to do was review their report and sign off on it."

"That *is* good news! Tell me about it." Kapono waited for Lai to respond, since she was the chief scientist.

"Okay," Lai began. "So you know that the problem is, the wormhole is gradually but constantly diminishing in size, which throws off our insertion calculations. We can adjust the spacecraft's radascan to continuously monitor the wormhole's size. Aileen will use that telemetry to update the insertion calculations in real time, so the approach vector is correct for the wormhole's size at any given instant."

Katherine nodded her understanding of the solution. "And you're certain that will work?"

"As certain as we can be without trying it for real, out in space," Lai replied. "We've run hundreds of computer simulations, with a 100 percent success rate. It's going to work." She smiled. "I'd stake my life on it!" *And I'll be doing just that.*

"Excellent! Great work, and perfect timing. You know that I've been trying to get our replacement ships expedited." Katherine clasped her hands on the tabletop and leaned forward. "The Oversight Committee is willing to consider my request. But they want to discuss it in person. So I'm meeting with the committee in Washington on the 17th. Having the insertion calculation problem solved will help our case."

"That's good news… I guess?" Lai said, a hint of concern in her voice.

"At least the committee's open to talking about it. And," Katherine added with a slight smile, "I can be pretty persuasive. It won't be easy, but I think I can get the delivery moved up."

"Katherine, I'd like to go with you," Lai proffered. "I think having the project's chief scientist there to cover the technical details and answer questions about them would be helpful."

Katherine considered Lai's offer. *Being able to answer any technical questions that might come up would be helpful… but it could also give certain committee members a target.* "I really appreciate your offer. But, are you sure you're up to it? You just got out of the hospital. Maybe Kapono could come with me."

"Oh, I know he'd do just fine," Lai said, looking at Kapono. "But I think the optics would be better with your chief scientist there to vouch for our readiness for a successful mission with the new ships." She smiled broadly. "And, I'm up for a road trip! I haven't been outside this base except for my aborted flight and extended stay in the hospital."

Katherine looked at Lai and returned her smile. "All right, then—we'll go pay the committee a visit. My assistant will make reservations for us. We'll fly into Reagan on the 16th—it's an early morning meeting the next day."

"Great! They won't know what hit 'em!" Lai joked as she and Kapono got up from the table. Lai reached for the door, but Kapono lagged behind.

"Lai, there's something I need to check with Katherine about. I'll join you in the lab in a few minutes."

"Okay, see you later," Lai replied as she left the office. Kapono closed the door behind her and sat back down at the table.

"Katherine, I was thinking... Lai deserves to know the score for her going on the next mission to the wormhole, don't you think?"

Katherine nodded. "Yes... you're right. I didn't want to hit her with that while she was in the hospital, but now that she's returned, I need to let her know." She looked at Kapono. "You know her pretty well. How do you think she'll take it?"

"Not very well, I expect. You know how important this project is to her, in the big picture but also personally. And I know she wants another chance after her aborted flight. But I think she'll understand that you had no choice."

"No... no, I don't have a choice." Katherine thought about the difficult meeting she'd had with Dr. Cheong several days ago, when the doctor had insisted that Lai be permanently grounded. Cheong had told Katherine that the extreme G forces from another trip into space and through the wormhole would probably be fatal to Lai.

"If you want, I can tell her," Kapono offered. *She might take the news better from a friend.*

"Thanks, Kapono, I appreciate your offer. But I'll tell her—it's my responsibility."

| 15 |

June 17, 2054

As the driverless taxi weaved its way through traffic toward the Capitol on yet another scorching summer morning in Washington, Katherine finished briefing Lai on the Prometheus Oversight Committee members. They'd already reviewed the makeup of the committee: two senators, one from each party; two House members, again one from each party; the Secretary of Defense; the Air Force Chief of Staff; and NASA Director de la Cruz. Senator Wilkes chaired the committee.

"Let me see if I have this, now," Lai said. "Chief of Staff Warner and Secretary Hudson are Neutral but tend to prioritize their missions when it comes to appropriations. And they tend to follow Wilkes's lead. Right?"

"Correct," Katherine confirmed. "And what about the senators and representatives?"

"All of them except Wilkes are Neutral, or slightly Positive. But they also tend to take their lead from the chair, Wilkes. Which brings us to her. You said she's Negative, right?"

"Right!" Katherine was pleased to see that Lai was listening carefully during their discussion at the hotel the previous evening, despite the dinner and drinks they'd enjoyed beforehand at Martin's Tavern. That was Katherine's favorite Georgetown hangout back when she worked for a defense contractor and visited Washington often. It had been a long time since either of them had enjoyed a night out, and Katherine thought they deserved it—especially Lai.

"Remind me… why is that?"

"Well, Irene—Senator Wilkes, I mean—and I go back a long way. We've crossed swords a few times. The last time was nearly three years ago, when I was being confirmed by the Oversight Committee to be the project director for Prometheus. Senator Wilkes didn't think I was the right person for the job." Katherine paused. "She lost. And she didn't take it very well. She won't be easy to convince today."

Lai shook her head. "I can't imagine why Senator Wilkes would object to your directing Prometheus." As Lai had gotten to know Katherine, she'd developed tremendous respect for her, both professionally and personally.

"Thanks, Lai. She… had her reasons." *Actually, she had her REASON—which had nothing to do with my ability to lead the project.*

"Well, I just don't get it. And what about Director de la Cruz? He's Positive, right?"

"Yes, but he's cautious. And political. He's agreed with me that the replacement ships should get high priority, but he probably won't fight for us against the wishes of the other committee members—especially Wilkes." *As long as Irene chairs the Senate committee that controls appropriations for NASA, José is going to do her bidding*, Katherine thought glumly as she remembered how her career had nearly been ruined by his loyalty to Wilkes. But she also recalled how he'd tried to atone for his deceit years ago by nominating her for project director on Prometheus, and also by introducing her to an influential aerospace executive at a conference 12 years ago.

"And thus, our strategy is…?" Katherine had covered it the previous evening, but that was after dinner and an extraordinary bottle of wine, and Lai wanted to be sure she was clear about it.

"We need to make the case that funding two more ships immediately is vital to the future of the United States and the rest of the world. We can't wait until next year, or even later, because the wormhole could disappear at any time. And it's a relatively small additional expense compared to the cost of the project to date. Also, we're very confident of success given how close we came with your mission, and we're certain we know how to prevent the problem from that flight—about which you can go into detail, if needed. Sound good?"

"Yes, ma'am!" The taxi pulled over to the curb and stopped near the visitors' entrance to the Hart Senate Office Building. Lai's eyes took in the boxy off-white building as she opened her door and stepped out into what felt like a steam sauna. She turned to Katherine, who was also getting out of the taxi, "I thought we were going to the Capitol?"

"This is part of the Capitol complex. It's where the Oversight Committee usually has its meetings." She noticed the look of disappointment on Lai's face. "You've never been to the Capitol building?"

"No. I was looking forward to seeing it."

"Tell you what... if this meeting doesn't take long, we'll head over there afterward and see if we can get in." Lai's face brightened. "Now, let's get through security and find the committee room."

Both women were dressed in what they jokingly called their "interview suits"—the same skirt suits they'd worn during Lai's interview with Katherine nearly two years earlier. As they walked through the swamp-like heat toward the visitors' entrance, they wished they'd worn something cooler. After making it through security without incident, they strode quickly across the central, light-filled atrium with its monumental Calder sculpture, their shoes tapping on the white marble floor. "This building is a *lot* more impressive inside than outside," Lai remarked as she gazed upward to admire the artistry of the black metal shapes, resembling mountains and clouds, of the huge sculpture.

"It's what's inside that counts, right?" Kathleen remarked, smiling as she glanced at Lai.

Lai returned Katherine's glance and nodded. "Yes... yes, it certainly does."

After crossing the atrium, they found the elevator bank that took them to the basement, where their meeting was being held. Since this was a Top Secret, closed-door meeting, it was in a small conference room instead of one of the large committee rooms used for public hearings. When they arrived at the room, a uniformed Capitol Police officer greeted them outside the door.

"Good morning, ladies. May I please see your government IDs?" the short, stocky officer said pleasantly but firmly.

"Of course," Katherine replied. She and Lai had already taken their IDs out of their purses on the way to the room. They held them out to the officer, who studied the cards for a moment and then looked up at the two visitors.

"Welcome, Dr. Etter, Dr. Shen. The committee members are expecting you. Please ensure your phones are turned off during the meeting," she reminded them as she opened the door for them. Katherine noticed the officer's name tag.

"Thank you, Officer Kabila," Katherine said as she stepped into the room, followed by Lai.

"Ma'am," the officer replied with a nod and a slight smile.

The two women pulled out their phones, turned them off, and took a quick survey of the room. It was small and sparsely furnished: two long dark wood tables facing each other, about eight feet apart—one with seven chairs, the other with two chairs in the center and one to the side. There was a young man sitting in the side chair with a pad and keyboard—*He must be the journal clerk*, Katherine assumed. There was a credenza along one wall with coffee, water, and trays of pastries and fresh fruit. The beige walls were decorated with prints of scenes from the history of the United States.

Katherine recognized the committee members, who were either sitting at one of the tables or standing, talking quietly in small groups. José de la Cruz noticed Katherine and Lai standing near the doorway and excused himself from his discussion with Chief of Staff Warner and Secretary Hudson.

"Katherine! It is so good to see you!" He smiled broadly as he walked over to them and gave Katherine a quick embrace. "And also a pleasure to meet you at last, Lai. Is it all right that I call you Lai?" He extended his hand.

"Of course, Director. It's an honor to meet you," Lai said, shaking his hand.

"Oh, but the honor is mine, Lai! What you did last March, risking your life for our country and the world—that was a heroic act. But, you were seriously injured. How are you feeling now?"

"Thank you, Director. I'm feeling pretty good now."

"Well, I am glad you could join us for this hearing. Please, help yourselves to refreshments if you would like; we will begin in a few minutes."

"Thanks," Lai replied. *Hmm... "hearing," not meeting.* She turned toward Katherine as de la Cruz rejoined the other committee members. "I'm going to get some coffee. Would you like anything?"

"Can you grab some water for me, please?"

"You got it!" Lai walked over to the coffee pot on the credenza and frowned. *Probably that DoD Standard crap*, she thought. *Oh well—better than nothing. At least it has caffeine.* She poured a cup of the hot, black liquid and a glass of water, and walked over to the table where Katherine was already sitting. All the committee members were now seated as well: Senator Wilkes in the center chair, with Chief of Staff Warner, Senator Craig, and Representative Sayavong to her right, and Director de la Cruz, Secretary Hudson, and Representative Bridgewater to her left.

"Let this hearing of the Prometheus Oversight Committee come to order," Wilkes announced as she tapped her gavel on its sound block. "I'll remind everyone that these proceedings are classified Top Secret." She looked at Katherine and Lai. "We welcome two senior team members from that project: Project Director Katherine Etter, and Chief Scientist Lai Shen. Dr. Etter and Dr. Shen, thank you for being here today," the senator said cordially. She looked to Lai to be in her late 50s, with sharp features, dark gray eyes, and black hair with silver highlights.

"We're glad to be here, Senator Wilkes," Katherine said, relieved that Irene seemed to be in a good mood. "We're grateful for this opportunity to talk in person with the committee about my request to expedite the replacement of the two ships that have, unfortunately, been lost."

Wilkes's cordial expression changed to a puzzled frown. "Dr. Etter, I believe there's been a misunderstanding." Katherine felt her neck tighten as the senator continued, "The purpose of this hearing is to make a final decision as to whether the Prometheus Project should be terminated."

What the fuck! Lai was shocked. She shot a glance at Katherine and saw that she looked surprised also.

"Senator, I—that was *not* what I was told when I agreed to attend this meeting!" Katherine protested. Lai noticed that Katherine appeared uncharacteristically flustered—and mad as hell. And she *was* mad as hell—for being deceived by de la Cruz. He'd deliberately kept the true purpose of the meeting from her. *And I walked right into Irene's ambush!* Katherine was angry at herself as much as at de la Cruz. *I should have known better than to trust him, and Irene!*

"Dr. Etter, this misunderstanding is unfortunate," Wilkes replied evenly. "But, surely you're not surprised that the committee would consider terminating the project, based on its disappointing record to date."

Before Katherine could respond, Secretary Hudson, a balding, heavy-set man in his 60s, spoke up. "Dr. Etter, the committee is extremely concerned about the lack of *any* success on Prometheus over the past three years. Instead, there's been only failed missions, destroyed or wrecked spacecraft, and a seriously injured scientist," Hudson said, looking at Lai during his last point.

Then Chief of Staff Warner, a middle-aged woman with short gray hair, attired in her Air Force general's uniform, piled on. "Those failures have reduced what we already knew was a low probability of success to near zero," Warner added. "Expending another $2.8 billion after getting no return on the $11 billion spent on Prometheus to date doesn't seem like a justifiable strategy, given the many urgent priorities for national defense."

Katherine, exasperated, raised her right hand. "If I could respond, please, Senator Wilkes?"

"Go ahead," Wilkes replied.

"Thank you. Secretary Hudson, General Warner... I don't deny that the project has had setbacks. But please consider that we are literally going where no human being has gone before—into deep space, one billion miles from Earth, to the only known stable wormhole in the galaxy, and ultimately to the future. Some setbacks must be expected with a project as ground-breaking as Prometheus. But with each setback, my team has quickly identified and corrected the problem, including the issue with the last flight. Dr. Shen can explain—"

"Yes, Dr. Etter," Wilkes interrupted, her voice sharp and cold. "It *is* your team. A team you selected, for a project on which you are the director. Thus the responsibility for its failures is *yours*. *You* are responsible for the two disastrous missions, for the loss of two nearly irreplaceable spaceships... and *you* are responsible for almost killing the project's chief scientist."

I've heard just about enough! Lai was outraged, and she spoke up before Katherine could respond to Wilkes. "Senator, I *volunteered* to go on the mission to the wormhole without a rescue ship. Dr. Etter tried to talk me out of it. It wasn't her fault!"

"Dr. Etter was ultimately responsible for the decision that almost cost you your life, Dr. Shen," Wilkes retorted. She paused. "But, we do need to examine *your* role in the project's failures." She turned her head in de la Cruz's direction. "Director?"

"Ah, yes, Senator," de la Cruz replied as he glanced at a holopad in front of him on the table, then looked up at Lai. "Dr. Shen, what was the cause of the explosion that destroyed *Chronos 1*?"

"Well, Director, as I've reported to the committee, there was a manufacturing flaw in the Quantum Drive activation circuits. That flaw caused a short-circuit, and an explosion, when the ship's Quantum Drive was activated for Trans-Martian Injection."

"I see. Why was the flaw not discovered during pre-flight inspections of the spacecraft?"

Lai felt a bead of sweat starting to run down her back. "Well, Director, it was, uh, an extremely tiny defect, microscopic in fact. Until the circuit failure in *Chronos 1*, we didn't know what to look for, and where."

"I see. And, who was responsible for inspecting the spacecraft?"

"That's the responsibility of Chief Engineer Meira Friedman, but she's advised by the Science team." Katherine grimaced inwardly, *I wish you hadn't added that last part, Lai.*

"And, Dr. Shen... who is responsible for the Science team, and overall technical direction of the project?"

Katherine didn't like where this line of questioning was headed; she turned toward Lai and whispered in warning, *"Lai!"* But it was too late.

"The chief scientist," Lai said quietly.

"And you are currently the project's chief scientist, are you not?"

"Yes, sir," Lai whispered.

"Dr. Shen, please speak up for the benefit of the committee," Wilkes demanded.

Lai cleared her throat. "I am the chief scientist for Prometheus," she said loudly.

"I see," de la Cruz continued. "And, regarding the failure of the *Chronos 2* mission—that was caused by an incorrect wormhole insertion formula, was it not?"

"Yes, Director, but—" Lai began to explain.

"And who developed that formula, Dr. Shen?"

Lai saw that trying to explain what happened to *Chronos 2* would probably be pointless. *But it's better that they focus the blame on me instead of Katherine.* "I did, Director."

"And therefore, Dr. Shen, *you* were responsible for the failure of both missions and the destruction of—"

Now Katherine had heard more than enough. *This isn't a hearing—it's an inquisition!* "Director, there's a logical explanation as to why the insertion formula was inaccurate, due to something Dr. Shen could not have anticipated. It was *not* her fault that—"

"Dr. Etter," Wilkes cut Katherine off, "Dr. Shen has accepted responsibility for her errors, and the impact of those mistakes on the project." She paused. "But now, let's talk more about *your* mistakes on the project." *Oh shit!* Lai thought as she glanced at Katherine, who looked even more pale than usual. "And I believe your biggest mistake was bringing Dr. Shen onto the project as chief scientist."

"Senator, respectfully, I believe that Dr. Shen was the best candidate available for that role, and she has served the project and her country admirably!"

Wilkes glared at Katherine, then at Lai, with contempt. "We have already discussed Dr. Shen's work on Prometheus and her contribution to its failures to date." She leaned forward as her eyes bored into Katherine's. "Now let's focus on how Dr. Shen was even in a position to cause those failures." Wilkes glanced quickly at the holopad in front of her. "You hired Dr. Shen against the strong recommendation of the FBI and Director de la Cruz. Is that correct, Dr. Etter?"

"Yes, Senator, but the director—"

"And you did so knowing *why* the FBI made its recommendation, isn't that true?" Katherine started to respond, but Wilkes talked over her as she glanced at her holopad. "Charged with 32 federal felony counts, including attempted murder, from a terrorist bombing at Stanford University; imprisoned at the Federal Correctional Institution at Dublin, California; and close association with suspected CCP agents, namely, her father and—"

"*Leave my parents out of this!*" Lai exploded as she shot out of her chair and added in her thoughts, *You fucking bitch!*

Katherine grabbed Lai's forearm and warned, quietly but firmly, "*Lai, sit down!*" But Lai wasn't in any mood to sit down, or be silent.

"You are out of order!" Wilkes shouted at Lai, rapping her gavel once.

"I haven't *begun* to be out of order, Senator!" Lai shot back, as Katherine again pleaded for her to sit down. "Katherine Etter is the *best* project director—*the best damn leader, period*—I've ever known! I don't know where Prometheus would be today if it weren't for her!"

She felt slightly dizzy and paused to steady herself, giving Wilkes an opening.

"Miss Shen, you will *sit down* and *be quiet* or I'll be forced to have you removed!" Wilkes shouted, her face reddening.

But Lai continued. "And as for me—I made a mistake when I was 19 years old. I paid for that mistake—yes, I did spend 60 days in prison. But I love my country, and my parents loved their adopted country! And I don't need to hear any more *lies* about their being agents, about their being disloyal in *any fucking way!*"

Wilkes rapped her gavel three more times. "*That will be all*, Miss Shen!" She tapped a button on her pad. "Sergeant at Arms, we need you in the room, right away!"

After a moment, Officer Kabila entered the room. "Yes, Senator?"

Wilkes motioned with her right hand toward Lai, who was still standing, breathing hard. "Escort Miss Shen from the room and keep her under guard until this hearing is finished."

"Yes, Senator." Lai wondered, *Is she going to cuff me?* But the officer merely opened the door for Lai and said, "After you."

As Lai went through the door into the hallway, she muttered in Wilkes's direction, "And it's *Doctor* Shen, you bitch."

Outside the room, Officer Kabila motioned to a padded bench on the opposite side of the hallway. "How about you have a seat over there, okay?"

"Fine!" Lai replied curtly. She sank onto the bench and buried her head in her hands. *What've I and my big mouth done now? There's no way they won't terminate the project after that tirade! When will I learn to shut the fuck up?* Then she looked up and noticed Officer Kabila staring at her. "*What?!*"

"Senator Wilkes can be a real bitch sometimes, huh, Dr. Shen." Her voice was filled with empathy, and kindness.

"Yeah," Lai managed a thin smile and nodded, "you've got that right, Officer."

Lai pulled her phone out of her purse and turned it on. She saw a message from Kapono: *How's it going?* She decided to not respond then; it would only be negative, and Katherine *was* very persuasive. *So, who knows, maybe...*

An hour passed while Lai worried and fidgeted with her phone. She was about to ask Officer Kabila about visiting the ladies' room when Katherine burst out of the conference room. Lai shot off the bench and went up to Katherine. "*What happened?*" She looked at Officer Kabila, who smiled and tilted her head down the hallway in a *get outta here* gesture.

"Let's find someplace to talk," Katherine told Lai as she started walking quickly down the hallway. Lai followed her, until they came to an empty auxiliary conference room. After they entered the room, Katherine pressed the *Occupied* button and locked the door, then sat down across from Lai at the dark wood conference table.

"I was able to convince the committee to allow the project to continue," Katherine began.

"Oh my god, it's—that's fantastic!" Lai exclaimed, overcome with joy and relief. "You did it, Katherine! *How?*"

"I got Sayavong, Craig, Bridgewater, and, to my surprise, Hudson, to see that the project is important enough to the United States, and the rest of the world, to keep it alive for now. That was enough to overrule Warner, de la Cruz, and... Wilkes." Katherine said the last name almost as an epithet. "But, hold on—it's not all fantastic." Katherine didn't look happy, and Lai slumped in her chair.

"What do you mean?"

"The project can keep going, but only to continue our research and ensure we don't lose the team we spent three years building."

"What about the replacement ships?" Lai asked, fearing the worst.

"We probably won't get them before late '55 or early '56, if then. And," Katherine added, frowning, "there's a condition."

"What is it?"

Katherine looked directly at Lai. "I need to get a new chief scientist."

Lai was devastated—but not surprised. "I—I understand, Katherine. It was all my fault, in there. I just don't know when—"

"No," Katherine interrupted, clearly upset—as upset as Lai had ever seen her. "You *don't* know when to shut up, Lai! You're a great scientist and wonderful person, but you've *got* to learn which battles you can win and which you can't win!"

"Yeah, I know. I'm sorry, Katherine. I let you down… I let everyone down."

"Hey," Katherine put her hand on top of Lai's. "It's all right. They were going to shoot you anyway. You just made it a little easier for them."

"Yeah, I suppose you're right." She composed herself. "Thanks. So, who's the new chief scientist? Kapono, right?"

"Oh, yes, of course. He won't like *how* he got the job again, but he'll understand. And he'll be glad you're there to help him."

Lai's head jerked up. "*What?* I'm still on the project?" she exclaimed, incredulous.

"The committee demanded that I get a new chief scientist. They didn't say anything about what I have to do with the *current* chief scientist," Katherine said with a sly smile.

Lai laughed harder than she had in a long time. "Wilkes will be really pissed!"

"I'm sure she will be—serves her right, the *bitch*." They gave each other a fist bump. "Oh, Lai, one more thing…"

"Yes?"

"Thank you for sticking up for me in there. I can't say it was the best time and place to say what you did, how you did, but it took guts, and I appreciate it." She paused. "And I appreciate *you*. I have your back. Never forget it."

"Thanks, boss. I *will* try to watch my mouth in the future. I promise!"

"Okay, good." Katherine straightened up in her chair. "Now we need to get those new ships."

Lai was confused. "I thought you said the committee didn't budge on that—it might be a year or two, or more?"

"That's right. But I have an idea how we might be able to get them a *lot* sooner."

Lai smiled. "What're you going to do—*steal* a couple of spaceships?"

"Not quite." Katherine got up from the table, pressed the *Unoccupied* button on the wall, and unlocked the door. "After we pick up our bags at the hotel, I want you to head back to Kansas on our scheduled flight tonight. I need to go to Dulles to catch a different flight. I'll call Kapono in a bit to update him." She opened the door as Lai followed her out of the conference room.

"Where are you headed... if you don't mind my asking?"

"Nice."

| 16 |

June 21, 2054

The rental car turned off Avenue Jean Lorrain onto the driveway for the hillside villa in Cap de Nice and pulled up beside a security kiosk that guarded an imposing black metal gate.

"Open driver's window," Katherine said as a male voice came from a speaker in the kiosk.

"Bonjour, comment puis-je vous aider?"

"En anglaise, s'il vous plait," Katherine replied to the AI security guard.

"Good day, how may I help you?"

"Good day, this is Katherine Etter. I have an appointment."

"Yes, Dr. Etter. Your voice print is verified. How long will you be visiting today?"

"I estimate an hour or so." *I'm pretty sure this will be a short meeting.*

"In that case, please park your car on the driveway by the front entrance. The house manager will meet you at the door."

"Thank you," Katherine replied as the heavy gate silently slid open. She navigated the Peugeot around the circular driveway and parked as she'd been instructed. As she walked up the flagstone path leading to the front door, she enjoyed the bright sunshine of a delightfully mild summer day in Nice. She was glad she'd chosen to dress lightly in a white cotton blouse and rosemary green linen skirt.

Katherine took in the xeriscaped grounds, then the villa's exterior. *This suits him.* Although small for a villa, its architecture was striking—rectangular shapes of white marble and dark gray stone, large expanses of glass, and inside, visible through the floor-to-ceiling windows, accents of light and dark wood and burnished metal. Aesthetically both modern and warm, and not ostentatious.

Katherine rang the doorbell. In a few moments, a slim, tanned, middle-aged man dressed in a gray polo shirt and black slacks opened the door and smiled. "Bonjour, Dr. Etter! I'm Henri. Please come in, he's expecting you," Henri said with a thick French accent as he opened the glass and metal door for Katherine.

"Bonjour, Henri—thank you." She stepped onto the marble floor of the foyer and looked around at the sparsely but tastefully furnished first floor. Then her gaze froze as she caught sight of the panoramic vista of the Mediterranean Sea through the wall of huge windows in the back of the villa. "Oh my! What a breathtaking view!"

Henri smiled, "Marvelous, isn't it? One never tires of it. But, please, come this way. He's on the patio, taking advantage of this glorious day." Henri led Katherine toward the large patio that stretched across the entire back of the villa, overlooking the sea. Several cushioned wood sofas and lounges dotted the patio. He approached a gray-haired man who was sitting on one of the sofas, facing the ocean. "Sir, Dr. Etter is here."

The man looked up, "Excellent. Merci, Henri."

Henri turned to Katherine. "Would you like something to drink? Iced tea, perhaps?"

"Iced tea sounds perfect, thank you, Henri." Henri headed for the wet bar as the man turned his head toward Katherine.

"Katherine, bonjour! Come and sit with me. It's been a long time." Katherine stepped around the sofa toward a loveseat next to the sofa as she remembered the distinctive accent: a blend of French, Jamaican, and American English.

"Bonjour, Arnaud. Yes, it has been a long time. It's good to see you again." Katherine had first met Arnaud Houde at an astroscience conference in Austin nearly 12 years ago, when she was a project director for Boeing Launch Services and he was still CEO and chief technology officer for InfiniTrek, the aerospace giant he'd founded nearly 50 years earlier. She'd been introduced to him at the opening reception, and they'd ended up talking for over an hour. She'd been aware of Houde's reputation as an exceptional, if somewhat eccentric, inventor and businessman, and of the many controversies that had swirled around him during his career due to his take-no-prisoners approach to business and life in general. For that hour, however, she decided to set those controversies aside and noticed his intelligence, his sense of humor, and his infectious smile and laugh. They'd stayed in contact with each other over the years, including some dialogue a few years earlier when NASA had awarded InfiniTrek the contract for the two Voyageur IV craft for Prometheus. InfiniTrek, and Houde, hadn't been told *how* the ships would be used—that was Top Secret. And thus, she needed to be careful during her visit with Houde.

"Forgive me for not getting up. My knees aren't what they used to be," Houde said with an apologetic expression. He was wearing a black polo shirt, casual black slacks, and sandals.

"No worries," Katherine replied with a slight wave of her right hand as she sat down on the loveseat a few feet from Houde. "Arnaud, your home is amazing!" She looked out at the deep blue Mediterranean and the surrounding hills. "And this view—it's gorgeous!" She noticed Houde's smile. *That's the smile I remember from 12 years ago.*

"Not hard to take, is it? When I decided a few years ago to return to France for my retirement, I thought first about returning to where it all started for me—Paris. Wonderful city. But," he said as he gazed at the afternoon sun glinting on the waves, "it has nothing like this." Houde had moved from Paris to Jamaica in his early 20s, then relocated to the United States ten years later to found InfiniTrek with his immense family fortune.

Henri returned with Katherine's iced tea and set the tall, frosted glass tumbler on the coffee table in front of her. "Thank you, Henri," Katherine told him. He nodded once and went back inside the villa.

Houde looked at Katherine, curiosity evident on his face. "So… what brings you all the way to Nice on this beautiful Sunday afternoon? I don't expect it was only to see how I'm doing in retirement and enjoy this view—wonderful though it is."

Katherine laughed. "Well, first, thank you for seeing me on a weekend; I appreciate it. Actually, I *am* interested in how you're liking retirement." She knew that Houde wasn't completely retired—he was still chairman of InfiniTrek and maintained an active interest in some of the other companies he'd founded. But she'd heard rumors that his health had deteriorated. She thought that might be behind his stepping back from almost all responsibilities in his many business ventures. "But, as you've surmised, there *is* another reason for my visit." She sat forward on the loveseat cushion and looked directly at Houde. "Arnaud, I need a favor. A big one."

Houde laughed. "Aha! I knew it wasn't just the view. Before we get to the favor, let me answer your first question." He paused and looked out toward the ocean. "Retirement has its pluses, and minuses. You know I've never been one to shirk hard work and long hours, and I've expected the same from those in my employ." Katherine nodded. "But over the last few years, it's become increasingly difficult for me to keep up that pace. You know, next month I'll be 84." He looked at Katherine. "I miss the work. I miss the excitement of invention, of breaking new ground, of taking risks." He paused and looked out again over the sparking water. "But, if it is time to slow down—shift out of hyperspeed, if you will—this isn't a bad place to do it."

"I understand."

"C'est bon. Now, about that 'big favor'... you've piqued my curiosity. I'm hoping the favor involves breaking some new ground and taking some risks." Houde smiled, and Katherine returned his smile.

"Well, in fact, it does, Arnaud." *Here we go—rolling for all the marbles...* "You know about the project for which I'm the director, and for which NASA procured two Voyageur IVs a few years ago."

"Of course. I trust you put them to good use?"

"Oh yes, we did. We were *this* close to success," Katherine said as she held up her right hand with its thumb and forefinger a quarter-inch apart. "And that involved breaking a *lot* of new ground, while taking some big risks. But, unfortunately, one ship exploded during a test flight—"

"No one was on board, I hope?"

"No, it was a non-piloted flight."

"That's fortunate. You know, InfiniTrek has had some of those, shall we say, learning experiences," Houde said with a wink. Although Katherine was only in her 20s then, she remembered the less-than-successful launch attempts of some of the first Voyageur spacecraft in the early 2030s. "What about the other ship?"

"That ship *almost* achieved our mission objective, but we had to abort at the last minute, and the ship was damaged beyond repair upon landing."

"Hmm," Houde looked thoughtful, and a bit suspicious. "That must have been quite a ride, to disable it enough that it couldn't land safely. We built considerable redundancies into Voyageur IV."

"It was," Katherine replied as she thought about how Lai was nearly killed. "But, as I said, there's a great deal of risk involved in our project."

Houde stared at Katherine, and his expression reminded her of the old line, *I know who you are, and I saw what you did!* "Yes, there certainly is," he said. "Exploring wormholes isn't for the faint of heart." Katherine's eyes widened slightly; she couldn't quite hide her shock. *How the hell does he know that? Those details are Top Secret! Was there a leak?*

"You're wondering how I know that, yes?" Katherine sat motionless, forcing herself to not react any further. "First, let me ease any concern about a security leak. There was no leak—at least, none that I know of. But, as you told me when we first met 12 years ago, I'm 'a bright fellow'," Houde smiled. "I know how to put two and two together, at least."

"What do you mean?"

Houde looked straight ahead, expressionless and motionless, for about 10 seconds. It seemed like an eternity to Katherine. Then he turned his head to look at her. "The two Voyageurs were ordered about one year after the Wagamese Wormhole was discovered. And almost all research on that wormhole is classified Top Secret—as is the Prometheus Project. Then, there's the matter of how the ships were spec'd: Quantum Drive, which is still experimental—*officially*, anyway; a deflector laser array; additional maneuvering thrusters; and, most interesting, a custom high-G command couch." He looked directly into Katherine's eyes. "Normal G forces for a Voyageur IV, even with Quantum Drive, are well under 10. The ship's standard seats can easily handle that. But I've read that the G force for traversing a wormhole can be 20 or more. Thus, I must conclude you're attempting to send someone into that wormhole. And you need another ship to finish the job."

Katherine cleared her throat. "Arnaud, you know I can't confirm or deny any of that. But I do need another ship to complete our mission. Actually, I need *two* ships."

"Oh, of course—the backup/rescue ship. But, from what you told me, the piloted mission had no backup ship, correct?"

"That's right. But some risks are unacceptable." *It should have been unacceptable to me the first time! I'll never risk someone's life like that again.*

"I understand. All right, then… two Voyageur IVs." Houde looked puzzled. "Why doesn't NASA procure them for you, as they did before?"

"They have… other budget priorities. The project can't get replacement ships through NASA for at least a year, maybe two." Katherine looked directly at Houde. "And that may be too late."

"Yes… you have no idea how long that wormhole will be around, do you?" Houde said with a sly expression. Katherine said nothing, and tried to not reveal anything with her face. Houde sighed. "Katherine, you're asking a very big favor."

"You're one of the wealthiest men on Earth, Arnaud! I know these ships aren't cheap, but surely—"

"It isn't a question of money. Well, not *completely* a question of money. These spaceships don't grow on trees."

"InfiniTrek doesn't have two Voyageur IVs available now, or in the near future?"

"I'd have to confirm inventory, but I expect any completed or nearly completed ships have already been spoken for." Then Houde's face brightened. "However, I know there's a couple of Voyageur IIIs that could be made available fairly quickly. Would those suffice?"

"I appreciate the thought, but we need the IVs. We've done all our development, testing, and missions with those ships. To start over now with Voyageur IIIs would cause an unacceptable delay." All that was true, but Katherine didn't want to tell Houde the main reason they had to have the Voyageur IVs: they were much more compact than prior Voyageurs, and thus they fit into the Atlas missile silos at the Prometheus base; the earlier Voyageur designs would not.

"Katherine, I'm sorry. I don't think I'll be able to grant you that favor," Houde said sadly. "If there were more time, it might be possible."

But Katherine wasn't going to give up—the stakes were too high for that. "Arnaud," she said quietly, leaning forward, "you share my view that positively influencing our long-term future is a key moral priority, is that right?"

"Yes, absolutely. I remember we discussed that when we first met."

Katherine sat up straight in the loveseat. "You know I can't give you any details about Prometheus. But, I will tell you this: if we are successful, we *will* positively influence humanity's future... in ways that you might not be able to imagine."

Houde sat silently for a few seconds, then he smiled. "The wormhole is a gateway to the future, isn't it? And, it's bi-directional!" He paused. "That's why you're doing this—to find out if and how the human race survives the ravages of climate change, the threat from AI, and so on, and bring that knowledge back to the present." Katherine struggled to maintain a poker face, but she was pretty sure she wasn't entirely successful.

"*That* is definitely breaking new ground, Katherine. And I can imagine the extreme risks to those involved." His face set in determination. "I'm not sure how, yet, but I *will* get you those two ships, as quickly as I can."

Katherine was overcome with gratitude and relief. She wanted to jump up and hug the elderly man, but thought better of it. Instead, she reached out and held Houde's left hand, which was resting on the sofa's armrest. "Arnaud, I don't know how to thank you! It's so generous of you."

"You're welcome, Katherine. But, you know, I pledged many years ago to give at least half my wealth to worthy causes." He looked at her. "I'm considerably behind on that pledge. This seems like a worthy enough cause to allow me to catch up a bit."

"Well, I'm overwhelmed." Katherine didn't want to spoil the moment, but she felt she needed to cover some important details. "How soon do you think they can be shipped?"

"Detail-oriented! I like that. The answer is, I'm not sure yet. I need to talk with the Voyageur Factory Manager in Louisiana. I may need to request some unnatural acts to get Prometheus to the front of the line." Houde winked. "I may be nearly retired, but I still have some influence. I'll have her contact you. You can provide her with any details she needs, such as the dimensions for the custom-fitted command chair."

"Excellent. Thank you again, Arnaud. This means everything to the project... and perhaps far beyond it."

"What's a few billion dollars, eh?" Houde chuckled. Then he grew serious. "Katherine, I do have a condition for my granting this favor."

Katherine felt a sudden burning in the pit of her stomach. *Oh crap, not more conditions!* "What, um, what is the condition?"

"Don't fret, it isn't extreme. If there's anything usable left of the two ships when you're finished with them, I'd like them returned to InfiniTrek."

The burning in Katherine's stomach subsided. "Well, of course. That's reasonable."

"Then it is done." Houde bent his head to speak into his watch. "Henri, could you please bring out the Dom Pérignon Brut '34." He looked up at Katherine and flashed a broad smile. "We must celebrate."

After a few minutes, Henri stepped onto the patio carrying a champagne bucket, stand, and two crystal flutes. He set the bucket and stand between Katherine and Houde, expertly opened the Dom Pérignon, and poured the pale effervescent liquid into the flutes.

"Merci beaucoup, Henri," Houde said. Henri nodded and returned to the villa. Houde lifted one of the flutes, and Katherine followed his lead. "To breaking new ground... and to the future. May it be worthy of our hopes, and our dreams."

"I'll drink to that," Katherine replied with a smile as she touched her glass to Houde's.

| 17 |

October 5, 2054

Lai stretched her arms over her head in an attempt to relieve her aching back, banged her fingers on a conduit, swore, and started rubbing her tight neck instead. She and Kapono had been sitting in the cockpit of *Chronos 3*, one of the two new Voyageur IVs delivered by InfiniTrek in August, since early that morning, preparing for Kapono's flight only two weeks away. It was late afternoon, and the weeks of 18-hour days they'd worked to get the ships and Kapono ready were taking their toll, mentally and physically. To complicate matters, the new Voyageurs had several updates compared to the earlier ships, including redesigned avionics and control panels. That meant re-programming Aileen and getting Kapono up to speed on the new controls. There was one big plus with the upgrades: a new AI-based Flight Simulator mode, which allowed fairly realistic practice missions without a separate Voyageur Flight Simulator—which the project couldn't afford.

Lai stifled a yawn and looked at the checklist on her holopad. "Let's run through the Manual Override simulation one more time, okay?" They'd already run that simulation three times that day. In that scenario, Aileen was offline due to failure of the primary *and* backup guidance computers, thus the ship would need to be flown manually. It was the most difficult task Kapono might face during his mission, although the odds he'd need to do it while in space were minuscule.

Lai remembered how difficult that scenario had been for her when she'd trained for her flight without benefit of the simulator.

"Oh joy," Kapono replied sarcastically. He fluttered his gloved fingers, as if limbering them up. "Ready when you are, Number One!" Lai had no idea why he called her Number One when they were working in the ship, but he seemed to enjoy saying it, so she rolled her eyes and plunged ahead.

"Primary and backup guidance computer failure... *now!*" Lai called out as she touched the appropriate button on the simulator control screen. Suddenly the simulated star field projected onto the forward windows, with the black hole that fronted the Wagamese Wormhole in the center, started yawing to the left. Kapono nudged the joystick that controlled motion within the x-y plane and the large thumbwheel that adjusted vertical movements, along the z-axis. Gradually the black hole shifted back to the center of the simulated star field.

"Good... good!" Lai encouraged him. He was doing much better than in his earlier attempts.

"'The Force is strong with this one!'" Kapono joked. *Doesn't he know any movies from this century?* Lai wondered, amused at Kapono's interest in ancient science-fiction movies and shows. But she didn't mind—after all, he was tolerant of her fondness for Shakespeare.

Then Lai noticed a slight yaw to the right. "K, watch the starboard yaw," she cautioned.

"See it," Kapono replied as he worked the controls. Now the simulated star field swung back to the left, until the black hole was almost out of view. "Oops—over-corrected. C'mon, you sleek Greek time machine!" Kapono said as he fought to get back on course.

"Watch the distance," Lai cautioned as she pointed to the proximity readout on the control panel.

"Thanks," Kapono replied. "Reversing Quantum Drive... now!" He tapped a button on the console in front of him and continued coaxing the joystick and thumbwheel to stay on course for the event horizon.

"Looking good!" Lai exclaimed. *This is his best run of this simulation yet—he's gotten further than ever before.*

"Thirty seconds to event horizon," Kapono announced. "Shutting down the Quantum Drive and switching to maneuvering thrusters." He punched the appropriate buttons on the console and continued working the manual steering controls as the simulated black hole appeared to loom closer and closer. "15,000 kilometers to event horizon!"

Suddenly the image projected onto the forward windows by the simulator showed that they were drifting away from the center of the black hole. Kapono tried several course corrections, but the drift worsened. Then the master alarm sounded and bathed Lai and Kapono in its flashing red light. *This feels like déjà vu all over again*, Lai thought glumly.

"I don't know what's wrong!" Kapono exclaimed. Lai checked the simulator's G force readout and saw it pass 10... then 15... then 20. She knew that if this weren't a simulation, Kapono would probably be unconscious now. Then the master alarm shut off and the simulated view of space disappeared, replaced by large red text: SIMULATION TERMINATED DUE TO MISSION FAILURE. Kapono slumped back in the command couch.

"Huh. I wonder what happened," he muttered dejectedly. "I thought I was on course based on the approach vector displayed on the console. I just don't—"

"*That's it!*" Lai exclaimed as she jolted upright in the co-pilot's seat and looked at Kapono. "The approach vector! You were using the vector that was computed right before the guidance computers went offline!"

"Of course!" Kapono said excitedly. "The vector has to be updated *in real time* to match the continuous shrinkage of the wormhole. The vector I used was a few minutes out of date." He shook his head. "Wow. It doesn't take much to throw off the insertion angle, does it?"

"No shit," Lai replied. "Well, there's got to be some way around that." Her brow furrowed in thought as she rested her chin on her right hand. "Hmm... what about... no, that won't work..."

"I have an idea," Kapono interjected. "Why don't we pick this up tomorrow morning? I don't know about you, but I'm beat. I think we'll have better success finding a solution after a good night's sleep."

"Yeah, you're right—I'm wiped, too," Lai replied wearily. "My back hurts... my *brain* hurts."

"Mine, too," Kapono agreed. He looked at Lai. "You know, I think it would do us good to get away from this for a while—take a little break."

Where are we going to find someplace out here in the middle of nowhere to take a break? Lai wondered. The base had a tiny gym with a treadmill, stationary bike, and some free weights, but that was it for recreation. "What do you have in mind?"

"Well," Kapono began with a far-away look on his face, "if we were in Maui, I'd suggest we head to Kaanapali Beach and go surfing. I'm biased, of course, but I think it's one of the most beautiful beaches in the world. And it's a great beach for novice surfers—or have you surfed a lot?" Kapono could tell from Lai's expression that she hadn't.

"No, not a lot of surfing. *No* surfing, in fact. But, I could enjoy the beach and watch you ride those bitchin' waves, bro."

Kapono grinned. "Hey, you know the lingo!"

"I know *some*," Lai confessed. "I've lived in California most of my life. I picked up some surfer-talk through osmosis. But... not many good surfing beaches in Kansas, huh?"

"No," Kapono agreed. Then he looked as if an idea light bulb had flicked on in his brain. "But, there might be something else..." He pulled out his phone and started tapping on it. "Yessss... that's it!" he said triumphantly as he slipped the phone back into his shirt pocket. "Let's go!"

"Go *where*?" Lai asked cautiously.

"It's a surprise," Kapono said with a sly smile. "Do you trust me?"

"Of course. But there'd better not be any surfing or horseback riding, or other such shit involved."

"No 'such shit,' I promise. This'll be fun!"

"We'll see," Lai replied with mock concern. She started climbing out of the co-pilot's chair, and Kapono noticed the Prometheus badge on the right shoulder of her uniform.

"You'd better change," Kapono said as he nodded toward her right shoulder.

"Casual or formal?" Lai joked.

"*Very* casual. I'll meet you at the elevator in, say, 15 minutes?"

Kapono was waiting by the elevator door as Lai hurried down the corridor toward him. She was wearing a black tank top, heather gray athletic shorts, and white jogging shoes. He did a double-take; he'd never seen her in anything other than business attire or her uniform.

"Hey, you said '*very* casual'!" Lai retorted as she noticed his expression. "I didn't bring many casual clothes with me."

"I did say that. You're perfect."

They rode up the elevator and stepped out of the small building into the fading late afternoon sunlight. It was cool for early October in Kansas—32 Celsius/90 Fahrenheit according to the weather app on Lai's phone. They made their way to a three-door garage that was partially concealed by a berm, about 100 feet from the elevator building. Kapono said into his phone, "Open my garage door," and the door on the left started to roll up. Lai knew the middle garage stall was for Katherine's car, from when she took Lai to the airport for their trip to Washington.

"What's the stall on the right for?" Lai asked.

"The ambulance," Kapono replied matter-of-factly. "I'm sure glad we had that when you returned from your mission."

Lai swallowed. "Me, too." Lai had learned that if they hadn't gotten her to the University of Kansas Hospital and its renowned trauma unit so quickly, she probably would have died. She saw the rear of Kapono's dusty hatchback as the garage door opened fully. "A *Prius?*" she exclaimed with surprise, and some derision. "It must be 20 years old!"

Kapono grinned as he grabbed a brush from its hook on the garage wall to clear the thick layer of dust from the rear window. "Twenty-six! Bought it in Lawrence when I joined the project. I figured a plug-in hybrid would be best—not many charging stations out here."

"How did you manage to get a garage?"

"That's one of the few perks of being chief scientist. Back when you had that role, I saw you weren't using the garage, so I just kept using it." He put the brush back on its hook. "You *did* know about the garage, right?"

"Uh, sure, yeah." Lai recalled that Katherine's assistant had told her about the garage space. She didn't care; she didn't think she'd need a car.

They climbed into the car and started off down the gravel access road, then after a few miles turned right onto US Highway 56. They drove through the remnants of Worden and kept going past the interchange with US 59, which headed north toward Lawrence. Lai had never been down this stretch of highway before. "So, you're not going to tell me where we're going?"

"Nope. But we'll be there soon."

After a few minutes, Lai saw a sign announcing they'd entered Baldwin City. She didn't see much of anything yet, except for a few buildings that appeared to be deserted. Then she noticed a stately Victorian house on her right, with a huge front porch and a sign saying "Three Sisters Inn" out front. But the sign was weathered, the windows boarded up. *Darn... it'd be nice to spend a night someplace other than the base... or a hospital.*

After a couple of minutes, Kapono turned left into the parking lot of a small, one-story building with a neon sign on the front: *Lar at Lan s*. Lai figured out that it had said *Lariat Lanes* at one time.

"*Bowling?* You have *got* to be kidding!"

Kapono grinned. "It's not a beach, but it'll take our minds off work for a while." He parked the car and then noticed a beat-up pickup truck parked by the front door. "Would you look at *that!*" he nearly shouted. "An F-150! It must be at least 30 years old—maybe 40!" It had a couple of tattered political stickers on what was left of its rear bumper and a "My Son Is In the Navy" sticker in the back window.

Lai shrugged. "What's the big deal? I see those on the road all the time."

"Not *gas* powered!" Kapono replied. "I haven't seen one of those in years!"

"I can leave you two alone, if you want," Lai teased. Kapono laughed, and they hopped out of the car and went into the bowling alley.

The small bowling alley, like the town, appeared to have seen better days. The carpet looked dirty and worn-through in spots, the paint on the walls was dingy, and some of the overhead lights were out. But Kapono saw that the 12 lanes gleamed. That was a good sign that someone there respected the game.

Lai noticed the place had a peculiar scent that she couldn't identify. "What do you suppose that smell is?" she asked, wrinkling her nose.

"All bowling alleys smell pretty much like this," he replied, smiling as he looked around the place. "It's a combination of the oil they use on the lanes, disinfectants, old shoes, stale cooking grease, and beer. Just think… a long time ago, when smoking cigarettes indoors was allowed, places like this would reek of stale smoke, too." Lai made a *yuk* face, feeling grateful she'd never had to live in those times.

The place was quiet; no one was bowling. In fact, it looked empty except for an older man who was sitting on a stool at a counter overlooking the lanes. There were a couple of beer bottles in front of him on the counter. He was wearing work boots, blue jeans, a faded denim jacket, and a dark blue baseball-style cap with "US NAVY VETERAN" in gold lettering on the front. Then Kapono noticed another man sitting behind a tall counter to their right. *Must be the manager.* He led Lai over to the counter. The elderly man had a bald pate fringed with thin gray hair. He wore rimless glasses and a medium-blue Oxford shirt with "Brunswick" and a small crown embroidered on the left chest pocket.

"Good afternoon, sir," Kapono said to the man. "We'd like to bowl, please." The man lifted his head and peered over his glasses at Kapono and Lai.

"Two, right? How many games?"

Kapono looked at Lai. "I think two will be enough, huh?" Lai nodded as she thought, *More than enough!* "Two games," Kapono said to the man. "And we'll need shoes." The man studied them up and down, went to the rack behind him, pulled out two pairs of shoes, and set them on the counter along with a pair of white socks.

"You're an 11," he told Kapono, "and she needs a 6."

"I'm a 5-1/2," Lai corrected him.

The man glared at Lai over his glasses. "Trust me, young lady—you want a 6."

Kapono whispered in Lai's ear, "Go with it." She rolled her eyes and grabbed the shoes. "How much for the games and shoes?" Kapono asked the man.

"$5.50 a game and $7 each for the shoes, and $4 for the socks for you. Plus tax. Pay when you're done." The man put a sheet of marked paper and a wooden pencil stub on the counter in front of Kapono.

"Uh, what's this for?"

The man peered over his glasses at Kapono, "You don't want to keep score, chief?"

Kapono chuckled, "Oh, sure! It's just that I've never had to do it myself—computerized scoring, you know?"

"Yeah, we had that." The man looked out toward the dark screens hanging over the lanes, "Broke a few years ago. Costs too much to fix."

"Okay, no problem," Kapono said, smiling. "I can figure it out—I'm a rocket scientist!"

The man stared at Kapono, in his Hawaiian shirt, khaki shorts and flip-flops, for a couple of seconds. "Sure, chief. Lane 6."

As they walked away from the counter toward Lane 6, they passed the old man sitting on the stool. Kapono approached him and said, "Thank you for your service, sir." The man lifted his head, stared at Kapono, then glared at Lai, mumbled something, and looked off toward the lanes. *Okee-doke,* Kapono thought. Then he looked in the direction of the restaurant and said to Lai, "Let's get some beers!"

"I don't like beer that much, and besides, we're supposed to be on duty," Lai protested.

Kapono stopped and looked at her. "I don't think one beer will hurt the project. Besides, you've *got* to drink beer when you're bowling—it's tradition!"

Lai relented. "Okay—one."

They walked through the restaurant doorway and stepped up to the bar, where an attractive 50-something woman with short, curly, salt-and-pepper bobbed hair was on duty. Her embossed name tag said *Eleanor.* "Good afternoon," she greeted them with a Yorkshire accent. "How may I help you?" Lai was taken aback. *Oh my god, she sounds just like my Stellar and Galactic Astrophysics professor from Cambridge!*

"I'll have a Tsingtao, please," Lai replied—that was her father's favorite beer.

Eleanor stared at Lai. "My dear, we have Coors, Budweiser, and light variants of those," she said with a pursed smile and a voice that was pleasant but edged with irritation.

Yup, exactly like my professor at Cambridge. "Coors Light, I guess."

"Make it two, please," Kapono said.

Eleanor took two bottles out of a cooler, opened them with a bottle opener, set them on the counter, and tapped a few times on the register on the bar. "That will be $17.48, please."

Lai reached for her phone, but Kapono waved his hand. "My treat." He pulled out his phone, clicked on its payment app, added a tip, and completed the payment.

"Thank you so very much," Eleanor said. "I hope you enjoy the bowling."

"Mahalo," Kapono replied as he and Lai grabbed their beers off the bar and headed for Lane 6. When they arrived, they set their beers down, selected balls from the rack behind them, then sat down and put on their bowling shoes.

"Damn, he was right—I did need a 6!" Lai admitted as she laced the black and red shoes.

Kapono chuckled. "I'm pretty sure he holds a PhD in Bowling Science," he said as he finished lacing his shoes. "Okay, let's bowl! Would you like to go first?"

Lai shook her head. "Oh no, you don't. None of that *ladies first* crap."

Kapono laughed. "Okay, then—here goes nothing!" He picked up his ball, stood motionless as he lined up for the roll, then hurled his ball down the lane. It hooked from right to left and slammed into the gap between the 1 and 2 pins, sending all of them flying. "Yessss!" Kapono exclaimed as he pumped his right fist.

"Wow, you're good at this! No wonder you wanted to go bowling."

"Nah, that was lucky. I haven't bowled in years." Kapono sat down at the scorer's table and marked an X for himself on the score sheet with the pencil stub. "You're up!"

Lai smiled half-heartedly, lifted her ball out of the return, walked up to the foul line, set the ball down on the lane, and gave it a push toward the pins. It rolled slowly down the lane until it veered to the left and went into the gutter. She turned around to see Kapono doing his best to stifle a chuckle.

"You haven't bowled before, have you?"

"How did you guess?" Lai replied sarcastically, her hands on her hips.

"I'm sorry, I didn't know. Could I give you a few pointers?"

"I think I may be a lost cause, but... sure."

Kapono got up and stepped onto the lane. "Okay, grab your ball and come over here."

Lai retrieved her ball from the return, and Kapono stood beside and behind her. He showed her how to position her body and arms, how to approach the foul line, and how to swing her arm so that it delivered the ball smoothly onto the lane. She appreciated his patience and liked his attention, and the feel of his body against hers. *Bowling isn't so bad after all*, she decided.

"Okay, try it again," Kapono said as he pushed a button on the return to clear and reset the pins. "Brand new start! You've got this."

Lai positioned herself on the lane and did her best to mimic the approach and follow-through Kapono had shown her. This time, the ball landed near the second lane marker to the right, bounced once, and sped down the lane until it hit the right side of the pin set, knocking down seven of them. She felt as if she'd just won a gold medal in the Olympics. She jumped up with a *whoop!*, thrusting both arms into the air as she turned around to see Kapono cheering her accomplishment as he stepped forward to give her a high-five.

"Not bad, for a *Chink!*"

What the fuck! Lai swung around in the direction of the voice. It was the man on the stool whom they'd seen earlier. He was glaring at her with obvious contempt. She started walking toward him, face flaming, but Kapono took her gently by her left arm.

"Hey," he said quietly, "never mind him—he's drunk. Let's bowl."

She looked at Kapono; she really wanted to give the guy a piece of her mind—or something else. "Yeah, all right, okay." She walked back to the ball return, trying to calm herself down.

"Now pick up that spare!"

"Huh?"

"Try to knock down the other pins. Maybe move your drop point a bit to the left."

Lai grabbed her ball from the return and lined up for the roll. She started moving forward, then she heard the man on the stool shout, "Goin' in the gutter, *Ching-Chong Chinagirl!*" She stopped short, dropped the ball onto the lane, and it curved slowly into the gutter. Lai swung around to face the man.

"*Fuck you, asshole!*" Lai yelled at him.

At the same instant, Kapono turned toward the man on the stool, angered by the epithets he'd hurled at Lai. *What the hell!* He jumped up from the scorer's table to go over to the man and... *do what?* He stopped. *No... that's not the way...*

Lai noticed Kapono getting up, and she turned to look at him. He was talking to himself, eyes closed, and she *thought* she heard him whisper, "... *thank you, I love you.*" Then he walked up to Lai and said, "Maybe it's not a good day for bowling after all. Why don't we get out of here?"

Now Lai was upset with Kapono. "I don't need to take that kind of crap! Who does he think he is?!"

He put his hands gently on her upper arms and said quietly, "We don't know what's going on with him. Maybe he's had a really bad day. Let's blow this pop stand, okay?"

Lai was mystified. *I just don't get him, sometimes!* But, despite her short-lived triumph on the lane, she'd had enough bowling for one day—or maybe a lifetime. "Yeah, okay. Let's get out of here." They changed out of their bowling shoes, put their balls back on the rack, and went up to the old man at the counter to pay.

"That didn't take long," he said. He peered over at the man sitting on the stool. "Did Klement give you any trouble? I think he's drunk again."

Lai started to reply, but Kapono said, "We, uh, need to get back to work."

"I see," the man said, looking at Kapono. He tapped his fingers on the register beside him. "So, $18 for the shoes and socks—you can keep the socks. No charge for the bowling. With tax, that's $19.67."

"Thank you, sir," Kapono said gratefully. He paid the bill with his phone.

"No problem. You have a nice evening, now."

"Thanks, you too." Kapono and Lai walked toward the door. Lai, still seething, looked back over her shoulder for one more glance at Klement.

It was almost dark, and the parking lot lights—those that were still working—bathed the lot in a soft orange glow. Lai said nothing as they walked to the Prius, climbed in, and Kapono pushed the Start button. Kapono glanced at her, saw the angered look on her face, and shut the car off. "Lai, what's wrong? Are you still upset by what that drunk said?"

After a few seconds, she replied, "Yeah, I know he was drunk. That doesn't excuse everything, though. He was a real jerk."

"Yes, he was. And I'm really sorry you had to go through that. But... is something else wrong?"

He's getting to know me pretty well. Lai turned to look at Kapono. "I just get sick and tired of having to take that kind of crap from people."

Kapono's eyebrows went up. "You've heard that type of thing before?"

"Hell, yes! Especially as a kid, through high school and into college." She paused and looked again at Kapono. "I guess you have no idea what it's like to be identified with a group that's despised by lots of people."

"No, I don't, personally," he said quietly. But he had some idea what it was like. He'd seen people he'd known treated as he'd just seen Lai treated—or worse. They included a boyhood friend who'd been tormented and bullied because of his religion, and his race. Enraged by the attacks on his friend, he'd gone after the bullies and intervened—with his fists. "I can imagine how tough it is, though."

"*Can you?*" Lai shot back. "It was hard enough being taunted and bullied as a kid, and a teenager, because of the shitty relations between the US and China. The fact I was born in California didn't seem to matter to those people—they saw me as the face of the so-called Chinese Menace." She paused. "It got worse after the American Security Act was passed. Suddenly it was like—like a fucking *patriotic duty* for some people to be hateful to Chinese Americans." She looked at Kapono. "So, no, it wasn't just one drunk asshole in a bowling alley. It brought back some bad memories. I hadn't heard that kind of shit in a while. I'd almost forgotten about it." *Almost...*

Kapono put his right hand on Lai's forearm. "Lai, I'm really sorry. Can you forgive me?"

Lai scrunched her face, puzzled. *"Forgive you? What for?" Well, maybe he could've punched out that drunk! I thought for a second he was going to do that. But, that wouldn't have solved anything.*

"For not being more understanding. And, for my responsibility for your pain, and that of others who've been through what you have."

HIS responsibility? Lai didn't understand where Kapono was coming from. But then, he often said things and acted in ways she didn't fully understand. *But, if all he wants is forgiveness from me...*

"Sure, I forgive you. Can we go back to the base, now? I'm pretty hungry."

"Mahalo. As for being hungry," he smiled at Lai, "I'm pretty sure there's a pizza place just down the road. And I'll bet they make a lot better pizza than we can get at the base."

Lai's downcast face broke into a grin. "I bet you're right! Let's go!"

Kapono started the car and headed for the parking lot exit. "But, you know… it's tradition to have beer with pizza."

"Okay—but only if they have Tsingtao!"

"Deal!" Kapono grinned as he turned left onto the highway, toward the center of Baldwin City.

| 18 |

October 17, 2054

Lai took her first bite of veggie pizza and chewed thoughtfully. "Gambino's pizza was definitely *way* better," she told Kapono, thinking of the delicious pizzas they'd enjoyed in Baldwin City almost two weeks earlier.

"Oh yeah—no comparison!" Kapono agreed while finishing a bite of his pizza. "I think the differences were the hand-tossed crust, the fresh veggies, and—for me—real sausage!" He grinned, "And of course, the beer."

"No Tsingtao, though!" But Lai had to admit that the craft lager, brewed nearby in Lawrence, that she'd had at Gambino's tasted pretty good.

Lai's pizza, and Kapono's with-everything pie, had come from the base commissary. They were lucky to have grabbed the last two pizzas before it had closed for the night. They'd worked all day and into the evening on final preparations for Kapono's flight in two days aboard *Chronos 3*. Now they were having a late dinner in Lai's quarters. Kapono had to check in with Haruto at 0830 hours the next day to begin the final pre-flight checks. Lai would focus on the final checks for the backup ship, *Chronos 4*. It had to be ready to launch in two days, also… just in case.

"I feel really good about your flight," Lai said after another bite. Kapono had performed three mission simulations flawlessly earlier that day, including the difficult Manual Override scenario. "Maybe third time's the charm!"

"Right!" Kapono said as he finished a bite of his pizza. "I feel good about it, too. I think I'm ready, and the ship is as ready as it'll ever be. Meira and her Engineering team have checked and rechecked everything."

"Well, we know what's at stake. This *has* to work," Lai said solemnly. "And, things are getting worse. Did you see the news today?"

"No, haven't had time. What's going on out there?"

"On my phone's news feed, I saw that the Atlantic Meridional Overturning Circulation has collapsed."

"*Completely* collapsed?" Shock was evident on his face.

"Yeah. And you know what that means." They both knew all too well what the long-predicted collapse of the AMOC meant. Climate around the world would be severely impacted, including much colder weather in the North Atlantic and parts of Europe. There was also the potential for catastrophic monsoons and flooding in the South Pacific, along with increased drought and heat in parts of North America.

"I do. Not anything good. Any other news—preferably *good* news?" Kapono realized that it was unlikely Lai would've seen good news in her news feed, since those feeds tended to focus on negative stories, but he could always hope.

"Well, no—not good news, anyway. I saw that Zambia invaded Malawi. There's concern that'll trigger a regional war in southeast Africa." Kapono knew that Zambia, suffering from decades of extreme drought, desperately sought access to water from Lake Malawi. It was just one of several conflicts raging around the world over access to increasingly scarce water and arable farmland, and over what to do about the 1.2 billion people who had become refugees due to rising ocean levels or intolerable heat.

Kapono shook his head, then looked at Lai. "I hope Earth of 100 years from now has figured out how to solve some of these problems."

Kapono decided to not think about the *otherwise* part of that statement.

"Me, too." Lai forced a smile. "I want to hear only *good* news from you when you return from the future, got it?"

"Understood, Number One! However, I *am* going to keep the winner of Super Bowl LXXXIX to myself. Maybe I'll place a little bet on the game next February."

Lai laughed, in spite of her concerns about everything going on in the world and the dangers Kapono would face during his mission. *It's not just about making it through the wormhole in one piece—it's getting BACK to the present.* Lai knew the quantum mechanics for a return trip were sound, but there were still a few uncertainties in her mind about exactly *how* to accomplish it. She hoped those remaining questions would be resolved within 100 years from now—*Maybe by me?* She took another bite of pizza.

"You know, K… it would be a *lot* easier if we'd just do that Love One Another thing like in my dream—make love the law," she joked.

Kapono looked at her with a thoughtful expression, "Well, maybe that's worth a try."

Lai laughed again, harder. "Kapono! I was *kidding!*"

"What's so preposterous about it?"

Lai's eyes and mouth opened wide. "Oh, come *on!* That was a stupid *dream!* I mean, have you ever heard about where people just loving each other can change the world?"

"Actually," he said with an odd expression, "I have—sort of."

"*Huh?*" Lai was used to Kapono saying weird stuff that she couldn't figure out, but that took the proverbial cake.

Kapono put the slice of pizza he was working on back into its box. "Have you heard of ho'oponopono?"

"Ho-oh-*what?*"

"Ho-oh-pono-pono. It's an ancient Hawaiian practice of apology and forgiveness… forgiveness of others, or of yourself."

"No, I've never heard of it." Then Lai's scientific curiosity kicked in. "What is it? How does it work?"

"It's pretty simple. There are some phrases—a mantra, if you will—that you say, once or several times. Saying this mantra helps cleanse your body of guilt, shame, haunting memories, ill will, or bad feelings that can keep your mind fixated on negative thoughts."

"Wow. That seems pretty powerful!" *If this ho-oh-whatever can help me with all that, especially the haunting memories, I've got to know more about it.* "What's the mantra?"

"There are four parts: Remorse, Forgiveness, Gratitude, and Love. You don't have to say the four parts in that order, but they're: 'I'm sorry. Please forgive me. Thank you. I love you.'"

Lai looked puzzled. "That's *it*? You just say those words, over and over?"

"Pretty much, yes. But there's a lot *behind* those words. Take 'I'm sorry,' for example. You say that when you realize that you've knowingly—or unknowingly—harmed someone or something, perhaps the Earth, and therefore you've harmed yourself. The core belief of ho'oponopono is that everyone and everything is connected. You say 'I'm sorry' to show that you're ready to make amends."

"Oh." *This seems like some mystical malarkey,* Lai thought. But she knew Kapono was an exceptional scientist, and she respected and trusted him. *It won't hurt to learn more about it.* "What about the next part—forgiveness, right?"

"Right. And forgiveness can be hard to achieve, especially in person." Lai nodded as she thought, *No shit!* "When asking for forgiveness, it must be sincere. Any 'yeah, but's' won't cut it—that's a sign you might be trying to find ways to let yourself off the hook or lessen your part in whatever happened. If that happens, you aren't ready for forgiveness. Your desire for forgiveness must be sincere and come from your heart. If it's impossible to ask forgiveness face to face, or over the phone—maybe the relationship is so far gone there's no way you can communicate, or the person has passed on—then you can silently ask for forgiveness. Does that make sense?"

"Yeah, it, uh, it does," Lai replied as she remembered some of her failed attempts to grant and receive forgiveness. *I don't see how asking silently could work, though.* "What about the gratitude part? Gratitude for what?"

"Gratitude toward another person, or maybe the Earth, for the lessons they've helped teach you. The lesson might have been especially difficult, or appeared negative, but sometimes we grow by leaps and bounds because of these experiences. We express that gratitude in a heartfelt 'thank you.' And feeling gratitude leads to the last step."

"Love?"

"Yes. We say 'I love you,' and if possible it's nice to express that love physically, with a handshake, a hug, by planting a tree—"

"Planting a tree?" Lai said with a hint of sarcasm.

"Well, whatever's appropriate. There are no rules on how to express love. If it's not possible to express your love in person, then you can imagine you're with the other person, hugging them or simply smiling at each other, while imagining you're holding hands."

"Okay… so, suppose I do all this, and the other person isn't receptive to it. What then?"

"Give them time. In any case, you know you've done your best. If they've passed on, or the relationship is too far gone and you're on your own, you've done what you could, and you're a better person for it. And, there's benefits beyond improving a relationship with one person. By practicing ho'oponopono, you can become more aware of how you affect others and the world around you. And that can lead to greater empathy and compassion."

Lai pondered what Kapono had said. "Where did you learn about ho'oponopono, K?"

"From my dad, when I was 14, I think." *And it's lucky for me I learned ho'oponopono when I did.* "Plus I had some lessons from a ho'oponopono master. It's a pretty common practice in Hawai'i, and there are similar practices in New Zealand, Samoa, and Tahiti."

Lai took a swig of water from her flask. "K, this all sounds wonderful. But, let me ask you… as a scientist, don't you want to see empirical evidence that it actually *works*?"

Kapono smiled at Lai. "Oh, I *know* it works. I mean, I use it every day, and I'm sure it's helped me in my relationships with others, and with the world in general."

"Ohhh!" Suddenly, Lai put the pieces of a puzzle together in her brain. "*That's* what you were doing in the bowling alley, with the drunk guy! And afterward, in the car with me. And, when we had lunch on my second day here—you said that mantra back then, didn't you?"

Kapono smiled again. "Yes, I did. I don't know how many times a day I say the mantra. I'll say it in the shower, or other times when I'm alone for a few minutes. You can say it anytime, anywhere. It doesn't have to be directed at one person, at one relationship, but it can be."

"But, when you use it like that, how do you know it's doing any good?"

Kapono thought for a few seconds. "Let me try to answer your question with an example," he began. "Many years ago, there was a clinical psychologist in Hawai'i, Dr. Hew Len, who was a practitioner of ho'oponopono. He worked at the Hawai'i State Hospital, in the ward for the criminally insane. This ward was reportedly so chaotic that not a day would go by without a brawl among patients, the nurses, and the rest of the staff. The environment was so destructive and depressing that the staff would call out sick a lot, and there was very high turnover.

"Dr. Hew Len would arrive at the ward each morning with a cheerful and tranquil disposition. He never made personal visits to the inmates—never did any therapy with them. He'd just walk through the ward, and he'd browse through the inmates' files from time to time. And, he used ho'oponopono to heal *himself*. His healing process involved thinking about the mindset of those patients and asking for forgiveness by connecting with them at a subconscious level."

"He doesn't sound like a hella good clinician!"

"I know, right? But strangely enough, things started to change in the ward. The prisoners and staff gradually got along with each other.

The inmates were less destructive, and the staff took more initiative to make the ward a better place. And the staff sick-outs and turnover plunged. During the four years Dr. Hew Len worked in the ward, many prisoners were released, and the staff performed their responsibilities dutifully again. Eventually, the ward was closed because there were hardly any inmates left."

Lai's brow furrowed. "Do you *believe* that story? It seems too good to be true."

"I do. But, as a scientist, I also believe in obtaining empirical evidence through experimentation. So, I decided to try to replicate what Dr. Hew Len had done—not in a ward for the criminally insane, of course."

"How did you do that?"

"By practicing ho'oponopono here, at the base."

Lai stopped chewing her pizza and looked at Kapono. "Really? What did you do, exactly?"

"Like Dr. Hew Len, I try to be cheerful and tranquil every day. And I say the mantra dozens of times a day, at least. Often it isn't directed at any one person. But I say it once a day for each member of the team." He smiled at Lai. "More than once a day for some people. I think it's been helping. But, what do *you* think? Have you noticed any results from my little experiment?"

Holy shit! Could that be why I've felt so good since I came on the project? "Actually, I *have* noticed something—something I couldn't explain, until now. I've never been on a project like this, with everyone under lots of stress, working long hours, confined to an underground base to boot, where people haven't been climbing the walls or even going at each other's throats after a few months. Everyone is just so... chill. And, I'm not the only one who's noticed that."

"Really?"

"Yeah. Katherine's mentioned it to me, and Meira and Haruto, and Major Goebel, too. They all said it was really weird. Like me, they've never seen anything like it. Katherine told me she started noticing it shortly after you joined the team. I didn't connect the dots—until now."

"So, there's some empirical evidence, eh?"

"Well, I can't deny the cause and effect of your experiment." She paused. "But... how does ho'oponopono actually *work*?"

Kapono looked at Lai for a few seconds. "Do you believe there's something beyond the physical?"

"You mean like, God?" Lai shrugged. "Maybe you've noticed, I'm not a religious person. My parents were, but it never took with me." She paused as she thought of something from her past—something she'd buried, or had tried to bury. *What the hell, I've told him just about everything else.* She took a sip from her water flask. "Remember I told you I went to Stanford?"

"Yes, of course."

"Well... that isn't completely true. After I was convicted and sent to jail, Stanford expelled me."

"Oh, Lai...!"

"When I got out of prison, I was... I was pretty messed up. I wasn't sure what I wanted to do. So, I hit the road... I borrowed my parents' car."

"Where did you go?"

"Nowhere in particular. I did some camping—Yosemite, Russian Gulch, Salt Point, a few other places. I spent a lot of time just driving, and thinking." She looked at Kapono with a sorrowful expression. "I was in a dark place, K... a *really* dark place." Kapono put his hand on top of Lai's; they were sitting on her bed, as it was the only sitting space in the tiny room other than her desk chair. "One day I was driving south down California 1—that's the highway that runs along the coast."

"I drove that route a few times when I was at Berkeley. Beautiful scenery!"

"Yes... it is. The section of road I was on ran along the edge of a tall cliff overlooking the ocean." Lai's voice grew quieter. "As I was driving, I had this thought that, uh, maybe it would be a lot better for me, and everybody, if I'd just turn the wheel to the right." Kapono's eyes opened wide, and his hand squeezed Lai's. "I saw a gap in the guard rail ahead—probably from a rock slide. *That looks like a good spot*, I thought." She took another sip of water. "Just as I was about to turn the wheel, I thought I heard a voice say, *Don't do it, Lai!*" She looked into Kapono's eyes. "I turned it anyway. At that instant, the motor stopped." She shook her head. "I have no idea how, or why. The battery had plenty of juice. The car just... died." She wiped her nose. "The car coasted onto the shoulder and stopped. I was shaking pretty bad. After a few minutes, I looked out over the ocean, and down at the shore below me. I saw maybe a dozen people down there, playing in the surf and the rocks." She looked up again at Kapono, her eyes brimming with tears. "I could've killed someone, K!"

"But you didn't!"

"No, I didn't. After I'd pulled myself together, I tried to start the car. It started right up. I took it to a mechanic two days later... he couldn't find a thing wrong with it." She looked at Kapono. "So, to answer your question—do I believe there's something beyond the physical? I guess I have to agree with Hamlet on that: 'There are more things in Heaven and Earth, Horatio, than are dreamt of in our philosophy.'"

Kapono smiled, nodded, and squeezed Lai's hand. "Yes, indeed. But, I thought it was '... *your* philosophy'?"

"Not in the First Folio edition," Lai countered with the hint of a smile.

Kapono smiled again, "You *do* know your Shakespeare. So, what did you do then?"

"I drove home, and the next day I started sending out applications to schools—I must have sent a couple of dozen." She smiled faintly at Kapono. "Three weeks later I got accepted at Minnesota. One of my father's friends, Dr. Hanwick, was the dean of the Physics department there, and he put in a good word for me. I got my bachelor's there two and a half years later."

"That's a good school, Lai."

"Yes, it is. And a beautiful state," she added, thinking of her family's cabin in the northern Minnesota woods. *Almost as beautiful as California.* She looked at Kapono. "K... this is another thing I haven't told anyone else about." Her faint smile returned, "So, now you've got all the dirt on me."

Kapono returned her smile. "*All* of it?"

"Okay, so, no—there's lots of other shit." *If he only knew all of that other shit, from the rape, and prison, and...* "We'll save that for another day... if ever!" She leaned back on the bed pillows that were against the wall. "Anyway, back to my dream... I can see how if everyone practiced ho'oponopono, it could make a difference—maybe a *big* difference. It would be really hard to make it happen, but who knows—maybe in time..." She grabbed another piece of her now-cold pizza out of its box. "But, the Jim Lovell hologram in my dream didn't say anything about ho'oponopono. He said that what happened was, love was the *law*. How the hell could *that* ever work?" She took a bite of pizza.

Kapono thought for a few moments. "The idea that love for others could be the law isn't as far-fetched as you might think. Did you know, for example, that kind of idea is mentioned in the Bible?"

Lai smiled, "As I said, I'm not a religious person. When I was a kid, my parents dragged me along to a few Christian services in Blackduck, when we were at the cabin during the summer. They were Buddhists, but they thought I should be exposed to other faith traditions. I don't remember much, except that after some of the services they had decent donuts."

"I wasn't very religious as a kid, either. But in college I audited a couple of classes on the world's religions. Pretty interesting stuff."

"Like...?"

"Well, Jesus told his followers that to love one another as He loves them is the greatest commandment, and He also told them that they must love their *enemies*. But specifically, regarding your dream... one of Jesus's followers, Paul, wrote that '...whoever loves others has fulfilled the law.' Think about that... sound familiar at all?"

"It *does* sound familiar... and I don't mean just from my dream. I've heard that before, someplace... maybe I took more from those services in Blackduck than the donuts."

Kapono chuckled, "Maybe!" He glanced at his pizza box but decided he'd had enough. "You said your parents were Buddhists. Did you learn anything about their faith while you were living at home?"

"A little. When I was young, I learned that Buddhists believe love is a boundless power that can heal any suffering, and that there's four kinds of unselfish love: loving kindness, compassion, joy, and, uh... equanimity. But, my understanding of Buddhism is pretty limited. I stopped practicing it in my early teens. My parents weren't happy about that. I thought I knew everything when I was 13, you know?"

"Yeah, I know that feeling," Kapono agreed, thinking about his rebellious years during his childhood, into his teens.

"Did you learn about other religions' take on love in your classes?"

"Yes, some. For example, in Islam, I learned that Muslims believe that God is so loving that He recreated His attribute of love as an instinct in us. Thus, true love is part of God's love, and it's our duty to love one another truly, as He loves us." He paused, lost in thought. "*Duty...* many duties are embedded in the law. Why not the duty to love one another?"

"I see where you're going, there, but I still think the whole idea of making Love One Another the law is impractical."

The words *unreasonable, illogical, impractical love* popped into Kapono's head. Then he remembered where he'd heard that phrase. "Lai, do you remember Daniel Bennett?"

Lai closed her eyes. "Yes, I remember Daniel Bennett," she said icily. *That hypocritical sonofabitch!* She opened her eyes and glared at Kapono. "Why did you bring *him* up?"

"Well, because... do you remember his Senate campaigns, and his presidential campaign in '28?" Lai nodded half-heartedly. "He made *love* a cornerstone of his message, which was almost unheard of in American politics. He talked about how we need to sow love, not hate, and love *everyone*—even our enemies. And he spoke about 'unreasonable, illogical, impractical love'."

"It didn't put him into the Oval Office, though, did it?" Lai said sarcastically.

"Well, no, I guess it didn't," Kapono admitted. "He did get a lot of support in the primaries and the nominating convention in '28, though. I just thought it was a remarkable message, for a politician. I brought it up because I thought it fits with what we're talking about."

"Yeah. Okay." Lai contemplated the congealed mass of cold veggie pizza in its box on the bed. "Kapono," she said sadly, looking into his eyes, "I hear everything you're saying, and I *really* wish that we could help everyone learn how to use ho'oponopono and base our laws on loving one another, but… I think there's just too much hate, too much intolerance, too many people trying to hurt and kill each other instead of loving each other, that I just can't see it working."

"Maybe not." Kapono thought for a few seconds. "But, you know, if we expect people to love others, we need to show love to them."

Lai pondered that. *That's sure true for me… in both directions.* "Yeah… you're right—as usual. But, we're not gonna solve this mess tonight." She attempted a smile, "Which means…you'll just have to get that ship to the future."

"Okay," Kapono said quietly. "But… it was a great dream, wasn't it?"

Lai sighed, "Yeah—it was."

Kapono sat up, "Speaking of taking that ship to the future… Sirai, what time is it?"

"Aloha! It's 0147 hours, bro."

Lai laughed, "Where the heck did you find a Surfer Dude Sirai voice?"

"hOS 12.1," Kapono replied as he jumped up from the bed. "I've got to get going. It's almost two; 8:30 is going to get here really fast."

"Oh, yeah—get outta here!" Lai ordered as she got up off the bed and opened the door for Kapono.

"You want me to put these in the trash?" Kapono nodded toward the pizza boxes on the bed.

"Nah, I'll take care of those—you get to bed."

"That's just what I'm going to do." He stepped around the bed and stood by the partially open door, facing Lai. "Thanks for the pizza, and the talk. I really enjoyed—"

Lai suddenly stretched up on the toes of her bare feet, grabbed the sides of Kapono's head, and pulled it toward her face as she gave him a deep, long kiss. *What the hell am I doing?!* She broke off the kiss, removed her hands from his head, and lowered her heels back to the floor. "I'm—I'm so sorry! I shouldn't have—"

Kapono smiled. "I'm not." He gently lifted her chin with his forefinger, leaned over slightly and pressed his lips to hers. Lai closed the door with a nudge from her left hand and turned the deadbolt.

| 19 |

October 19, 2054

"CapCom, this is *Chronos 3*," Kapono's voice came clearly from the main speaker in the Flight Control room. "I'm just under 100,000 kilometers from the wormhole, and Aileen reports everything looks good. And, you were right, Lai—it's an amazing sight!"

The Prometheus team members gathered in Flight Control were hearing about events from 90 minutes ago—that's how long it took radio signals to travel the one billion miles between the wormhole and Earth. Despite the time delay, Katherine and Haruto had decided to use audio communications for Kapono's entire flight, to better track its progress and obtain details that could be important if a rescue mission were needed.

Haruto chose to not respond to Kapono. If everything went as planned, he'd be through the wormhole long before he'd receive a reply from the base. Instead, Haruto turned in his chair at the main mission console to address his teammates crowded into the small room: Katherine, Lai, Chief Engineer Meira Friedman, and Captain Kyle Otterman, the astronaut on loan from NASA who would command a rescue mission in *Chronos 4* if it were needed. Otterman, and everyone else on the Prometheus team, hoped that his help wouldn't be needed that day. Commander McDowell from Flagstaff Station was connected to Flight Control via audio link. The observatory was tracking *Chronos 3* with its optical and radio telescopes.

"So far, so good," Haruto said. "We should get a few more reports from Kapono before G forces make it difficult for him to talk, but then Aileen will keep us updated."

Lai was nervous, unconsciously tapping her right foot on the gray tile floor. As Kapono's updates came in, she was reliving in her mind her experience in *Chronos 2*. *But this time, it's going to work—I know it will. Kapono's got this.*

"Just passed 50,000 kilometers to the wormhole—ETA 2 minutes 15 seconds. Aileen will be reversing the Quantum Drive shortly." Everyone in the room was riveted to Kapono's voice coming over the speaker, with the realization that by now he could be 100 years in the future. That was their hope, at least.

"ETA 2 minutes, Quantum Dr—"

BANG!

Everyone in Flight Control jolted when they heard the sharp, metallic burst from the speaker—it sounded like a gunshot. At the same instant, the audio from *Chronos 3* went dead. By force of habit, Haruto started to call the spacecraft, but he stopped when he realized it would be pointless. Instead, he switched his microphone to the Flagstaff Station channel.

"Flagstaff, did y'all hear that?" he said urgently, but calmly. "Can y'all tell us what your telemetry showed in the last 15 seconds?"

"CapCom, we did detect what sounded like some type of impact. We're running the telemetry through AI analysis now," McDowell replied, his voice equally calm but tinged with concern. "We should have results in a minute or two."

This is going to be a long two minutes, Katherine thought as she turned to Captain Otterman, an 18-year veteran of the Air Force and NASA with hundreds of hours of space flight experience. "Captain, could you tell anything from what you heard? I know it's not much to go on."

The lanky, blond-haired astronaut, wearing a blue NASA flight suit, thought for a moment. "As Commander McDowell said, it did sound like something hitting the ship—a micrometeorite, perhaps.

But, that's a guess, and there's no way for me to tell what effect it had, other than we know both primary and backup communications were affected."

"But, the ship has a deflector array to take care of those!" Lai countered.

"That's true, Lai," Otterman replied. "But it can deal only with objects in the ship's path. There's a chance that a micrometeorite could approach the ship laterally, such that the deflector couldn't reach it. Given the ship's speed, the window of vulnerability is extremely small. But, it exists. I hope that's not what—"

"Flight Control, this is Flagstaff," McDowell's voice said over the speaker. "The AI analysis on the telemetry is complete."

"Go ahead, Commander," Katherine said, trying to keep her voice steady.

"The conclusion from the analysis is that the sound we heard came from an object, most likely a micrometeorite, striking the side of the ship and passing through it." His voice seemed strained. "The analysis shows there were *two* impacts with the ship, a tiny fraction of a second apart. That supports the conclusion that the object passed through the ship. Based on the time interval between the impacts, it appears the object struck the ship at a speed of about 70 kilometers per second, at an angle of between 30 and 35 degrees."

"Understood," Katherine said. "Is there any way to tell *where* on the ship the impacts occurred?"

"Yes, there is." It sounded like McDowell cleared his throat. "Based on acoustic analysis, coupled with the apparent damage to primary and backup communications, we believe the object passed through the cockpit, very close to the command couch." There was an audible gasp in the room. "There's a high probability that, in addition to the communications consoles being knocked offline, both guidance computers were damaged. Also... the AI analysis calculated a 98.5 percent probability that the impact caused a total failure of cabin integrity." He paused. "If Dr. Ailana survived the impact, he may not have life support for very long."

Lai put her hands over her mouth and tried not to cry out.

"Thank you, Commander." Katherine was having trouble speaking. "Is there any visible sign of the spacecraft?"

"There's nothing visual right now, and nothing on radio telescope. But it's hard to make out something the size of a Voyageur IV at this distance, especially with the visual and electromagnetic interference from the black hole. We're not giving up, though. We'll let you know if we see anything."

"Thanks again, Commander, and thanks to your team. We'll sign off for now, but we'll keep this channel open for any updates."

"Understood. Our thoughts are with you and your team there. Signing off."

Katherine looked around the room. "Opinion, please... based on what we heard from Flagstaff, is it *possible* that Kapono survived the impact?"

"Absolutely," Otterman said as Haruto and Meira nodded in agreement. "It appears the odds aren't in his favor, but I can tell you I've personally beaten the odds several times in my career."

Katherine smiled. "That's what I wanted to hear, Captain." She looked at Haruto, "How long will it take to get *Chronos 4* ready for liftoff?"

"An hour and a half—two hours, tops. Right, Captain?" Haruto replied as he looked at Otterman.

"I agree. With all the pre-flight work you and Lai did on the ship in the past few days, it won't take long. I'll get suited up right away and start the final checks from the cockpit," Otterman said as he stood up.

"I can help Haruto and Meira with the final checks here," Lai offered.

"Thank you—all of you," Katherine said as she looked around the room of determined faces. "Kapono needs our help. Let's bring him home."

"T-minus five minutes," Haruto reported the countdown status to Captain Otterman in *Chronos 4* and the team members in Flight Control. "Everything shows Green here, Captain. What about on your end?"

On *Chronos 4*, Otterman rechecked the displays around him. "Looking good, here, CapCom. Aileen, can you provide an overall flight status, please?"

"All ship's systems are nominal. Quantum Drive electrostatics are at 99.983 percent efficiency. Local weather is grand: clear skies, temperature 29 Celsius, and wind is from the south-southwest at 7 kilometers per hour and is of no concern. FAA confirms that a ground stop is in effect within a 500-kilometer radius of the base."

"Excellent, thanks, Captain and Aileen," Haruto replied. He turned around to the other team members in the room. "Everything is Green for launch in T-minus 4 minutes 12 seconds. Openin' the silo hatch now." He lifted a safety cover on the silo hatch switch and flicked it to the OPEN position.

On *Chronos 4*, Otterman watched as the silo hatch doors slid open and a deep blue, late afternoon sky appeared in the round opening above him. *Today is a good day to fly.*

"T-minus 3 minutes," Haruto reported. "Switchin' the spacecraft to internal power." He pressed the three buttons that freed *Chronos 4* from the umbilical cables that connected it to the silo. "*Chronos 4*, please switch your guidance computers to—"

"Flight Control, this is Flagstaff Station!" Commander McDowell's voice blared over the main speaker. "Please come in!"

"Commander, this is Katherine Etter. Do you have an update for us?"

"Yes, Dr. Etter. About two minutes ago, our optical telescope recorded what looked like a *very* large explosion next to, or perhaps within, the black hole that is the entrance to the wormhole. Also, our radio telescope readings jumped off the scale. And now, the black hole—" He seemed to turn away from his microphone, "*Is it con-*

firmed?" then returned to the mic. "It's confirmed—the black hole is gone."

Lai was incredulous. *Gone?? I always knew this day would come, but why now? Why NOW?!*

Haruto shot a glance at Katherine, who closed her eyes and nodded. "Holdin' countdown at T-minus 2 minutes 10 seconds!" Haruto called out.

"Commander, is there any sign of *Chronos 3?*" Katherine asked, hoping beyond hope.

"No, Dr. Etter. That was a tremendous blast, whatever it was—too large to be from the spacecraft. If the ship were anywhere near the black hole, it would have been destroyed instantly." He paused. "I'm sorry, Dr. Etter. We'll keep monitoring the area for the next few days, just in case."

"Thank you, Commander. Signing off for now." Haruto closed the channel.

No one spoke for several seconds. Then Lai said what everyone was thinking. "Maybe he made it through the wormhole!" she said with all the enthusiasm and hope she could muster.

Katherine put her hand on Lai's shoulder. "Yes... maybe he did. Maybe he's safe, somewhere in the future." *But, if he did make it to the future... with the wormhole gone, he's never coming back.*

| 20 |

October 21, 2054

After 36 hours with no sign of *Chronos 3*, Katherine reluctantly took action to have Kapono declared missing and presumed dead. The details of his disappearance could not, of course, ever be revealed to the public.

Meanwhile, the Prometheus Oversight Committee had notified Katherine that the project had been terminated, effective immediately, and a Top Secret congressional inquiry had begun. One by one, the project's team members cleaned out their workspaces and quarters and sadly bid farewell to their teammates who remained at the base. A small team led by Haruto and Meira would oversee the return of the base to the Air Force and the surviving Voyageur IV to Infini-Trek. Some team members had already been reassigned to other projects: Major Goebel with the Air Force, and Captain Otterman and a few others with NASA. Others, including Katherine and Lai, didn't know yet what the future held for them... although Katherine expected there would be some rather unpleasant congressional hearings in her immediate future.

Lai unlocked the door to Kapono's quarters using the key Katherine had given her. She'd asked Katherine if she could take care of sending Kapono's personal effects to his father, and Katherine had gratefully granted her request. Katherine had already called Kapono's father to let him know about his son being declared missing and presumed dead. That was always a difficult duty, but Katherine was especially sorrowful that she couldn't give Kapono's father any details about his son's contributions to the project, his bravery, and most of all how he had sacrificed his life in an attempt to save humanity.

Lai had never been in Kapono's quarters. After she opened the door and turned on the overhead light, she stopped in the doorway, transfixed by what she saw. The wall opposite the door featured what looked like a large window overlooking a beautiful, sunny beach. *Kaanapali Beach?* It was only a holographic screen surrounded by a white wooden frame, but it was so realistic that Lai thought she could almost hear the waves crashing onto the beach. The walls of the room were painted sky-blue. That color and the simulated window gave the room a cheerful, tranquil feeling. There was also a colorful surfboard mounted lengthwise on the wall opposite the bed; it stretched nearly the entire width of the wall. *How the heck did he get that down here?* Seeing these reminders of her recent conversations with Kapono caused her to remember how much those talks meant to her—how much *he* meant to her—and how much she missed him.

Lai saw Kapono's holopad sitting on the desk under the simulated window. Katherine had given Lai permission to check it, in case there was anything Kapono's father might want. She sat down at the desk and noticed a framed photo on it. The photo showed a Polynesian man and woman who appeared to Lai to be in their late 30s. The man looked a lot like Kapono, with the same brown eyes and broad nose. The woman wore a serene, kind smile. A boy of about four years old stood in front of them. The photo reminded Lai of a photo on the desk in her quarters. That one showed a happy nine-year-old girl with black hair and green eyes, and her proud parents behind her. She wiped her eyes with her sleeve and made a mental note to include the photo on Kapono's desk in the package she'd send to his father.

Lai touched the power button on the pad and entered the passphrase that Katherine had given her. She saw three objects in the center of the home screen; they were named "For Dad," "Last Will and

Testament," and "For Lai." She saved the "For Dad" object and the will document to her cloud drive to send to Kapono's father, then she said, "Open 'For Lai'." A video player popped onto the screen. Lai noticed the video was paused about one-sixth of the way through. "Resume," Lai said.

Lai smiled when she realized the video was from one of the old *Star Trek* shows that Kapono loved. *But,* she wondered, w*hy would he leave this, of all things, for me?* She'd watched enough of the show with a college roommate that she recognized one of the characters: a brown-haired, 30-something man in a tight green V-necked shirt with gold braid—*Captain Kirk*, she recalled. He was talking with an older man with black hair, wearing a blue shirt—*Dr. McCoy, I think*—about someone named Scotty who apparently had been charged with murder on a planet called Argelius. Captain Kirk was clearly upset about the situation; he went over to a short, bald man in a black jacket and trousers and asked him about other suspects in the murder. The man replied that the other suspects would be located and questioned, but the outlook for Kirk's friend—*the man in the red shirt must be his friend, Scotty*, Lai realized—was grim. Then Kirk asked the bald man, "What is the law in these cases?" A distinguished-looking man, with gray hair and a salt-and-pepper beard, wearing a flowing black and silver tunic, stepped forward from the background, smiled and said gently:

"The law of Argelius is *love.*"

"Pause!" Lai felt what seemed like an electric shock course down her spine, and a line from one of her favorite Shakespearean plays popped into her head—*"... the lightning in the collied night..."* She realized she'd seen that scene before—probably as a frosh at Stanford, 17 years ago. And with that revelation, the last missing puzzle piece of her dream dropped into place.

She watched the entire video. She learned that on Argelius, loving others was *literally* the law and had been for hundreds of years, since their "Great Awakening." There was so little crime that they had no need for criminal investigators; they had to bring one in from another planet to deal with the murders that the Scotty character was accused of—which, as it turned out, were committed by an entity that lived on the fear of others. *Huh,* Lai thought, *I've known some people like that.*

Now she understood why Kapono had left her that video. *He doesn't give up easily! But, it's just an old TV show! Argelius is a figment of someone's imagination. It's not real... it could NEVER be real.*

Or... could it?

Lai sat at the desk for several minutes, engrossed in thought as the events of the past few days swirled around in her mind...

Remorse, forgiveness, gratitude, and love...
Love is a boundless power that can heal any suffering...
It is our duty to love one another truly, as God loves us...
Whoever loves others has fulfilled the law...
Unreasonable, illogical, impractical love...

To Lai, the idea *did* seem unreasonable and illogical... and so very impractical. But it was clear that Kapono believed in it. *And if anyone knows about love, he did.*

Suddenly, Lai knew what she had to do, or at least *try* to do—something Kapono would have wanted her to do. But it could mean asking for help from someone she despised. *I have no choice... I can't do this all by myself.*

| 21 |

October 29, 2054

Ben was bored. And that made him very happy. His being bored meant that those under his protection were safe. Thus, over the nearly 25 years he'd served in his current profession, he strove to make each day as uneventful—as boring—as possible. Today was such a day—blissfully boring. But, although Ben was bored, he remained vigilant, focused, and alert.

He was sitting at a small built-in desk in the butler's pantry of the old town house, wearing what he always did while on duty: a black suit, white button-down long-sleeved shirt, and dark necktie. Above the desktop was an array of nine flat screen monitors in a three-by-three grid. Each monitor was fed from a camera in one of five zones around the outside of the town house or the four zones inside the house. His seasoned eyes continually swept the monitors, looking for anything out of place. His teammate was keeping watch outside—a pleasant duty on a warm, sunny day in late October. They took turns alternating between indoor and outdoor surveillance duties.

Suddenly Ben's boredom was shattered by the motion detector alarm for Monitor 5, which covered the northeast half of the fenced back yard. Ben canceled the alarm and squinted intently at the monitor screen, but he saw nothing amiss.

"Chickadee Two, this is Chickadee One," he spoke into his headset microphone. "Motion detected on Monitor 5, but visual is negative. Please recon and report."

"Roger, Chickadee One," his teammate's voice came through his earpiece. Ben continued surveying all nine monitors as he paid particular attention to Monitor 5. He soon saw his fellow agent enter the camera's field of view.

"Chickadee One, everything looks good here, nothing—wait! I see movement in the shrubs!"

"Checking..." Ben zoomed Monitor 5's camera into the hydrangeas in the left corner of the back yard—a perfect cover for... *what?* "I see it, Chickadee Two. Approach with caution."

Ben looked closely at the monitor as the other agent drew her Glock from its holster and stepped carefully toward the shuddering shrub. Suddenly, the trespasser sprang from under cover of the dense bush and raced across the yard. "Chickadee Two, you'd better go after that vicious bunny!" Ben laughed as the rabbit disappeared under the fence into the neighboring yard.

"I wish we could take out those damn shrubs," she replied, clearly annoyed as she shook her head and holstered her pistol.

"You know what Mr. B would say about *that*."

"Say about what?" A bald, elderly man in a bathrobe, silk pajamas, and slippers stood in the butler's pantry doorway.

"Oh, nothing, Mr. B. Hannah just scared off a rabbit hiding in the hydrangeas. Another red-letter day for the Secret Service," Ben chuckled.

"You never let anything get by you, not for 20 years," the old man said as he stepped into the pantry and put his hand on Ben's shoulder. "That's why I sleep so well at night. Carry on, Benjamin."

"Yes, sir, Mr. B," Ben replied as the man shuffled out of the pantry and the adjoining kitchen, into the living room. *That's right, nothing gets by me—and nothing ever will.*

Then Ben noticed on Monitor 3 a woman approaching the gate of the ornamental black iron fence surrounding the small front yard of the town house. He checked the time: 13:29. *Right on time.* He appreciated the visitor's punctuality.

"Chickadee One to Chickadee Two, our scheduled visitor is approaching the front door; please provide backup."

"Roger, Chickadee One," Hannah replied as she began to move into position to discreetly cover the front entrance of the town house.

Of course, Ben had done a thorough background check on the visitor when she'd first requested to meet with Mr. B, but there was no harm in being extra cautious. He stood up from the monitoring station and went into the living room as the doorbell chimed.

"Mr. B, your 1:30 appointment is here."

"Thanks, Benjamin. I hope she doesn't mind my being dressed like this."

"I'm sure she'll be fine with that, sir."

Ben stepped from the living room into the front foyer, disabled the locks and alarm on the hardened front door, and opened it. A short, 30-something woman dressed in a dark gray skirt suit looked up with wide eyes at Ben, who towered over her with his powerful six-foot-nine frame.

"Uh… hello. I'm Lai Shen. I have an appointment to see the president."

"Good afternoon, Dr. Shen. He's expecting you. Please come in." Ben showed Lai into the foyer and guided her into the living room. He was glad for the 3D scanner with facial recognition built into the front door frame, so he didn't have to subject visitors to a search.

"Hello, welcome to my home! Please, sit and get comfortable." The old man smiled as Ben escorted Lai into the bright living room and motioned to a loveseat across from the sofa where the man sat. "Please forgive me for not getting up, and for this robe. I haven't been feeling 100 percent lately—nothing contagious, not to worry."

"Good afternoon, Mr. President," Lai said. "It's an honor to meet you. Thank you for seeing me." Ben noticed that she seemed nervous. *Well, not unusual for someone meeting a president for the first time.*

"My calendar isn't exactly bursting with urgent business," the old man joked as he winked at Ben. "But, you know, it's been a long time since I was in the White House. Benjamin and other folks call me Mr. B. How does that sound to you?"

"That's fine, Mr. Pres—I mean, Mr. B."

The old man took stock of the woman sitting stiffly in front of him, with both of her feet planted on the floor and her hands clasped on her lap. "Benjamin tells me you've come a long way to see me today. How can I help you?"

Lai shifted uncomfortably in the loveseat. "Well, sir, I..." She paused, then cleared her throat. "Mr. B, I... uh... I need your help to save the human race."

The old man sank back in amazement into the sofa cushions and studied Lai's face. *She looks dead serious!*

"Oh? Is that all?" The old man smiled, not from amusement but from how implausible it seemed that this woman he didn't know—indeed, that *anyone*—would come to him of all people with such a request. But he wanted to be courteous to this woman who'd come a long way to see him, and he was genuinely curious to find out what she had in mind to "save the human race." "Well, you've got my attention. Let's talk about it." He turned to Ben, "Benjamin, could you please ask Anton to bring us something to drink?" Then he looked at the mysterious woman who wanted his help... *saving humanity?* "Would you like some tea?"

"No, thank you, sir. Coffee, black, if you have it. I'm not fond of tea."

"Coffee lover, huh? I like you already! Benjamin, ask Anton for two black coffees, please—and the pot, too. We might be here a while!"

Bright mid-afternoon sunlight streamed through the living room windows of the old, red brick town house in the Charlestown neighborhood of Boston. Anton wheeled a small serving cart into the living room; the cart carried two bone china cups and an insulated coffee pot.

"Here you are, Mr. B," Anton said to the old man seated on the sofa. "You wanted your coffee black, also—right, ma'am?" he asked Lai.

"Yes, that's great, thank you." Anton poured coffee into both cups and handed one to the man and one to Lai, then set the coffee pot on the low table between the two of them.

"Thanks, Anton," the old man said as the red-haired house manager nodded and returned to his office adjacent to the living room. "If it weren't for my accent, you wouldn't think I'm a Bostonian, liking my coffee black as I do. I must admit I'm addicted to the stuff. It's one of my few vices—that I'll admit to, anyway," he said with a wink as he took a sip of coffee.

"I guess I have the same addiction, Mr. B." Lai took her first sip of coffee. *This is incredible! The guy may be a sonofabitch, but he knows his coffee.* She set her cup on the coffee table, and the man did the same with his cup.

"So, Dr. Shen... or may I call you Lai?" the old man asked.

"Lai is fine, Mr. B."

"Okay. Then please call me Daniel."

"Uh, okay, sure." *That's just a bit too familiar for me for where I'm at right now.*

"Great. Now, let's talk more about what you said before Anton came in. You said something about my helping you 'save the human race.' Did I hear that correctly?"

"Yes, sir, you did. I know it must sound ridiculous. You probably think I'm crazy."

Daniel smiled. "Oh, not at all. Believe me, I've heard lots of crazy things in my life. Trying to save the human race isn't one of them." He folded his hands on his lap. "But I *am* curious as to how you plan to accomplish that worthy goal, and why you came to *me*, of all people, for help."

Lai looked down at her coffee cup on the table, then looked into Daniel's eyes. "Well, that, sir, is, as they say, a long story." She bit her lower lip. *Might as well get this out there right now, before we go any fur-*

ther. "But, sir, I have to tell you... I wasn't sure I wanted to come here today, to ask for your help."

Daniel cocked his head slightly to the side. "Why is that, Lai?"

She took a deep breath. "Because of what you did to my parents, and to me, and to millions of other Americans of Chinese descent, and many other Americans!" she burst out, with palpable bitterness and anger in her voice. "I don't understand how someone like you, who's championed racial and social justice, could do something like that! And, I don't know if I can ever forgive you for it."

Daniel was momentarily stunned, but he closed his eyes and nodded when he realized what Lai was talking about. "The ASA... you're referring to the American Security Act, aren't you?"

"Yes." Lai tried to control her anger, but it was conspicuous as she glared at Daniel. "Do you have any fu—any *idea* what that law did to many loyal Americans? *It destroyed their lives!*" she nearly shouted as she thought of her parents. *If it weren't for Daniel Bennett and that fucking law, they'd be alive now*, Lai seethed. Ben suddenly appeared in the doorway to the living room and stared warily at Lai, then looked at Daniel.

"It's okay, Benjamin. We're just having a conversation, here. Nothing to worry about."

"Yes, sir," the Secret Service agent replied, sounding as if he wasn't entirely convinced. But he returned to the kitchen and his monitors. Daniel turned back to Lai.

"Lai, I... yes, I know that the ASA ended up hurting many people. And for that I am deeply, truly sorry. That was *never* the intent of that law. It was supposed to help *protect* America, and Americans. But," he said sadly, "it was exploited by a few people—evil people—to their own ends." *I thought I could keep them in check... I was wrong.*

"You *must* have realized that could happen with a law as sweeping as the ASA!" Lai shot back, exasperated. "I mean, I'm a *scientist*, not a politician, but even I know there are lessons from history that should have given you some *clue* as to the dangers of that kind of law." Her memory flashed back to what she'd read about President Roosevelt's infamous Executive Order 9066 during World War II and Senator McCarthy's *Enemies from Within* speech from the mid-20th century.

"Yes, Lai," Daniel said quietly. "I was aware of the risks. In fact, I spoke out about them as vice president. I knew the American Security Act was flawed." Daniel paused, then looked into Lai's eyes. "But when President Pendamai had to resign in early '36 and I was sworn in as president, I was faced with a terrible choice." He took a sip of his coffee. "The ASA was coming up for a final vote in Congress. So was ratification of the Toronto Climate Agreement." He leaned forward. "I believed that the Toronto Agreement was the country's, and the world's, last hope to fight climate change. But, we didn't have enough votes for passage. I was offered a deal: the ASA for the Toronto Agreement. I took it." He paused for a few seconds. "I wish now I hadn't."

Lai glared at Daniel. "Well... we make our choices, and then we have to live with them. As it turned out, the Toronto Agreement didn't matter. We're toast, anyway."

"What do you mean?" Daniel said with a puzzled expression.

"I know about the RAND study, and the others."

"Oh. I see." Daniel looked down at his coffee cup, then looked up at Lai. "Is that why you're here today? The Prometheus Project didn't work out, and you're going to try something else?"

Now it was Lai's turn to be surprised. And her surprise jolted her thoughts away from her anger and bitterness toward Daniel and back to the reason she'd come to Boston to see him. "You *know* about Prometheus?"

Daniel smiled slightly. "The president asked for my advice on it late last year, so he authorized my access to the project files." *But, he didn't take my advice,* Daniel thought as he recalled the president's decision to not expedite the replacement for *Chronos 1*. "Also, Benjamin and the Secret Service did a thorough background check on you before your request to meet with me was accepted."

"Oh, of course. Well... that will make my story a *bit* shorter."

"And I'd like to hear it," Daniel replied. "I bet it's a good one."

"I guess you'll be the judge of that, sir."

Daniel smiled. "All right, then! But, before you begin, let me warm up our coffee—we may need it," he said as he reached slowly for the coffee pot on the table in front of them.

"Here, let me get that," Lai said as she jumped up from the loveseat and reached for the coffee pot.

"Thank you." He looked at her as she poured the coffee. "I read every word of the Secret Service's report on you. You're quite an exceptional woman, Dr. Shen," he said with a kind expression.

Damn, I'm starting to like this old man!

Lai spent the next 45 minutes telling Daniel how she came to be there that day, starting with her friendship with Kapono and segueing into what he'd taught her about forgiveness and love, which led to the idea of working to embed love for others in the law. It turned out Daniel knew a little about ho'oponopono, as one of his friends was a practitioner. She also shared some pertinent details from the project, including her aborted trip to the wormhole, and her dream. After telling Daniel about that dream, she stopped and took a sip of coffee.

"A pretty crazy dream, huh?" Lai asked Daniel, who had been listening attentively during Lai's long story.

"Crazy? I don't know about that." He smiled and looked directly at Lai. "Think how many people thought the Camp David Covenant of '35 was an impossible dream. And then there was the man who, almost a century ago, had a dream that many people thought was crazy at the time. He dreamed that, one day, his children would live in a nation where they wouldn't be judged by the color of their skin, but by the content of their character." His voice began to rise in volume and intensity, until he sounded to Lai more like the Daniel Bennett she'd seen on old videos of his campaign speeches. "And he dreamed of the day when 'all of God's children, black men and white men, Jews and Gentiles, Protestants and Catholics, would be able to join hands and sing in the words of the old Negro spiritual: *Free at last! Free at last!*

Thank God Almighty, we are free at last!'" Daniel paused to catch his breath. "Dr. King's so-called crazy dream has yet to be fully realized, but we've made considerable progress in the past 90-plus years. So... maybe yours is not so wild a dream after all, eh?"

Lai smiled slightly, "Maybe not."

"But, you haven't answered my other question: why ask *me* for help? You know, I'm 85 years old—I'm not exactly a spring chicken."

"That's a big plus, as I see it, sir. My parents taught me to respect and treasure the wisdom and experience of elders. But, to answer your question... my friend Kapono told me about you—about how you've emphasized the importance of love, even loving one's enemies, during your life, particularly during your Senate and presidential campaigns. He—and I—thought that was extraordinary. Plus, you're an excellent public speaker." Lai thought of his little speech a few minutes earlier and the videos she'd watched while preparing for many hours for her meeting with Daniel Bennett—and confirming that he was the best person to help her. "I *suck* at that—if you'll forgive the expression. I'm a scientist, not a politician or evangelist. And," she added, "the fact you're a former president of the United States doesn't hurt, either."

"I see you've done some homework," Daniel said with a smile. "And, about what you said about my talk about love during my campaigns... signing the ASA into law isn't my only regret from my time in the White House. Looking back, I wish I'd done more to advocate for love during my seven years as veep and one year as president."

"Well, here's your chance to ease that regret." Lai paused for a few seconds. "I read that you once said something about how our fire of rage should get us working to do things that will affect meaningful change."

Daniel nodded and smiled, "That's right."

"Well, I don't know about you, but I've got that 'fire of rage' about what's happened to this planet, and what *will* happen if we don't do something about it. We've tried many things to reverse course; they haven't worked." She paused. "One thing we haven't tried yet is to wholeheartedly embrace love for each other, even for our enemies." *I bet RAND Corp didn't factor THAT into their algorithms.* "That's what I'm going to work toward, with everything I've got. But," she admitted, "it won't be nearly enough. I need help. I need *your* help, Daniel."

Daniel flashed a smile. "I thought you said you're not an evangelist, Lai. You're doing a pretty damn good imitation of one right now."

Lai's cheeks flushed. "Thanks. But, it's one thing to sit here and talk with you. It's another thing to get up in front of lots of people."

"That's a skill that can be learned." Then Daniel thought about something his late friend Aida Pendamai had asked him to do—which he *didn't* do—while talking with her late one night at the White House almost 19 years ago. He raised his head to look at Lai. "Do you believe in second chances?"

Lai was momentarily taken aback by the question. Then a memory flashed through her mind of a devastated young woman who'd just been released from prison and soon thereafter would try to end her own life, and her lips formed a slight smile. "Absolutely."

Daniel, remembering Lai's background report, returned her smile and nodded. "One of my favorite prayers is from Saint Francis of Assisi. Have you heard of him?"

"I can't say I have—I'm not a religious person."

"Well, his prayer goes something like this: *Make me an instrument of peace. Where there's hatred, let me sow love. Where there's darkness, let me sow light.* That's really what you're talking about doing: becoming an instrument of peace; sowing love and light where there's hatred and darkness." Lai nodded, and Daniel smiled. "I would be honored to join you on your quest, Lai, and help you however I can."

She was overcome with relief and gratitude. "Thank you, Daniel!"

"But… there *is* one thing we need to talk about: this idea of making 'love one another' the *law*." He took a sip of coffee. "Dr. King believed that 'love is the greatest force in the universe'—and I believe that, too. But he also believed that, while law can influence moral behavior, you can't *legislate* morality. And since you researched me before coming here, you may have seen that I've said that *you can't legislate love*. And that's what we're talking about doing, right?"

Lai wracked her brain for a response; then she remembered something Kapono had told her. "Are you familiar with the teachings of the Apostle Paul?"

Daniel nodded, "Yes, I am."

"Then you probably know that Paul said that 'love is the fulfillment of the law'."

"Yes, in his letter to the Romans. But, Lai, he wasn't talking there about loving others literally being the law."

"How do you know? Did you ask him?" Lai asked with a wry smile.

Daniel chuckled, "No, of course not. But biblical scholars generally agree on what that passage means."

"Did *they* ask Paul what he meant?"

Daniel laughed. *It's obvious she hasn't studied the Bible much, but...* "You're a persistent woman!" He thought for a few seconds. "Here's the deal... if love for others *did* become ingrained in the law, I'd be okay with that. But I think there's little chance of it happening."

Lai nodded, "That's what I told Kapono. His hope, and his faith in what might be possible, were greater than mine."

"I wish I could have met him." Daniel studied Lai's face for a few seconds. "He meant a great deal to you, didn't he?"

Lai cleared her throat. "Yes, he did."

Daniel sat up straight on the sofa. "All right, tell you what... let's go for it—making love for others the law. And even if we're not successful getting that done, I think we can do a lot of good just by sowing love and light wherever we can. What do you think of that?"

"I think... that sounds great, Daniel." Lai thought for a few seconds. "So... where should we start?"

"Good question!" Daniel closed his eyes and lowered his head, deep in thought. Then his head popped up and he smiled at Lai. "Do you know the saying, 'Don't start by trying to feed the whole world—just feed a small country'?"

"No, I haven't heard that one."

"It means to start small. That's what we need to do—have one success that serves as an example for others. Do you remember the friend I mentioned, the one who's a practitioner of ho'oponopono?" Lai nodded, and Daniel grinned, "He's the governor of Hawai'i."

Lai's face brightened. "Oh, that's perfect! Hawai'i's fairly small, many people there are familiar with ho'oponopono, and you have a friend in leadership!"

"All right, then! I'll call him and get a meeting scheduled as soon as he's available." He paused and looked at Lai. "When you came here today, you said you weren't sure if you could forgive me for the ASA. And I can understand if you're not able to do that right now. Will it be a problem?"

"No, sir. I understand now why you thought you had to do it, and I respect that you had a difficult decision to make. But... forgiveness may take a little while, yet."

"Okay, then." He called toward the kitchen, "Benjamin!" The tall agent appeared in the living room doorway.

"Yes, Mr. B?"

"I'll be going on a trip with Dr. Shen pretty soon—probably in the next couple of weeks."

"I'll start making preparations, sir. Where are we going?"

"Honolulu!"

| 22 |

November 10, 2054

As Ben drove the white Subaru into the visitor parking lot of Washington Place, Lai peered out of the side window from the back seat and admired the graceful white Greek revival mansion. "It's gorgeous!" she exclaimed to Daniel, who was sitting with her in the back seat.

"Isn't it? You're in for a treat." Daniel had visited Hawai'i's historic executive mansion next to the Capitol building in Honolulu many years ago, before another home was built for the governor and Washington Place became a museum. He was glad that Governor Peleke had suggested they meet at the old executive mansion instead of his mundane office at the Capitol.

Ben parked the wagon, hopped out, and opened the driver's side back door for Daniel while visually sweeping the parking lot. He wasn't at all pleased that Daniel had requested minimal Secret Service protection for the trip to Hawai'i, which meant Ben was the only agent protecting the former president. As Daniel climbed slowly out of the wagon, he noticed Ben taking in every detail of their surroundings.

"You worry too much, Benjamin," Daniel gently chided the tall agent. "It's a beautiful day in Hawai'i, and we're visiting the governor. There must be Capitol Police all over the place."

"I do worry, Mr. B," Ben replied, "but never too much." Daniel smiled and patted Ben on his back. They joined Lai and walked together down the sidewalk leading to the side entrance of the mansion. Daniel wore a gray tropical-weight sport coat and slacks and a white Oxford shirt, Lai a short-sleeved dark green dress, and Ben his usual black suit.

"How do you know Governor Peleke, Daniel?" Lai asked as they walked.

"Kaleo and I go way back. I campaigned for him when he was first elected to the House in '26, back when I was a senator—and we were both a lot younger!" he laughed. "He campaigned for me during the primaries in '28, and for President Pendamai and me in '28 and '32. And, I was an advisor for his first run at the governor's mansion in '50."

A Capitol Police officer met them inside the entrance. "Welcome, President Bennett," the officer said, smiling warmly. "And you must be Dr. Shen," he added, looking at Lai.

"That's me!" Lai replied.

The officer exchanged greetings with Ben and then said to all of them, "Please follow me; the governor's expecting you." He led the three visitors through the main hall of the historic mansion. Lai was spellbound as she walked past the first-floor parlors with their Victorian-era furnishings, and the paintings that depicted the history of Hawai'i and the Hawaiian kings and queens who'd lived in the mansion. "Here we are," the officer announced as they arrived at a white room that was surrounded on three sides by floor-to-ceiling multipane windows and decorated with cushioned wicker furniture and a grand piano.

Lai contrasted the sunny indoors lanai with the windowless, drab underground base she'd called home for the past two years. *This is like heaven!*

Daniel, noticing Lai's expression of delight, smiled and whispered to her, "I thought you might like this."

A medium-height man with graying black hair, wearing black slacks and a navy Hawaiian shirt with hibiscus flowers, stood up from one of the sofas and walked over to them. "Aloha!" he said with a warm smile. He turned toward Daniel and extended his arms. "Daniel! It's been—forever!" The two men embraced.

"It has been, Kaleo. Thank you for seeing us. And, congratulations again on your victory last week!" Daniel was referring to the gubernatorial election one week ago, when his friend had been elected to a second consecutive term by the largest margin in Hawai'i's history.

"Thank you, Daniel. I'm grateful for and humbled by the support and love of the people of Hawai'i. I guess I must be doing something right!" he laughed. Then he turned toward Ben, "Benjamin, it's great to see you again! How are you?" They shook hands.

"Likewise, Governor. I'm well, thank you, sir. I'm doing my best to keep this man out of trouble," Ben replied as he smiled slightly and shot a sideways glance at Daniel.

The governor laughed again. "Daniel never was one to follow directions, was he? I hope you can join us for this discussion."

"I'd like that, Governor—thank you," Ben replied.

Then Kaleo turned to Lai, "Dr. Shen! It's a great pleasure to meet you. Daniel has told me so much about you." They clasped each other's hands.

"Thanks, Governor, the pleasure is mine. And please—it's Lai."

The governor nodded, "And I'm Kaleo, okay?" He motioned to the sofa and chairs behind him. "Let's sit down and talk." They sat down, and Lai noticed a coffee service on the low table in front of them, along with what was probably the most wonderful aroma she'd smelled in many years.

"Is that what I *think* it is?" Daniel asked Kaleo.

Kaleo smiled and nodded, "Island-grown Kona coffee. You know I wouldn't deprive you of that, my friend." He reached for the pot and looked at Ben and Lai. "Would you like some of the world's best coffee?"

Ben declined, but Lai wasn't about to pass it up. "Oh yes, please!" Since the huge reductions worldwide in coffee-suitable land and coffee yields in the past decade due to climate change, finding genuine coffee of *any* kind was increasingly difficult, and very costly—to the point where real coffee had become a luxury for most people. Kaleo poured coffee for the three of them, and Lai savored her first sip. *This is even better than the coffee at the Prometheus base and Daniel's place. I've gone to heaven twice in one day—not bad for a non-believer!*

Kaleo took a sip of coffee, set his cup back on the table, and looked at Lai. "Lai, Daniel told me when he asked for this meeting about your idea for encouraging people to love one another through the law. And I must say, I think what you and Daniel are trying to accomplish is extraordinary. I don't have to tell you, we need a lot more love and forgiveness in the world."

"Thank you, sir... sorry—Kaleo. But I can't take credit for the idea. It came from a Hawaiian friend named Kapono."

"Ah, I see. And Kapono was the one who taught you about ho'oponopono, is that right?"

"Yes, he did." Lai smiled, then nodded once. "And much more."

"Daniel told me you and your friend worked on a secret project for the federal government, and he's been declared missing?"

"That's right." Lai wished she could tell Kaleo more about Kapono's contributions to Prometheus, especially how he'd sacrificed his life for the future of humanity, but that was out of the question.

"I am so sorry for your loss," Kaleo said sadly, and then he looked into Lai's eyes. "But, please remember, he lives on in your heart, and in the hearts of everyone who loves him. And you honor him through your efforts to 'sow love and light'," he turned his head toward Daniel and smiled, "as Daniel likes to say."

"Thank you," Lai replied, trying not to tear up from Kaleo's kindness. *He doesn't sound like any governor I've ever heard! He sounds more like a counselor, or minister.*

Kaleo sat up straight on the sofa. "Now, about your idea... I'd appreciate it if you could share with me the whole story of how you and Daniel came to be here today. Then we can discuss how I can best help you. Is that okay with you?"

"Sure, I'd like to do that."

Over the next hour, Lai gave Kaleo as many details as she could about how and why she decided to push her skepticism and doubts aside to use love as a lever to prevent the dire predictions of humanity's fate from becoming reality. Daniel contributed details about his meeting with Lai at his home nearly two weeks earlier. Kaleo listened in rapt attention and asked many questions. After Lai and Daniel had finished their story, Kaleo had one remaining question.

"Lai, Daniel... I understand and agree with everything you've said. You know that I'm a practitioner of ho'oponopono, and your mission to encourage love and forgiveness is close to my heart." He looked at Lai. "I don't know if Daniel told you, but I was a practicing clinical psychologist before being elected to Congress in '26."

"No, I didn't know that." *That explains a lot!* Then Lai remembered something from her discussion with Kapono over pizza in her quarters, right before he disappeared. "Did you ever work with Dr. Hew Len?"

Kaleo smiled, as if recalling a fond memory. "I did! I first met him at one of his seminars when I was in high school. I learned about ho'oponopono then, and he encouraged me to pursue a degree in psychology. He was my ho'oponopono master during college." His smile faded. "He passed away not long after I graduated from the University of Hawai'i. He was a wonderful mentor and friend."

Kaleo looked down at his folded hands for a few seconds, then looked up at Lai and Daniel. "But, here's my question... why must love for others be embedded in *law*? Isn't it enough to promote love and forgiveness for each other?"

Daniel started to respond, but Lai spoke first, frustration evident in her voice. "We've *tried* that. Many great people have tried that, over thousands of years—for instance, Jesus Christ, the Apostle Paul, the Dalai Lama, and many other religious leaders of many faiths. Also leaders like Mahatma Gandhi, Dr. King, Harriet Tubman, Nelson Mandela..." she paused and looked at Daniel, "... and Daniel Bennett." Daniel smiled; he felt honored to be included in Lai's list. "And many, many more. *It didn't work.* They tried telling everyone to love one another; that loving each other is our God-given duty; that loving one another is the fulfillment of the law. Where did that get us?" She looked directly at Kaleo. "Not every place in the world is as wonderful as Hawai'i, Governor."

Kaleo shook his head. "Hawai'i does relatively better than other states and countries, but we still have far too much crime—over 3,000 violent crimes each year. I hear what you're saying. But you're advocating replacing all laws with *one*: love one another. Is that right?"

Lai nodded. "Yes, that's the idea."

"But... how would that work?"

Lai hesitated; she needed time to think. She hadn't thought through those important details. She had been acting on faith, and hope. Now she realized that wasn't nearly enough. *I'm getting in way over my head here. Help!*

Then Daniel spoke up. "Think about it... for one thing, it's a lot *simpler*. How many pages are in Hawai'i's Criminal Code, my friend?"

"Thousands! But, 'love one another' can't cover *every* type of crime—can it?"

"Why not?" Daniel posed. "If you show love to someone, you won't knowingly hurt them. You won't steal from them. You won't lie to them or cheat them. No... you'll be kind to them. Protect them. Share with them. Be honest with them." Lai was astonished. Daniel had pushed back with her on the idea of making Love One Another the law. Yet now he was advocating for it.

"Okay, okay!" Kaleo held up his palms. "I can see where it *might* be possible that one-size-fits-all could work, as far as the law goes. But, what about *enforcement* and *corrections*? I think we're talking about a complete overhaul of Hawai'i's criminal justice system, aren't we?"

Daniel nodded, "Yes, I think you're right." He glanced at Lai, then turned back to Kaleo. "We never said it would be *easy*. It will take time. There'll be considerable re-thinking needed for law enforcement, in the judicial system, and in corrections, and education for people in those agencies, and for the general public. And I mean, a *lot* of education. It would be a seismic shift for the people of Hawai'i." He paused, and smiled. "But, Kaleo... if it works here, in Hawai'i, it can be a model for the country, and the world!"

Kaleo thought for a few seconds, then looked at Lai. "I don't know if you're aware of this, but the governor of Hawai'i has quite a bit of power—much more than in most other states. I've always chosen to use that power discreetly... to guide, to teach—and sometimes to nudge a bit, when necessary. So, Daniel... what you said about a lot of education being needed doesn't scare me. It actually *appeals* to me." He paused and smiled. "And it *really* appeals to me that Hawai'i could be at the forefront of a worldwide movement... 'a light for the world,' as Aida used to say—right, Daniel?"

Daniel smiled from the memory of the late president. "That's right." He straightened up in his chair and looked at Kaleo. "So, what do you think? Will you help us realize this dream?"

"I think... it's worth thinking more about. And talking more about." He looked at Lai and Daniel. "I'd like to include a few others in this discussion—people who'll be essential if we move forward, and whose counsel I value highly: the lieutenant governor, the House speaker, the Senate president, and the attorney general. Would you return to Honolulu to meet with them, and me, as soon as we can arrange something?"

Lai was overjoyed. "Certainly!"

"That would be great, Kaleo," Daniel added. "We'll be glad to come back here whenever you give the word."

"Excellent," Kaleo replied. "First, I'd like to talk with each of them individually, to brief them and get their input. Then I'll schedule a meeting for all of us. It could take a couple of weeks to get that done. Is that okay?"

"Definitely," Lai replied, "whatever works best for you." She looked at Daniel with a wry smile, "Our schedules are more flexible than yours, Kaleo—right, Daniel?" Daniel laughed and nodded.

Kaleo stood up, and the others followed suit. "Great. I'll have my assistant get back to you to schedule the next meeting." He shook hands with the three visitors. "Lai, it was truly a pleasure to meet you.

Daniel and Benjamin, it's always good to see you. Benjamin, take good care of 'The Enforcer,' okay?" Ben looked puzzled, but Daniel laughed at the reference to the nickname one of his football coaches at Stanford had pinned on him long ago.

Back at the parking lot, Lai stopped Daniel before he got into the wagon. "I want to thank you for your help in there. I had *no* idea how to respond to Kaleo. I know you're not completely on board about making Love One Another the law."

"You're welcome, but you need to give yourself more credit, Lai. What you said when he asked about that was inspired. You've done some homework!"

"Thanks. Homework's one thing I was always pretty good at."

"Anyway, no need to thank me for helping you. We're a team—we're in this together. We'll 'fight the good fight,' and… we'll see what happens." Daniel looked at Ben, who was nervously scanning all around the parking lot as they stood beside the wagon. "We'd better get going before Benjamin blows a gasket."

They climbed into the wagon, and Ben headed for the exit. Daniel turned to Lai, who was sitting with him in the back seat. "Can I ask you a personal question?"

"Sure."

"These flights between Boston and Honolulu aren't cheap. And if this movement takes off, we could do lots of flying around the country, and maybe to other countries. Are you okay with that?"

"Thanks for thinking about that—I appreciate it. But, no, that won't be a problem for me." Lai decided to not mention that she was a multimillionaire. She'd inherited her parent's Bay Area home, the lake cabin in Minnesota, and a significant amount of money. She'd sold the home when she joined the fusion project at Lawrence Livermore. Plus, she'd had almost no expenses while working on Prometheus. "Oh, speaking of travel… I'm going to make a side trip to Maui tonight and tomorrow before heading back to the mainland. I'll meet up with you back in Boston, okay?"

"Maui?" Then Daniel remembered something Lai had told him when they first met. "Oh, yes—I understand." He patted her left hand. "Have a safe trip."

"Thanks, you too."

| 23 |

November 11, 2054

Lai turned the rented Jeep into the short driveway, stopped behind an old Honda hatchback that was in the carport, turned off the motor, and took in the front of the small, one-story home. *What a cute house!* It was painted creamy beige, with white and sage trim. There was a large lanai with a bronze-colored metal roof and white railings across the entire front of the house, and a gable with a big window above the porch. The home's multi-pane windows and French doors were open to the island breeze. A few small palm trees decorated the front yard. Lai had noticed that all the trees in the area were fairly small—then she realized that none were more than about 30 years old.

Lai hopped out of the Jeep and walked around it toward the open front door. She heard barking, and then a big golden lab ran around the corner of the house, dashed up to her, and started pawing her white cropped pants and purple sleeveless blouse with muddy paws while he licked her hands. "Uh, hi there… aloha?… down boy!" she said as she tried, unsuccessfully, to discourage the dog's friendly greeting.

Then a short man with weathered skin, wearing a straw fedora, sweat-stained white T-shirt, and khaki shorts came around the far corner of the house. "Akela, come!" he commanded. The dog immediately left Lai and retreated to the man's side as he walked up to Lai.

"I'm so sorry!" the man apologized as he looked at Lai's muddy pants and blouse. "He usually doesn't do that with strangers." He smiled, "He must really like you. He's very perceptive about people."

"Don't worry about it," Lai replied as she brushed off most of the dirt. Then she looked at the man's face—an older version of the face she'd seen on the photo on Kapono's desk.

"You must be Lai. Sorry about these clothes—I was working in the garden and lost track of time."

"No problem, sir. Yes, I'm Lai Shen. It's good to finally meet you, Mr. Ailana," she said as she extended her right hand.

He checked his hands, which were encrusted with garden dirt. "I need to wash these," he said. "Let's go inside so I can clean up, and we can talk. And please, call me Keone." He motioned with his right hand toward the open front door and followed Lai onto the lanai and then into the living area; Akela joined them. "Please, be comfortable," Keone said over his shoulder as he went into the galley kitchen to wash his hands. "I just need a couple of minutes."

"Thanks—take your time," Lai replied as she looked around the small living area. There was a small upholstered sofa, a wood chest with a padded top, a square coffee table, a modest round glass bistro table with two chairs, wood shelves built into a corner with knick-knacks and a tiny TV, and some potted plants. Two large ceiling fans with wooden blades carved like palm fronds rotated slowly overhead. A staircase with painted wood railings led to a loft; Kapono's surfboard was mounted on a wall in the loft. There were a few prints on the living room walls, and a framed photo sitting on one of the corner shelves. Lai realized it was the same photo Kapono had on his desk at the base.

Keone emerged from the bedroom sans hat, wearing a blue Hawaiian shirt with a palm tree pattern. "Okay, let's try that again—aloha!" he said as he joined Lai in the living area and extended his right hand, which Lai shook. "Can I get you something to drink?"

"Do you have any Kona coffee?" Lai thought of the incredible brew she'd enjoyed the day before at Washington Place.

"I do! And I'd be glad to make some for you. Or, how about iced coffee?"

Lai liked that idea; it was a warm day for November in Maui. "That would be great, thanks!"

Keone went into the tiny kitchen to get the coffee. "Thanks for coming all this way to see me. That's a long trip!" Keone said as he worked in the kitchen.

"It was no trouble. I had a meeting yesterday in Honolulu, anyway."

"Ah! Did you get in any sight-seeing?" He came out of the kitchen carrying a tray with two glasses of ice and a glass pitcher and set the tray on the coffee table. He poured coffee into the glasses as Lai sat down on the sofa.

"Not really. But, my meeting was at Washington Place—that was *amazing*." Keone handed Lai a frosty glass, took one for himself, and sat down on the cushioned chest next to the sofa. Akela padded over to Keone and lay down on the wood plank floor.

"It's beautiful, isn't it? I took a tour through there several years ago. I didn't know it was used for meetings, though."

Lai savored her first sip of the iced Kona coffee. "Well," she confided, "my meeting was with Governor Peleke and former President Bennett." She smiled, "I guess they have some clout."

"I'd say!" Lai realized, *Kapono and his dad have the same smile.* "You have some important friends. I know you and my son were working on some high-security stuff, but I'd be interested to hear about your meeting if you'd like to tell me about it… if you're *allowed* to tell me about it."

"Sure, I'd be glad to do that, sir." *That's only right—I wouldn't have been there at all if it wasn't for Kapono.*

"But, before you do that, I wanted to tell you… I appreciate your sending me my son's personal effects, including his surfboard. That was very kind of you, Lai."

"It was no trouble, sir. I was glad to do it. It was the least I could do… considering everything he did for me." The way Keone nodded, it seemed to Lai as if he *knew* all that his son had done for her.

"So... Kapono told me that he met you while working on that secret project that he couldn't tell me anything about, is that right?"

"Yes, that's right. He started on it a few months before I did. When I got there, he was the first to welcome me, and was really kind to me."

"That's Kapono," Keone said, smiling.

"Yes," Lai agreed as she returned Keone's smile. "And in time, we became friends." Lai wanted to tell Keone how much Kapono meant to her, but she wasn't sure how to go about it. *Oh, hell—just get it out there*, she decided. "Actually, your son was my *closest* friend. He helped me in so many ways. He taught me about ho'oponopono... and a lot more." She started tearing up. *Dammit...* "And, uh..." she looked up at Keone, "... eventually, we became more than friends. He meant the world to me, sir."

Keone looked at Lai with sympathy, understanding, and kindness. "Yes, I know, Lai. Kapono told me about you, several months ago. Not by name. But he told me he'd met someone who worked on the same project he did. Someone he loved very much. That was you, of course. He said he couldn't tell you he loved you because he was your subordinate, then you were his." He paused as he noticed tears starting to trickle down Lai's cheeks. "I wanted to be sure you knew that, in case he didn't have a chance to tell you himself."

"Thank you. He... he did tell me, right before he went missing." She thought back to her last night with Kapono—*The best night of my life*. Then Lai realized she was being incredibly selfish; she looked at Keone. "But, how are *you* doing? I only knew Kapono for a couple of years. It must be so hard for you."

"Oh, Akela and I, we're doing okay," Keone said softly. "Some days are worse than others." He looked down at the old lab, snoozing at his feet. "I know Akela misses him. Kapono raised him from a pup. I think he's still waiting for him to walk through that door and take him to the beach to play in the surf." He paused. "It was, uh, such a surprise when I got the call from Dr. Etter. I didn't realize that project was so dangerous." He paused again and cleared his throat. "Dr. Etter couldn't give me any details, but she told me that Kapono gave his life for his country, and in fact for the whole world. I really miss him, but I'm very proud of him." He looked at Lai. "And I'm so glad that he found you. He'd been looking for someone like you for a long time."

Someone like me? Someone as messed up as I am—or was, at least? "What do you mean?"

"Kapono was picky. He was waiting for just the right woman—someone 'whose heart was filled with love,' he said. That was you."

Lai shook her head. "I don't know, Keone. I'm pretty messed up. Kapono helped me a lot with that, but I kind of doubt—"

Keone leaned forward. "Lai—listen to me. Kapono was good at knowing what was inside people. And I know he was right about you. I can tell your heart is full of love—for him, and in general." He reached out and grasped her right hand. "You know, it's hard to be one's best self when you're in pain. I know about that. And Kapono knew. He went through some tough times when he was young."

Lai remembered her lunchtime talk with Kapono on her second day at the base. "Are you talking about when his mother—your wife—died in the fire in '23?" she asked softly.

"Yes. I don't know what Kapono told you about that."

"Not much, except that he wasn't quite five years old, and it was really hard on him—and you."

"It was. And because he was so young, I think it was a lot tougher for Kapono. He was very angry, at everyone and everything—at the Earth—for taking his mother from him. He got into lots of trouble when he was a boy, into his teens. He skipped school a lot—ran off to the beach to surf or just hang out... sometimes with the wrong people. He got into a lot of fights. If he hadn't been a minor, he probably would've wound up in jail."

Lai was astonished. *That isn't the Kapono I knew!* Then she was upset with herself. *I dumped all my baggage on Kapono, but I never took time to find out what he went through when his mother died!* "Kapono didn't tell me any of this. But, he did mention that you taught him ho'oponopono when he was—I think he said 14. Did that help him?"

"Yes, it did. I introduced him to ho'oponopono and got help from a master to work with him on it. It helped him with his anger and helped him to forgive the Earth—and himself. There was more to his transformation than ho'oponopono, but it helped him a lot. It can help you, too, Lai."

"I think it's already helped me. And it's partly the reason I came to Hawai'i, for the meeting yesterday in Honolulu. Did you really want to hear more about that?"

"Yes, I'd like that."

Lai shared with Keone the long story of how her dream and Kapono's encouragement had led her to ask Daniel Bennett for help to base the law on the simple but powerful idea of Love One Another, and how Governor Peleke has shown interest in making Hawai'i a test case for the concept. When she was finished, Keone leaned back against the wall and considered what he'd heard.

"That's quite a story, Lai. What you've done to take an idea from a dream and try to make it reality, to help the whole world... you should be proud of that. I'm so excited about what you've done so far, and what could come from your efforts."

"Thanks, Keone. But, I had lots of help—from your son, from Daniel Bennett, and now, I hope, from Governor Peleke. And, as the old poem goes, '... I have promises to keep, and miles to go before I sleep.'"

"I understand. But, remember, you're not alone in this." He smiled in a way that made Lai feel as if he knew something that she may not. "And I don't mean only President Bennett and Governor Peleke."

| 24 |

18 October, 2135

Sumati Patel gazed out of the window wall of her 22nd floor office, looking at the city's sun-drenched skyline and the busy plaza below. She was thinking about the report she'd just finished reading from the pad on her small glass desk. Then her thoughts were interrupted by a chime from her phone.

"Madam President, your 2:30 is here," a woman's voice announced from the phone.

"Thank you, Charlotte. Please send her in." Sumati got up from her desk and walked over to the door in her dark blue saree with gold trim as the visitor entered the office. "Hello, Doctor! It's good to see you again. Thank you for coming," Sumati said warmly as she shook hands with the visitor and motioned to the small round glass table next to her desk.

"It's good to see you, too, Madam President," the slender, elderly woman, dressed in a black pants suit and blue blouse, replied as she and Sumati sat down across from each other at the table.

"How is your son?" Sumati asked.

"He's well, thank you. He's busy working on the designs for the replacement bridges for Perth. He'll be going there soon to supervise their construction."

"That's good news—Perth really needs those bridges. And your daughter-in-law—how is she? She's in the Peace Corps, is that right?"

"Yes. She's on holiday now but will be starting an assignment in West Texas soon."

Texas... THAT will be challenging—and not a little hazardous. "I wish her safe travels. Please convey to her my gratitude for her service."

"I will, Madam President—thank you."

Sumati leaned back in her swivel chair. "So... it's happened."

"Yes. The Wagamese Wormhole appeared in the constellation Triangulum Australe at 2:52 this morning. I was three minutes off on my prediction."

Sumati smiled, "Only you would mention such a small difference, Doctor." Then her expression became serious. "I read your report on the Prometheus Project. I understand that the first attempt to travel to the future will be made just over five years from now, is that right?"

The doctor nodded, "Yes—1,945 days from now, to be exact. But, as you saw in the report, that attempt will not succeed. However, nearly six years from now—on 26 September, 2141—a second attempt will be made."

"And we're not sure if that attempt will be successful, correct?"

"That's right, Madam President. Apparently, the ship was damaged by a micrometeorite. It may or may not have entered the wormhole. If it did, we don't know the condition of the spacecraft, or if the pilot survived."

"If it did not enter the wormhole, observers on Earth of the past would have been able to track it, would they not?"

The doctor hesitated for a few seconds. "Shortly after the ship was damaged, the wormhole was destroyed by a tremendous explosion. If the ship didn't enter the wormhole, it would have been destroyed by the blast."

Sumati looked at the doctor with a puzzled expression. "Do we know what caused the explosion?"

"There's only one way it could have happened. We did it."

Sumati's look of puzzlement changed to shock. "What do you mean, *we* did it?"

"I believe that, somehow, a powerful explosive device, most likely a nuclear warhead, was sent into the wormhole—*our* end of the wormhole—to purposely destroy it."

"But, the Council hasn't even discussed doing that!" Sumati countered.

"Not yet. But obviously, it will. And it's clear that their decision will be to destroy it."

Sumati considered what the doctor had just told her. "Why would we do such a thing?"

"To prevent anyone from using the wormhole to travel through time. Specifically, to prevent the pilot of the second Prometheus mission, Dr. Kapono Ailana, from returning to the past. That was his mission: to learn what happened to Earth in the future and bring knowledge of the future back to the mid-21st century in hopes of resolving some of the immense problems Earth faced then." The doctor paused. "And, Madam President, as chief physicist, I must tell you that I think it would be a mistake to allow that to happen. A mistake that could threaten the future of the entire planet. You may recall the discussions I've had with the Council's science committee on that subject."

Sumati nodded slowly, "I do. So, you are in favor of this decision that the Council made—*will* make—to destroy the wormhole?"

"Yes, Madam President. But with one provision."

"And, what is that?"

The doctor set her face in determination. "We *must* give Dr. Ailana every chance to make it safely through the wormhole. After that, we should destroy it."

"But, Doctor, according to your report on the Prometheus Project, Dr. Ailana had a near-zero chance of surviving the micrometeorite impact, correct?"

The doctor closed her eyes and nodded once. "Yes, that's true. And if he did survive the impact, he may not have made it through the event horizon before the wormhole was destroyed." She leaned forward. "But there is a *chance*, however slim, that he will arrive here six years from now. We *must* give him that chance, Madam President."

Sumati looked sympathetically at the doctor. "But, if we wait six years, isn't there a chance that someone from the present will attempt to travel back in time, for what they believe is a very good reason?"

"Yes, it's possible—but unlikely. The wormhole is almost three billion kilometers—two billion miles—from Earth. With spacecraft available today, it would take nearly two years to reach it. And the ships that could make that type of voyage are, as you know, in very short supply."

"Yes, I know," Sumati replied. "Thus I don't know how we could hope to mount a rescue mission for Dr. Ailana."

The doctor nodded solemnly. "I agree. We won't be able to send a ship to help him. All I ask is that we give him every chance to reach Earth on his own—if he can. If his ship's Quantum Drive survived the micrometeorite strike, it's possible he could make it to Earth. And if he does," the doctor smiled slightly, "we can cross that bridge when we come to it—can we not?"

Sumati thought in silence for a few seconds. "I don't know, Doctor. Given the very low odds of his reaching Earth—of being alive at all—I think it would be prudent to destroy the wormhole as soon as we can, to prevent anyone from attempting to reach the past and endangering the present—and our future." The doctor started to respond, but Sumati finished her thought. "We could launch a probe carrying one of our asteroid-buster warheads now, and within two years the wormhole will no longer be a threat."

"But, Madam President, that would in itself change the past!" Sumati looked quizzically at her. "History records that the wormhole was destroyed on 20 October, 2054—that's 26 September, 2141 in our time. We must hold to that timeline to avoid changing the future in some unanticipated, and possibly tragic, way. Most importantly, we *must* allow the first Prometheus mission to happen, and to fail. Do you understand why?"

Sumati didn't understand. But then she recalled what the report she'd just read had said about that mission, and its aftermath. "Oh! Yes, of course... I do understand. So, we need to wait about three years before launching the probe, to allow that mission to happen, yes?"

"That's right, Madam President—at *least* three years. But I believe we need to wait *four* years before launching the probe, to allow Dr. Ailana's mission to happen and give him a chance to reach the future, and Earth."

"I don't follow you, Doctor. I understand the importance of allowing the first mission to fail. But why can't we simply destroy the wormhole right after that flight—before Dr. Ailana's mission?"

Time travel is a sticky wicket, the doctor thought. "It's complicated, Madam President. But the net of it is, *we don't know* what will happen if Dr. Ailana does *not* make that attempt. History could unfold in a much different way... with serious consequences for the entire world."

Sumati nodded, "I think I understand what you're saying."

"Also, the exact timing of the wormhole's destruction is important."

"How so?"

"We know that the Prometheus team was going to launch a rescue mission for Dr. Ailana. We must destroy the wormhole about two hours *after* Dr. Ailana's accident, but no later than that. That will give Dr. Ailana time to get a safe distance from the wormhole, if he can, and will avoid jeopardizing the rescue ship." She paused. "And, Madam President, I believe there are reasons other than trying to protect history and Earth's future for us to make every effort to save Dr. Ailana's life."

Sumati smiled knowingly, "Are you thinking of our Guiding Principle?"

"Yes, I am," the doctor replied, returning Sumati's smile. "And, one other thing."

"What is that?"

The doctor's eyes began to glisten. "Respectfully, Madam President... I think you, and the Council, owe me one." She turned her head to look out the window toward the plaza below. "And you all certainly owe *her* one."

Sumati smiled and nodded. "You're right—we do owe both of you more than we could ever repay." She looked down at the tabletop as she thought for a few seconds, then looked up at the doctor. "All right... I will ask the Council to wait four years before launching the probe with the warhead. And we'll carefully time the detonation as you've suggested. We will give Dr. Ailana... Kapono... every chance to come home—albeit a much different home than he's used to."

"Thank you, Madam President," the doctor said gratefully. *And he WILL make it, somehow... I know he'll find a way.*

| 25 |

November 23, 2054

Governor Peleke leaned back in his brown leather swivel chair, pausing to reflect on the past four hours of spirited discussion in the Capitol's executive conference room. He looked at the other people sitting with him around the beautiful koa wood table. "All right, I think we have a plan. Sirai, please read back the action items we've agreed to," he said to his holopad on the table in front of him.

"Kaleo, here are my notes on the action items," Sirai began. "Step One is to educate the people of Hawai'i on LOA, that is, Love One Another. That effort will be led by Daniel Bennett and Lai Shen, with assistance from House and Senate members as they communicate with their constituents."

House Speaker Kitagawa interjected, "To minimize the time and effort needed from House members, I'll recommend to them that they simply include LOA as a topic in their town hall meetings."

Senate President Elefante nodded, "That's a good idea, Lisa. I'll do the same with the senators."

Sirai continued, "Step Two will be an assessment of public sentiment toward LOA, to be started no later than June 1, 2055 and completed by August 1, 2055. Details on how the assessment will be conducted are to be determined. If the results are positive, the legislature will draft an amendment to Hawai'i's Constitution and begin deliberations in both chambers."

Kitagawa turned toward Elefante, "Brandon, if we get to that point, the House can draft the amendment, if that's okay with you."

Elefante looked relieved. "That's absolutely fine with me. As I've explained, I have some reservations about this entire idea."

Lieutenant Governor Kapela looked at Elefante, who was sitting across the table from her. "Brandon, I don't think any of us is ready to *commit* to LOA. But I think we've agreed today that it's worth investigating—that's what the education and assessment phases are for. If those don't pan out, we won't be moving forward with an amendment. The people of Hawai'i will decide how far this goes."

The Senate president nodded, "Okay—you're right, Jeanné. Let's take it slow and see what happens."

"Step Three," Sirai continued, "directs the attorney general's office to begin researching, no later than next January, what would need to change in Hawai'i's criminal justice system to implement LOA. The attorney general will deliver her report to Governor Peleke no later than December 31, 2055."

Attorney General Swenson nodded, "That'll work. We'll need at *least* a year for that analysis. There would be a *lot* of changes needed."

Elefante exhaled with a short whistle, "You can say that again, Danica!"

Kaleo looked at Swenson, then Elefante. "No one said this would be easy. But we've all agreed it's worth the attempt, right?" Everyone at the table nodded or voiced their agreement.

"And finally, Step Four: if the proposed amendment is passed by the Senate and the House, they will work with the secretary of state to author the ballot measure. Realistically, that would happen no earlier than November 2056," Sirai concluded.

"That was a good summary, I think," Kaleo said, as he looked around the table. "Does anyone have any questions or revisions?" There were none. "Great. I recommend we reconvene for a checkpoint in mid-January. Does that work for you, Daniel and Lai?"

"Works for me!" Daniel replied. He smiled at Lai, "Are you okay returning to Honolulu in mid-*January?*"

Lai turned toward Hannah and grinned, "I think we can manage that—right, Hannah?" Hannah gave a thumbs-up. The Secret Service agent was grateful that Governor Peleke had gladly approved Daniel's request for her to sit in on their meeting. As someone with a graduate degree in Public Policy, she'd found the discussion about transforming Hawai'i's criminal code fascinating.

Daniel turned to Kaleo, "What do you think about having a rally at the same time? I think it would be a good way to jump-start the education process."

Kaleo thought for a few seconds. "That's a good idea, Daniel. Perhaps we could have it here, on the Capitol grounds. I'll ask my staff to look at dates and get back to you by, let's say, mid-December—all right?"

Daniel looked at Lai, and they both nodded. "Perfect. Thanks, Kaleo," Daniel replied for both of them.

Kaleo stood up. "Everyone, thank you for your input and counsel. We've taken the first step toward a future that I believe could be of tremendous benefit to Hawai'i." The state government officials said goodbye to each other and left the conference room, leaving Daniel, Lai, and Hannah with Kaleo.

Daniel stood up and shook hands with his friend. "Thank you for your leadership, and your help, Kaleo. This was a big step forward."

"My pleasure. That went better than I'd hoped!"

"I'd like to return for your inauguration in December, if that's okay with you." Daniel thought he'd better ask Kaleo about it, since having a former United States president participate could cause security headaches.

"I'd love it if you could be here, Daniel," Kaleo said happily, and then his expression became somber. "I just wish it would be on a day other than December 7."

Daniel nodded his understanding, then he turned to Lai and Hannah. "I need to discuss something with the governor—if you have time, Kaleo. Could you please excuse us for a few minutes? Capitol

Police can escort me out of the building, if that's okay with you, Hannah—and Kaleo?" They both nodded.

Lai looked at Hannah. "Should we wait outside?" It was a picture-perfect late November day in Honolulu.

"Sure!" Hannah replied enthusiastically. "We'll be right outside the main entrance, Mr. B."

Lai and Hannah said goodbye to Kaleo and made their way out of the Capitol building. They stopped next to a reflecting pool on the plaza near the main entrance. "I wish you could've seen Washington Place," Lai said to Hannah. "It was beautiful." Lai didn't think much of the modern building that had replaced Hawai'i's iconic Iolani Palace as the state Capitol some 85 years earlier. To her, the current Capitol building looked too much like many of the other uninspiring public buildings built in the mid-20th century.

"Well, buildings are buildings," Hannah replied. "But, how about this weather! I could get used to this!"

"For sure! You've *got* to come back here with Daniel and me in January." In the few weeks Lai had known Hannah Ochrankyne, they'd become close friends. They had something in common: both had attended Stanford University. Except Hannah had graduated from there, following in her mother's footsteps, then earned a master's degree in Public Policy there. *Other than that*, Lai reflected, *we're much different.* Lai was in awe of Hannah. While in high school and then at Stanford, she'd been a world-class swimmer and had won one gold and two silver medals at the 2052 Olympics—again following the same path as her mother, who was one of the greatest Olympic swimmers of all time. And on top of that, Lai thought her friend could easily be a professional model. She was five-ten with the statuesque figure of an elite athlete, curly brunette hair, brown eyes, and a beautiful smile. But Hannah chose to join the Secret Service after the Olympics. She'd been on Daniel's detail for nearly two years.

"I'd love that, but it'll be Ben's turn," Hannah said with disappointment. Ben and Hannah alternated road trips when only one agent accompanied Daniel.

"Yeah, but you're a *lot* more fun! Ben's great, but he's so... serious. And, so tall!" She looked Hannah up and down. "You're only *one* foot taller than me!" Lai felt bad for Hannah when they went jogging in Boston; Daniel insisted that Hannah accompany her. Lai figured that Hannah had to throttle back to half-speed, at least.

Hannah looked at Lai with a mischievous smile. "You can *not* tell anyone I told you this, but... under that big, gruff exterior, Ben's a pussycat."

Lai laughed, "I won't tell a soul!"

Then Hannah's smile disappeared. "Ben loves Mr. B so much. He's been on his detail for over 20 years. Ben will probably be with him until... well, you know." Lai started to reply but saw Daniel and a Capitol Police officer approaching.

"Here you are!" Daniel called to the women. "Sorry to keep you waiting." Daniel thanked the officer, who headed back to the Capitol building.

As they started walking toward the parking lot, Daniel looked at Lai. "I just had a call from an old friend of mine—Jim Kassenbaum. He was a senator from Kansas, from the other side of the aisle. But our political differences—and there's *lots* of them—never got in the way of our friendship. That's based on mutual respect, and love." He paused, remembering something painful from years ago. "Jim voted against the American Security Act. He called it 'an abomination against the Constitution, human decency, and God.' He begged me to veto it." His voice grew quieter. "I wish I'd listened to him. Anyway, Jim retired from the Senate a few years ago—he couldn't take the rancor anymore. He wanted to do what was best for the people of Kansas, the United States, and the world. He got fed up battling those with other agendas. He's on the Kansas Board of Regents now. I told him the other day about Love One Another, and he's really excited about it. He's invited us to present on it in Lawrence as soon as we can get there." Daniel stopped walking, and Lai and Hannah stopped beside him. "So... what do you think?"

Lai considered it. *Kansas... not the first place I'd choose, besides Hawai'i, to go public with LOA. But, what the hell, why not?* "Sure, let's do it! It'll be interesting to see how LOA plays in the Heartland of America, huh?"

"My thoughts exactly," Daniel replied. "Great. I'll tell Jim and we'll get it scheduled—I'm thinking early next month." They resumed walking toward their car. "Oh, one more thing... I was thinking it would be good to get the word out about LOA, a trial balloon if you will, and see what kind of reaction we get."

"Yeah, okay, that's a good idea," Lai agreed. "How do we do that?"

"For instance, we could do it on one of the Sunday morning news shows—maybe this Sunday, remote from Boston. I still have contacts at the networks; I can see who might be interested."

"Well, okay," Lai replied cautiously. "Uh... you'll do the talking, right?"

Daniel smiled at her, "If you insist. But I think you're going to feel compelled to say *something*. You're quite irrepressible, you know."

Lai laughed, "That's me—Ms. Irrepressible!" Then she noticed a grin on Hannah's face. "Okay, what's so funny?"

Hannah wiped the grin off her face, but she was still smiling. "If you and Mr. B go to Kansas in December—that'll be Ben's turn. Then for Hawai'i in January..."

"Oh, you lucky lady!" Lai exclaimed happily as she gave Hannah a high-five.

| 26 |

December 2, 2054

Lai looked up at the Gothic stone facade of stately Budig Hall as she, Daniel, and Ben approached the three large, arched doorways of the main entrance. Once again, Daniel had insisted on the minimum Secret Service detail for the event at the University of Kansas, and it was Ben's turn for the road trip.

It was a cool, cloudy, drizzly day in Lawrence. Daniel turned to Lai and remarked, "Not nearly as nice as the weather in Honolulu, eh?"

Lai replied with a slight smile, "No, it isn't... but Kansas has its charms."

After they'd entered the building, Lai led the way to the auditorium, the largest of three in the hall, for their presentation. She'd visited the University of Kansas a few times for symposia; the last one was in the same auditorium they'd use for their event. They found the entrance and walked into the auditorium at stage level. The event was to start in just over 15 minutes, and Lai noticed that the bowl-shaped room, which could seat 1,000 people, was already about half full. There were even a few people in the balcony. Ben walked over to the Kevlar-lined podium he'd shipped to Lawrence for the event and began to inspect it. Daniel had protested using the hulking bulletproof podium—*Benjamin, this is at a university, for gosh sakes!*—but Ben had prevailed.

Daniel saw his friend Jim Kassenbaum and walked over to him to say hello. As Lai stood next to Ben and the podium, she realized she had nothing to do for a couple of minutes, so she pulled out her phone and started checking email. There were quite a few unread emails; she skimmed through them until she saw one that caught her eye. *What the hell?* she scowled as she read it.

Ben noticed Lai's expression. "Is everything okay?"

Lai looked up from her phone. "Just another hate email from the 'Lai Shen Fan Club'." She'd gotten several emails since she and Daniel had gone public with Love One Another on *Face the Nation* the previous Sunday. Most were supportive, but a few were like the one she'd just read. She handed her phone to Ben, who read the email that was on the screen:

> *Hey, you fucking commie bitch - I saw you on tv. I know your working with the ccp to destroy America, just like your traitor father did. You and other Chinese devils like you must be and will be stopped!*

"A real day-brightener, huh?" Lai said with a grimace.

Ben handed the phone back to Lai, his face expressing both sympathy and concern. "I'm sorry you have to deal with people like that. Could you please forward it to me?"

"Of course," Lai replied. "Forward current email to Ben Abwao," she told Sirai. Ben had asked Lai to forward suspicious communications to him or Hannah for investigation by the Secret Service. Their job was to protect Daniel. But Lai understood that if someone did act on a threat against her, they might endanger him also. And she was grateful for Ben and Hannah looking out for her safety, too.

Ben nodded once, "Thank you, Lai."

Daniel and Kassenbaum walked over to Lai and Ben. "Lai, let me introduce you to my friend, Jim Kassenbaum." Kassenbaum extended his right hand to Lai, and Lai shook it.

"It's great to meet you, Senator. Daniel's told me a lot about you."

Kassenbaum smiled at Lai. "It's been a while since I was in Congress. My friends call me Jim. And it's a pleasure to meet *you*, Lai. Daniel's told me about you, and how you two met. That's quite a story!" Kassenbaum turned toward Ben and extended his hand. "Benjamin, it's been a long time! Great to see you again! How are you?"

Ben shook Kassenbaum's hand. "I'm well, sir, thank you." Then Ben's phone beeped. "But, if you'll excuse me, there's something I need to attend to." He walked off the stage and started climbing the staircase to the right of the stage, toward the balcony.

"Jim, thank you for sponsoring us here today to talk about LOA," Lai said. "Daniel and I really appreciate your help introducing it to the people of Kansas." *I've spent so much time here in recent years, it's beginning to feel like a second home.*

"I'm grateful you could come," Kassenbaum replied. "I'm excited about what you and Daniel are trying to do—'sowing love and light,' and advocating for including the duty to 'love one another' in the law. The world desperately needs more love and kindness, and forgiveness. I'm glad to do whatever I can to help you."

Daniel grinned and patted his friend on the arm. "I'm going hold you to that, Jim!"

"Do you have everything you need?" Kassenbaum asked.

Daniel grabbed the top of the armored podium with his left hand. "Between Benjamin and the university's audio-visual team, I think we're set."

"Good! I'll let you two get ready—we'll start at 10:30, and I'll introduce you, okay?"

"That'll be great, Jim. Thanks for doing that," Daniel replied.

Kassenbaum stepped off the stage, leaving Daniel and Lai alone by the podium. Lai checked her phone—*four minutes to go.* She scanned the auditorium and saw it was nearly full—*mostly students and faculty,* she surmised. Then she noticed several people with handheld cameras in the back of the main floor. "Uh, Daniel... why are all those cameras back there?" she asked as she pointed toward the back of the hall.

Daniel looked in the direction Lai was pointing. "Oh, good! They're from the major networks and news channels; Jim and I tipped them off about the event. They should give the LOA movement quite a boost, publicity-wise." Daniel noticed Lai's surprised expression, and he smiled. "'Go big or go home.'" He looked at his watch. "We'd better sit down, it's almost time." They took their seats behind the podium. Shortly, Kassenbaum strode from his seat in the front row up to the podium, to polite applause from the audience.

"Good morning, students and faculty, members of the Board of Regents, and guests of the university. My name is…" Kassenbaum began. He quickly introduced the purpose of the event and the two presenters, Daniel and Lai, but he took time to go into detail about his relationship with Daniel—which Daniel appreciated. *Thank you, my friend! That's going to fit right in.* And then he turned it over to Daniel, who approached the podium, exchanged an embrace with Kassenbaum, and stepped up to the microphone.

"Thank you all for coming today," Daniel began. "You may have noticed we have several representatives of the media with us." He raised his head to look toward the back of the main floor. "Welcome! I mention our friends from the media because, I don't know about you, but it's getting hard for me to watch the news lately." He paused and looked around the auditorium—a sea of mostly young faces. "These are tough times. We, as a country, and as a planet, face many difficult challenges. Sometimes they may seem insurmountable. It can be hard to even get out of bed some mornings. It is for me—and not just because I'm 85 years old!" Lai smiled as she heard a smattering of laughter from the audience. *I can't wait to hear where he's going with this*, she thought.

"But, here you are—students and faculty of the University of Kansas—seeking truth… seeking insights that can help us solve our many problems. You are the future. You are our light, and our hope." He paused again. "But these rough times can wear us down. And when we're in pain, it's hard for us to be our best selves." Lai raised her eyebrows; she was surprised, but pleased, to hear Daniel echo Keone Ailana's wise words.

"We often have different opinions about how best to deal with the challenges we face today." Daniel looked at Kassenbaum, sitting in the front row, and they exchanged smiles. "Jim Kassenbaum will tell you we've had many disagreements over the years; some of them were real doozies. But, that's good—we need diverse perspectives, different angles for attacking these issues." He swept the audience with his eyes again. "But sometimes the pain we feel causes us to treat people who have different opinions as our *enemies*, rather than as fellow Americans... fellow citizens of the world... fellow human beings." He paused to take a sip of water. "Have you noticed that many people seem angry all the time? It's easy, and understandable, to be angry about what's happening in our country, and the rest of the world. But it's been said that when someone's been angry for a long time, they get used to it. And it becomes comfortable, like old leather. And, finally, it becomes so familiar that they can't remember feeling any other way. And that anger, and hatred, and intolerance, make it hard for us to come together to solve our many problems."

Daniel looked around the large auditorium. "I know you represent many faith traditions. As you may know, I'm a Christian. One of my favorite authors is the Apostle Paul. In his letter to the Colossians, Paul exhorted the citizens of Colossae to '... put on love,' because it's 'the perfect bond of unity.' And oh, we *do* need to be more united in these United States of America, and across the world."

With that preamble, Daniel segued into the Love One Another movement—its purpose, its foundation in faith traditions, the connection to ho'oponopono and similar practices, and its stretch goal of embedding love for others into the law. Lai noticed that the expressions of people in the audience varied from intrigued to surprised. *Many of them probably didn't expect to hear this, especially from a former politician and president. But those who know him aren't surprised.* As Daniel continued, Lai noticed his voice was increasing in intensity and volume.

"I realize that many of you—maybe *most* of you—think this idea of embedding 'love one another' in the law is pretty crazy. A close friend of mine thought that, too, not long ago." He turned his head to glance at Lai, and he smiled. "And when you think about it, it *is* crazy. But, you know, *love* is crazy. And not just crazy; as I first said many years ago, love is *unreasonable, illogical, and impractical*. But, I submit to you: if you love your country, if you care about its future, and the future of the world, then it's not so crazy, or unreasonable or illogical." He paused again. "Think about what *patriotism* means—it means *love of country*. And you *cannot* love your country if you don't love your country*men* and *women*—yes, even those who *disagree* with you... even those whom you might consider to be enemies." Daniel paused and looked into the audience, from one side of the auditorium to the other.

"We are at our best when we give the ultimate sacrifice to put one another, and our communities and our country, ahead of ourselves. That's what love means. And, love says that *each person* has dignity, and worth. It's about looking at someone and understanding that *my* destiny is interwoven with *their* destiny. And it truly is—we're all in this together." Daniel took another sip of water.

"You may be thinking, putting love into the law would be incredibly difficult. It would take a long time, require lots of changes in how we think about the law, how we enforce the law. And that's all true. But, as the Chinese philosopher Lao Tzu said, 'The journey of a thousand miles begins with one step'." Lai smiled. *Now he's quoting Chinese philosophers!* Daniel continued, "It will not be easy. To succeed, we must be consistent and unyielding in our advocacy of love. That means, for example, when someone says, '*fuck you*,' which I've heard a lot in my life, my response—and your response—must be, '*I love you*'." Lai noticed many people in the audience smiling and nodding.

He paused. "I've been accused for many years of leading a conspiracy—a conspiracy of love. To that charge, I gladly plead guilty," he said as he raised his right hand. "I ask you today to consider joining Lai and me in that conspiracy, as impractical and crazy as it may seem. Think about it. And please share with us your thoughts and ideas at our website, LOAinLaw.com. And now," he said as he turned to look at Lai and motioned with his left hand for her to join him at the podium, "Lai and I will try to answer any questions you may have. Thank you. I love you."

As the audience gave Daniel a standing ovation, Daniel stepped out from behind the podium, Lai left her chair to stand beside him... and Ben's head was about to explode. He tried using his eyes, head, and hands to signal Daniel to move back behind the armored podium, but he was too wrapped up in the Q&A to notice. Ben visually scoured the people remaining in the auditorium and didn't see any obvious threats, but he kept sweeping the auditorium with his eyes as Daniel and Lai answered questions.

Many of the questions were directed to Lai. The questioners seemed interested in getting her perspective as a scientist, as someone closer to their age, or as a member of a racial minority in the United States who'd faced persecution in recent times. To her surprise, she answered the questions easily. *I must have learned more from my talks with Kapono, Keone, and Daniel than I realized,* she thought.

Daniel noticed the ease with which Lai answered the questions and connected with the audience. *People need to hear more from her. After all, this was her idea!*

After about 25 minutes, there were no more questions, and the remaining attendees filed out of the auditorium. Ben had come down to the stage, and Daniel went over to him. "Benjamin, I'm sorry about not staying behind the podium. I know you're just trying to protect me, but I could tell this was a friendly crowd, and, well, nothing happened!"

Ben didn't look appeased. But all he said was, "We just never know for sure, Mr. B. All it takes is one crazy person to ruin your whole day."

Lai chimed in, "And not 'crazy love,' either."

Daniel chuckled. "No, I expect not."

Then Kassenbaum walked up to them and thanked Daniel for his presentation. As they were talking and Lai was listening to their conversation, she saw someone coming down the stairs from the balcony, heading toward her. He was wearing a faded denim jacket and a dark blue baseball-style cap with "US NAVY VETERAN" in gold lettering, and he was calling out to her, "Miss Shen! Miss Shen!" *Shit! It's the guy from the bowling alley,* Lai realized. *What the hell does he want?* Ben was standing a few feet from her; she was about to signal him to intercept the man, but she stopped herself, her cheeks flaming from shame. *What the hell am I DOING? I'm telling everyone to love one another, and I can't even love one person!*

But Ben was already moving to block the man. Lai held up her right hand to Ben in a "stop" signal and said, "It's okay—he's an old friend." Ben stopped, nodded, and backed off. Lai walked to the edge of the stage to meet the man—*Klement,* she remembered. "Hello, again!" she said pleasantly. "How can I help you?"

He removed the cap that covered his short gray hair. "Miss Shen, I... uh... maybe you remember me from the bowling alley, a couple of months ago?"

Lai nodded. "Yes, sir, I do." He seemed to Lai to be grief-stricken, and close to tears.

"I saw you were going to be here today, and I just had to come and tell you, uhm, how sorry I am about how I acted back then. I said some terrible things. I don't know what got into me." He wiped his nose on his jacket sleeve. "I know I was really upset about my son," he continued. "He was on the *Enterprise* when she was hit by that missile. He and a lot of other sailors were killed." *Oh my god!* Lai remembered that, a little over a year ago, a Chinese missile had crippled the giant aircraft carrier as it was on patrol in the South China Sea; over 900 men and women had died. China had claimed it was an accident and had formally apologized, but the incident had nearly started a war. "I don't know if you can ever forgive me."

Lai took both of his hands in hers. "I'm so sorry about your son, and his shipmates! Of course I forgive you, Klement. It's Klement, right?"

Klement's expression became calmer. "Yes, miss—Klement Sedlák."

Lai looked into his eyes. "Mr. Sedlák, I have a favor to ask of you: can you please forgive *me?*"

Klement looked puzzled, but that look vanished as he remembered something Daniel had said. "Well, sure, of course!"

Lai released his hands. "Thank you. Now, how are you doing, Mr. Sedlák?" She remembered what the bowling alley's manager had said about Klement's drinking.

Klement expression changed; he smiled happily. "Oh, I'm doing a lot better now! After how I treated you, I knew I needed help. My friend Freddie—he's the manager at the bowling alley—helped me get into AA. I haven't touched a drop in over a month! Oh, and you can call me Klement."

Lai beamed at him, "That's wonderful, Klement! I'm so happy for you! And, my name is Lai."

Klement nodded, "Okay, Lai. And, I wanted to tell you, I really liked what you and President Bennett said today. I'm going to remember it and try to practice it."

Lai took Klement's right hand in her hands. "That's good to hear, Klement. I'm glad it was helpful to you. And I want you to know… I love you."

Tears started trickling down his face. "Oh, thank you, Lai!" He reached out and hugged her, and she hugged him. Then he stepped back from the embrace. "I'm really glad I came here today. But, I need to get back to my farm. Could you please tell President Bennett how much I liked his talk today?"

Lai nodded, "I'll be glad to do that. I'm so glad you came here today. Have a safe drive home; I'll keep you in my thoughts. Oh, could you say hi to Freddie for me?"

Klement put his cap back on. "Thanks for that, Lai. And, sure, I'll tell Freddie." He looked around the near-empty auditorium. "Say, where's the fella who was with you at the bowling alley?"

Lai tried to not show her sadness as she replied as honestly, and hopefully, as she could. "He… I think he's in a better place, now."

Klement's face fell. "I'm really sorry to hear that. He seemed like a good guy. It was nice of him to thank me for my service. Not many people do that."

Lai smiled and nodded, "Yes… he was a good guy."

Klement started heading for the exit. "You and President Bennett take care, now!"

Lai waved at him, "Thanks, we will!" Then she remembered something… something she should have done a long time ago, but hadn't. *Damn.* She checked the stage, saw that Daniel and Ben were alone together by the podium, and went over to them. "Daniel, could I talk with you for a minute?" She looked at Ben.

"I need to find the AV team and get the podium packed up," Ben said. Daniel and Lai walked over to the other side of the stage.

"What's up?" Daniel asked. "Hey, by the way, you were great on the Q&A!"

"Thanks, Daniel. And your talk was—perfect!"

"Thank you. I've still got it, huh?"

"Absolutely!" Then Lai grew serious. "When we first met, you asked me to forgive you for the American Security Act. And I told you I wasn't ready to do that yet."

"Yes… I remember."

"Well, that was incredibly selfish and inconsiderate of me. Of *course* I forgive you! I should have forgiven you a long time ago. I hope you can forgive *me* for not telling you sooner."

Daniel looked into her eyes. "Thank you. Of course I forgive you. But, I knew you'd already forgiven me," he winked. "You just forgot to tell me. It's been a busy five weeks."

Lai smiled and nodded, "It sure has."

Daniel put his right hand on Lai's shoulder. "'Love is patient'."

Then Lai suddenly realized there were others she needed to forgive—and ask forgiveness from. "Daniel, I'm going to make a side trip before returning to Boston. I'll be back there in two or three days."

"Where to, if you don't mind my asking?"

"California—the Bay Area." *I think… I need to check on that.* "I'm going to see a former high school classmate, and also someone I knew at Stanford." *And then, Cambridge… probably better if I fly to London out of Boston.*

"Reunion time, eh? Hey, I'm going to Kaleo's inauguration on December 7. Would you like to come with me? We could meet up in San Francisco and fly together to Honolulu—maybe on the 5th?"

"Sure, I'd love to go with you—thanks for asking me. Let me know your itinerary and I'll get the same flights to Hawai'i and back to Boston."

"Great, I'll do that. I hope you have a good trip to California."

"Thanks." *I hope it's going to be a good trip, too. This is going be hard... really hard. But, I've got to do it.*

| 27 |

December 4, 2054

Lai sat in the driver's seat of her rental car as it hummed eastward down Highway J1 through California's Central Valley, which was awash with green from torrential rains that fall. As she looked out at the farm fields that stretched in all directions, she thought about her meeting two hours earlier with Tony, the man who as a high school senior had raped her after they'd left their prom. She'd located him through his parents, who still lived in San Jose. They'd been happy to hear from her and glad she was going to reconnect with their son. They knew nothing about the rape; Lai had never told anyone about it, except Kapono.

That went okay... considering, Lai thought. Tony had been shocked to see Lai at the front door of his small ranch-style home in Campbell. But after he'd recovered from that surprise, he told her he was glad she'd come and suggested they go across the street to a public park to talk—his wife and two young children were at home. Lai agreed, and they sat at a table in the park and talked for over an hour.

It was hard just looking him in the eyes at first, Lai remembered. Seeing Tony again resurfaced her shock, her panic, and her terror during that night seventeen and a half years ago... and also the depression, flashbacks, sleepless nights, nightmares, and feelings of misplaced guilt and shame she'd experienced for a long time afterward. She knew why she was there, sitting with Tony in the park. But the words she had come to say... words she'd planned to say... refused to flow from her mind to her lips.

Then Tony spoke in the awkward silence. He tearfully told Lai that he was sorry and ashamed about what he'd done—that the rape had haunted him his entire adult life. *You and me both*, Lai remembered thinking. He told her how grateful he was that she'd never reported his crime to the police. He was 18 years old at the time, and a rape conviction would have ruined his life... although he admitted he more than deserved that fate. He said he'd tried to contact her two years ago to apologize, but she seemed to have disappeared. And she had—deep below the Kansas prairie. After seeing her on a news story about the event in Lawrence, he was going to try again to reach out to her—then she appeared at his front door. Then, he told Lai that he knew what he'd done was unforgivable.

No... not unforgivable, Lai remembered thinking as she'd looked at Tony's anguished face. *I may not be able to ever forget, but I can forgive.* And then the words flowed, and she told Tony she forgave him. Tony's look of surprise, relief, and gratitude was like a balm for Lai's soul. And although Tony was taken aback when Lai asked him to forgive her, he readily did so. Then, after catching up on each other's lives since high school, they promised to stay in touch.

But as the red Hyundai sedan turned right onto California 33 and approached FCI Mendota, she thought, *This could be a lot tougher. How will he react to seeing me? And will he accept forgiveness from me, and grant me forgiveness?* But then she remembered what Kapono had told her: *Give them time. In any case, you know you've done your best... you've done what you could, and you're a better person for it.* The car turned into the prison's visitor lot, and Lai steered it into a parking space. *Let's see what happens...*

Lai waited at one of the square steel tables in the visitation room of the medium-security prison. She was wearing the same dark green dress she'd worn for her meeting with Governor Peleke at Washington Place. After a few minutes, a guard entered the room with an inmate, who was dressed in standard prisoner's garb: a blue chambray shirt and dark blue denim pants. Although the man had long black hair and a full beard, and he'd aged 15 years since Lai had last seen him, she recognized him instantly.

"You're the last person I ever expected to see here," the man said roughly as he sat down at the table across from Lai. The guard stepped back to stand about eight feet away. "I was surprised as hell when I heard you wanted to be added to my visitors' list." He glared at her, "Why the fuck are you here, anyway?"

"Hello, Jared," Lai said as pleasantly as she could manage, given his hostile greeting. "Thanks for seeing me. How are you?"

Jared scowled, "Oh, I'm doing fucking great, Lai. Having tons of fun here in the middle of nowhere, behind 12-foot-high razor wire for the past 15 years."

Lai nodded empathetically, "I can understand. I spent some time at Dublin."

"Two whole months in a women's prison, huh?" Jared scoffed. "Big fucking deal!"

This is going to be even harder than I thought. Lai wanted to tell Jared about how it *had* been a 'big fucking deal' for her... about how she and her parents had suffered because of his betrayal; about her physical and psychological abuse in prison; about how prison had changed her into the callous, detached person she'd been until recently; and about her suicide attempt after she'd been released from prison. Then she thought, *No—that's not why I'm here.* With great effort, she pushed her pain aside.

"As for why I'm here, I wanted you to know... I forgive you, Jared. And I hope you can forgive me for taking so long to tell you that."

"I don't want, or need, your forgiveness, Lai!" Jared almost spat the words. "I was fighting for a righteous cause! I thought we were *friends*, working for the same cause! And then you *betrayed* me!"

I betrayed HIM? Lai had testified against Jared in court, as part of the plea bargain agreement to have the 32 felony counts against her reduced to a class A misdemeanor. But she was incensed that he'd equated his deceit about the firebombing of Hoover Tower with her testimony in court. She was about to respond in kind to Jared's angry words. But then she remembered something else Kapono had told her: *When asking for forgiveness, it must be sincere. Any 'yeah, but's' won't cut it—that's a sign you might be trying to find ways to let yourself off the hook or lessen your part in whatever happened. If that happens, you aren't ready for forgiveness.* She closed her eyes for a moment and took a deep breath before responding.

"Jared, I *was* fighting for the same cause you were—but not in the same way that you did. And, I did think of you as a friend. I'd like it if we could be friends again. That's why I came here today."

Jared glared at Lai for a few seconds. "I saw you on *Face the Nation* the other day with Bennett, talking about that Love One Another stuff. It shocked the hell out of me. How the hell could you cozy up to that *fucking asshole*—the guy *responsible* for the American Security Act?"

"I can understand how you feel about Daniel Bennett. I felt the same way, before I met him and got to know him. He's a good man, Jared. I understand now why he believed he had to sign that bill, and why he regrets that decision. And, I've forgiven him."

Jared shook his head, "I don't think I could ever do that. And I don't understand how *you* could do that, after what that fucking law did to your parents!" Lai started to respond, but Jared continued, "I thought you were a physicist. What's this LOA shit all about? I switched off *Face the Nation* after I saw you sitting there with Bennett."

Lai noticed by the large clock on the wall that her visitation time was almost over, so she gave Jared a short version of the story behind the Love One Another movement, skipping over details such as her relationship with Kapono. After she finished, she asked Jared, "What do you think about that?"

"Huh," he shook his head once. "Good luck with that. What you're trying to do—you and Bennett—it's never going to happen… not in this fucked-up world."

Lai smiled slightly. "I thought the same way about it not long ago. But someone close to me convinced me that encouraging people to love one another is the only way we're going to get out of the mess we're in. And, it helped me a lot personally, too."

"A guy?"

"Yes… a really great guy." Lai noticed an almost imperceptible softening in Jared's expression.

"Well… you deserve that." He looked down at the table for a moment, then raised his head to look at Lai. "You know, I always liked you, Lai—even though you testified against me. And I'm glad you came out of this okay." He paused. "I don't know what's going to happen to me when I get out of here. I might get early release in a few months. I was a semester away from graduating, but it's been so long, I don't think any school will accept my credits from Stanford."

Lai was elated to see a glimmer of consideration and kindness from Jared. "Jared, you're a hella intelligent man—a talented man. I *know* you're going to make it when you get out of here. And I'm pretty sure at least some of your coursework can be accepted at another school." Lai and her father had researched that question when she'd applied to other schools after being expelled from Stanford. "Just remember that there are people, like me, who care about you, and who love you. And if I can help you in any way after you get out, let me know." She took a piece of paper with her email and phone number out of a slit pocket in her dress and held it out for the guard to examine. He nodded, and Lai handed it to Jared. "*Anything.*"

The guard stepped toward Lai and Jared. "Visiting time's over."

Jared looked at the piece of paper, then looked up at Lai and stared at her for a few seconds. Then he stood up. "Thanks for, uh, coming to see me," he said quietly.

"You're welcome, Jared."

The guard led Jared out of the room. He glanced over his shoulder at Lai as he went through the door, into the corridor leading to his cell.

| 28 |

January 20, 2055

Lai peered out at the large crowd that was gathering around the ornate, round open pavilion that she, Ben, Daniel, and Governor Peleke were standing in. *Wow, there could be a few thousand people already! Governor Peleke is a popular guy in Hawai'i—I'm glad he's supporting us.*

Lai was standing beside Ben, who was almost two feet taller. She craned her neck to look up at him. "How many people do you think there are?"

Ben, who like Lai had been scanning the crowd, thought for a few seconds; he'd been trained in estimating crowd sizes. "I'd say it's at least 3,500—maybe as many as 4,000." And, it was growing by the minute. Ben was worried, as usual. Although both he and Hannah had made the trip to Honolulu due to the potentially large turnout and outdoor venue, they were the only Secret Service agents there. Fortunately, there were Capitol Police officers on hand for crowd control and security—Governor Peleke would be making the opening remarks.

Ben's keen eyes swept the venue on the lush grounds of the iconic Iolani Palace, adjacent to the state Capitol building. Although the palace and grounds were picturesque and historic, the site was far from ideal, security-wise. The speakers would be standing in the *Keliiponi Hale,* also known as the Coronation Pavilion, in the middle of the palace grounds. The area behind the speakers had been cordoned off, and there was a backdrop screening the speakers from that area. But that still left nearly 240 degrees of open ground for Ben and Hannah to monitor. They were glad they were able to use the armored podium here—the same podium that was used in Lawrence.

Lai checked her phone—*five minutes to show time.* She stepped over to where Daniel was talking with the governor and waited until there was a break in their conversation. "Good morning, Governor... sorry—Kaleo!" Lai said cheerfully. She was in a happy mood. The broad news coverage of the event in Lawrence had generated strong interest in Love One Another across the United States and also in a few other nations. She'd been busy building the movement's social media presence, and she and Daniel had appeared on morning and weekend news shows for the major networks and news channels. She'd been interviewed on CNN several years ago regarding the fusion project at Livermore, but that didn't prepare her for the intensity of the media attention they were enjoying now. *Not exactly enjoying—more a "pain and delight" thing,* Lai thought. Daniel was in his element, of course, both on the news circuit and speaking at events like the one in Lawrence and that day in Honolulu. Lai was glad to leave the public speaking to Daniel while she focused on the behind-the-scenes work, which was quickly becoming overwhelming. Daniel knew some experts in managing efforts similar to his and Lai's crusade, and he'd lined up interviews with several candidates for when they returned to Boston. And friends such as Katherine Etter, who was still unemployed, had volunteered to help with LOA in any way they could.

"Aloha, Lai!" Kaleo replied. "It's a beautiful day to officially kick off the LOA movement in Hawai'i, isn't it?" And it was—bright sun with only a few clouds in the sky, about 70 Fahrenheit, and the crowd seemed energized and in a good mood.

"Yes, it is!" Lai replied. "And thank you again for all your help and support, including for today's rally. We wouldn't be where we are today without you."

"You know I believe in what you and Daniel are doing. I'm glad to help in any way I can." Then he saw his press secretary motion to him. "I'm sorry, I need to attend to something. I'll be right back." He left Lai and Daniel to walk over to the staffer.

"Are you all set?" Lai asked Daniel, having no doubt that he was. But she noticed an odd expression on his face. "Is something wrong?"

"Uh, yeah. I... my voice isn't doing so well," Daniel replied in a raspy voice, and then he coughed once. *That cough wasn't very convincing. And he seemed just fine 15 minutes ago*, Lai thought. "It must be from that cool, dry air in Minnesota," he added. They'd stopped in the Twin Cities en route to Hawai'i to make the rounds of local news shows and speak at Lai's alma mater.

"Oh, that's a shame!" Lai said skeptically. "Maybe you could keep it short—just hit your main points." She knew that Daniel could keep talking for a long time once he got going.

But Daniel looked at her with an apologetic expression. "Lai, I don't think I can get up there and talk today. You'll need to speak for us."

Lai was not at all on board with that idea. *Oh hell, nah!* "Daniel, you know I've never done *anything* like that before!" She glanced over her shoulder at the crowd—people were still arriving. "There's *thousands* of people out there! And, I don't have anything prepared! Maybe you could, uh, gargle some warm salt water, or something?"

Daniel put his hands lightly on her shoulders and looked into her eyes. "Lai... you need to do it. You'll be fine. You don't need anything written down—just speak from your heart."

Kaleo's press secretary, Thomas, walked up to them. "Are you all ready? The governor's about to make his opening remarks."

Lai started to respond, but Daniel told Thomas, "Yes, we're ready." Noticing Lai's panicked expression, he held her shoulders more firmly and told her, "*You're ready*. I'll be right beside you."

Lai heard Thomas's voice over the loudspeakers as he introduced Governor Peleke: "Aloha, ladies and gentlemen! Would you please welcome..." She felt an odd sensation, as if the world were spinning around her, and she wasn't sure where or when it would stop. Then she realized, *I guess it stops with me.*

Kaleo was warming up the crowd, giving a brief introduction to the LOA movement and the idea being considered to base Hawai'i's laws on Love One Another. Then he turned around toward Daniel and Lai, standing behind him. "And to tell you more about this idea and how it could benefit the people of Hawai'i and the world, I'm delighted to welcome my friends, Daniel Bennett and Lai Shen!"

There was polite applause. Lai looked apprehensively at Daniel; he smiled at her and said quietly, "You've got this."

Lai walked slowly up to the podium and pulled the microphone down to her face with her shaking hands; Daniel took a couple of steps to stand behind her. "Aloha! I'm... uh..." Then she realized that most people in the crowd could only see the top of her head. *Dammit!* She pulled the wireless mic off its stand and side-stepped to the left of the podium. Daniel moved out from behind the podium to stand at her left side.

"There—that's better!" There was good-natured laughter from the crowd. "Let's try that again... Aloha!" *ALOHA!* the crowd shouted in reply.

Ben was, as Daniel sometimes kidded, about to have a coronary. "Chickadee One to Chickadee Two!" he said quietly but urgently into his headset. "Did you know about Mr. B not speaking today?"

Hannah's reply came through his earpiece, "No idea. Must be a last-minute change."

"My name is Lai Shen. I'm so happy and grateful to be here with you today, on this beautiful day in Honolulu. Thank you all for coming." She looked to her left. "I'm here with my friend, Daniel Bennett. Maybe some of you know who he is." There was considerable laughter from the crowd. Daniel smiled as he thought, *Using humor—good! You're doing great, as I knew you would.*

Meanwhile, Ben was trying to catch Daniel's attention. Finally, Daniel noticed Ben trying to signal him, and he shot the agent a *What?* look. Ben motioned with his eyes, head, and left hand for Daniel to move to his right—behind the armored podium. After a moment, Daniel caught on, rolled his eyes, nodded, and shuffled behind Lai to stand behind the podium, to Lai's right. Ben nodded approvingly and exhaled a sigh of relief. He didn't like the fact that Lai was still out in the open, but he didn't know what he could do about that. Having Lai's face hidden behind the podium as she was speaking wasn't a practical option. *I'll have to arrange for a step stand from now on.*

"But, you don't know who *I* am," Lai continued in a quiet but steady voice. "So if it's okay with you, I'd like to take a few minutes and tell you a little about myself, how I came to be here with you today, and why Daniel and I are working with Governor Peleke and other leaders to propose to you, the people of Hawai'i, a new approach to law, and law enforcement—one based on love, and forgiveness." Daniel could see that the crowd was listening attentively. *She's got their attention.*

"I have to tell you, it feels kind of weird for me to be up here today, talking with you about love. Because not that long ago, I was anything but a loving person." The crowd was dead silent. "I was an angry and bitter person, resentful and hateful toward those whom I thought had wronged me or my family. I had no need or time for friends, or for love." Lai paused, searching for the right words. "A wise man named Nelson Mandela once said, 'People must learn to hate.' Well, I learned how to hate a long time ago. And over the years, through lots of practice, I got *really* good at it—so good that my two favorite words were 'Fuck you!'" There was a smattering of laughter from the crowd, and Daniel, thinking of when he'd first met Lai, smiled for a second.

Lai looked over the thousands of people in the crowd and cleared her throat. "But Dr. Mandela also said, '... if they can learn to hate, they can be taught to love.' And luckily for me, that's true. I was taught to love by a wonderful man, from Maui. His name was Kapono. He taught me the importance of Remorse, Forgiveness, Gratitude, and Love. That may sound familiar to those of you who know about ho'oponopono." From the knowing nods and smiles Lai saw throughout the crowd, it was clear many people *did* know about ho'oponopono. "Kapono understood that I was a bitter, angry, hateful person because I was in pain. I'd been hurt badly by several people over the years. But, I didn't realize that hatred is a disease that afflicts the hater more than the hated. My anger, and my hatred, had poisoned my soul." Lai paused to take a couple of breaths. *I thought this would be hard... but it feels pretty good!*

"Kapono taught me about ho'oponopono. From him, I learned the importance of forgiveness—of others, and... for myself." She glanced to her right at Daniel, and he smiled in response. "I learned how to be more grateful, and thankful. And I learned the importance of showing love to others... even those who've hurt me, or those close to me."

Daniel was beaming. *She's come such a long way. And now, standing up in front of this huge crowd, baring her soul... she's such a different person than when I met her just three months ago.*

Then Daniel noticed something—*someone*—moving in the crowd in front of them, about 10 rows back from the pavilion. They were coming toward the podium. Ben had noticed the movement, too. He stepped closer to Daniel and Lai and started to ask Hannah to check it out. But before he could finish, the person stopped, raised his right arm, and pointed a pistol directly at Lai. "*Death to Chinese devils!*" he yelled. Then he pulled the trigger.

As the man shouted and fired three shots—*POP! POP! POP!*—Daniel did the only thing he could think of: he bent his left leg at the knee and toppled over on top of Lai, knocking her hard to the concrete floor of the pavilion. At the same instant, Ben leaped from his position a few feet from the podium and fell on top of both Daniel and Lai. A few people in the crowd had already taken the shooter to the ground, with frantic shouts of, "Get the gun! *GET THE GUN!*" Hannah and two Capitol Police officers rushed to help restrain the man and put him into handcuffs.

In the pavilion, there was an eerie silence. Although Ben didn't see any wounds on Daniel or Lai, he pushed a button on the phone on his belt that would automatically send Emergency Medical Services and both Secret Service and FBI backups to his location. Daniel was face down on top of Lai, and Lai was also face down and appeared to Ben to be unconscious. Daniel was moaning softly; Ben risked turning him over. As he did, he saw a large, ragged circle of blood on the back of Lai's white blouse, and a similar circle on Daniel's chest. And then he saw a bullet hole, in the middle of Daniel's chest. Blood was oozing freely from the wound. "Mr. B! *Mr. B, can you hear me?*" Ben cried. He quickly checked under Lai to make sure she hadn't been hit by another bullet.

Ben heard Hannah's anxious voice in his earpiece, "How are Mr. B and Lai?"

"He's been shot once in the chest, but he's breathing. Lai's unconscious but not wounded. EMS and backups are on the way."

Governor Peleke approached, with a woman beside him. "I'm so sorry about this! Capitol Police have the suspect in custody." He tilted his head toward the woman next to him. "Dr. Rochelle is an ER physician—she's offered to help."

The doctor, who was carrying a large first-aid kit that one of Peleke's staffers had retrieved for her, crouched down beside Ben. "What's the situation?"

Ben looked at the doctor, grateful for her help. "President Bennett was shot once in the chest. Dr. Shen wasn't hit, but she's unconscious—she hit her head pretty hard."

"Is there anything else you need?" Peleke asked Ben.

"EMS is on the way, also FBI and Secret Service backups. I think we're good until EMS arrives, unless Dr. Rochelle needs anything."

Peleke put his hand on Ben's shoulder. "Okay. I'll get out of the way, but Thomas and I will right over there if you need anything."

"Thank you for finding Dr. Rochelle, Governor." Peleke stepped away to confer with a police captain.

As Ben worked with the doctor on Daniel, the people still on the palace grounds were standing with their hands or arms linked, in concentric circles around the pavilion. The people in the outermost circles faced outwards, forming a protective barrier. Some were stunned into silence; some were crying; others were praying.

Then Lai regained consciousness; she noticed her back felt wet. She had a large, bloody welt on her forehead where it had slammed into the pavilion floor, and a throbbing headache to go with it. As Daniel was being treated by the doctor, Ben gently helped Lai to sit up. "Wha... what happened, Ben? I thought I heard shots! Is Daniel..." She turned her head and saw Daniel lying face-up on the pavilion floor with the ugly red splotch on his chest, his head supported by Ben's rolled-up black jacket. "*Oh my god!*" Lai gasped, her right hand covering her mouth.

Then Daniel opened his eyes and looked into Ben's worried and distraught face. "Benjamin..." he said weakly.

"Mr. B, you just lie still—EMS will be here soon."

Daniel nodded once. "How's Lai?" Lai shifted to a kneeling position at Daniel's side so he could see her.

"I'm fine, Daniel! Don't worry about me!" She started crying, "You shouldn't have done that! *Why the hell did you do that?*"

Daniel attempted a smile. "It... it seemed like a good idea, at the time." He noticed the blood on Lai's forehead. "That's... a nasty bump on your head... sorry about that... I'm not as spry as I used to be." They heard the EMS siren in the distance, growing steadily louder. Daniel looked again at Ben. "Benjamin... listen to me."

Ben leaned down closer to Daniel's face. "Yes, Mr. B?" Daniel coughed once. Ben glanced at Dr. Rochelle, who said nothing but met his eyes with an expression he'd seen once before—when he was helping a doctor tend to a fellow agent who'd been mortally wounded.

"This... this is on me," Daniel gasped. "You and Hannah did everything right... everything you could, to protect Lai and me. Don't give... give it another thought."

Ben grasped Daniel's right hand. "We're going to get you fixed up, Mr. B. Then we'll have a talk about following Secret Service directions better, okay?"

Daniel smiled faintly. "Sounds like a plan." Then he looked at Lai. "I'm so proud of you. You... you were doing great up there. You're... a natural."

Lai held Daniel's other hand. "I don't know about that, Daniel. We need you... *I* need you! I can't do this without you!" She tried to stop crying, as she knew her tears wouldn't help, but she was having trouble holding them back.

Daniel gripped her hand. "You *can* do it, Lai... I *know* you can. I believe in you. I heard you today... you're ready... everything you need, you have in there," he said weakly as he lifted his hand and pointed toward her heart. "*Trust in yourself.*" Then his hand dropped back. "Remember... 'love never fails'."

He closed his eyes as a paramedic touched Lai on her shoulder. "Excuse us, ma'am," he said as he gently supported her by her right arm and helped her stand and step away from Daniel so he and his partner could do their jobs. Lai felt numb as she watched the paramedics and Ben carefully lift Daniel onto a stretcher and take him to the ambulance, as if she were in a dream—a terrible dream. A line from *Hamlet* popped into her head: *"O God, I could be bounded in a nutshell and count myself a king of infinite space, were it not that I have bad dreams."*

Hannah entered the pavilion, walked up to Lai, and touched her arm. "Ben's going with the paramedics in the ambulance. Why don't you drive there with me. We'll get that bump on your head taken care of, and get everything else checked out, too." she said gently.

"Yeah... okay," Lai whispered.

Hannah saw the devastated look on Lai's face and wrapped her arms around her friend, holding her tightly. Lai rested her head on Hannah's shoulder as they held the embrace for several seconds. Then Hannah said, "I thought you might want this," and Lai saw that Hannah was holding a black jacket with *FBI* in large yellow letters on the back and smaller letters on the front.

"Thanks, Hannah." As Hannah wrapped the jacket around Lai's shoulders, she finally realized why her back felt damp. She walked with Hannah toward their SUV for the drive to the hospital, thinking only about Daniel as they moved slowly through the green palace grounds.

I'm sorry... please forgive me... thank you... I love you.

| 29 |

November 13, 2057

Lai stepped out of the dark bedroom and closed the door quietly behind her. She walked down the short hall into the dimly-lit living room, switched on the holographic fireplace, and collapsed into an old, overstuffed leather recliner.

What a three years it's been! Lai closed her eyes and felt the warmth from the fireplace sink into her exhausted body. She'd decided she needed a break, her first in over two years, from her nearly non-stop schedule of meetings, rallies, and travel. She was recharging for a few days at her lake cabin in the north woods of Minnesota.

The efforts in Hawai'i to make Love One Another the law of the land had taken a long time and considerable work by Lai, Governor Peleke, Keone Ailana, and many others, but had been successful. The proposal had been put to a statewide vote one week earlier, and it had passed overwhelmingly. Lai realized it could take years to implement, but the referendum was an important first step.

As she relaxed in the comfy recliner, she also thought about how the LOA movement had been gaining support in other states and nations. There were organized efforts underway in two dozen other states, including Lai's home state of California, Daniel's home state of Massachusetts, and also Columbia, Georgia, Kansas, Minnesota, New York, Puerto Rico, and Utah, among others. Daniel's friend—now Lai's friend—Jim Kassenbaum had helped tremendously in those efforts. Elsewhere in the world, support for LOA was surging in over

25 nations, including Australia, Brazil, Canada, France, Israel, Italy, Japan, Kenya, Mexico, New Zealand, South Korea, Sweden, Taiwan, Thailand, the Netherlands, the Philippines, the Republic of Palestine, the United Kingdom, and Ukraine. Lai was overwhelmed by the support she'd received from religious leaders of many faiths: Christian ministers, imams, rabbis, and Buddhist monks and nuns, among others.

Lai hoped that Kapono would be proud of her for overcoming her disbelief and shortcomings to lead the LOA movement. She didn't know if LOA would ultimately be successful in saving humanity from itself, but she felt at peace with her efforts, at least.

She'd almost dozed off when her phone buzzed. She grinned when she saw *Katherine* on Caller ID. Lai hadn't talked with her for a few weeks. She'd been out of work since Prometheus had been shut down, but she'd been helping with LOA and also had taken advantage of the time off to fall in love and get married. "Accept call," Lai told Sirai. She noticed it was a voice-only call, most likely due to the poor 8G reception in the boondocks of northern Minnesota. "Katherine! How the heck are ya?"

"I'm doing great, Lai! How are *you*?" Lai smiled at the joy in Katherine's voice. *She sounds happier than she's been in years! Married life must agree with her.*

"I'm good, thanks. I'm just really tired. I'm chillin' at the cabin for a few days."

"I *bet* you're tired, zipping all over the world for the last three years! And on that—congratulations! I heard about the referendum being passed in Hawai'i. You must be so happy about that. I know you worked very hard to make that happen. And I know what it means to you. I've been praying for you, and for the success of LOA."

"Thanks, Katherine. I *am* happy about that—and grateful for all the support and love I received from all over Hawai'i—and from friends like you." Then Lai thought of who else would be happy about the referendum. "I just wish Daniel could've been here to see it happen," she said sadly.

"Yes, I wish that, too. He was an incredible person, wasn't he?"

"Yeah... he sure was." *I can't believe that three years ago, I despised him... and he sacrificed his life for me.* Then Lai decided to put the past aside and focus on her friend in the present. "But, hey, how's everything with you?"

"I have some good news—I got a job!"

"That's great!" Lai exclaimed happily. "Tell me all about it!"

"It's with InfiniTrek. I'm the new program director for the development of the Voyageur V for the Europa mission!" Lai was ecstatic for her friend. She knew that NASA's planned mission to Europa was the hottest project in the astroscience world. It would be the first non-classified use of technologies such as Quantum Drive that had been proven during Prometheus. Katherine had told her Senator Wilkes and José de la Cruz had been working behind the scenes to block her from any job with, or connected to, NASA or the Department of Defense. "So, I get to work closely with José de la Cruz again."

"How's that working out?"

"Oh, José is his usual charming self. But I'm watching my back."

"Good! I'm surprised he and Wilkes didn't block you from this job, too."

"So am I. But I had some unexpected help. I really thought my chances of landing the job were slim to none. Then all of a sudden, I got the call that it was mine."

"What happened?"

"It was the darnedest thing. I found out that Arnaud Houde submitted an unsolicited recommendation for me to the Hiring Committee." Katherine paused. "He died two days after I was told I got the job."

"How about that... two spaceships, and now a job. He must have really liked you." Lai recalled what Katherine had told her about the high-stakes meeting with InfiniTrek's founder in Nice and her introduction to Houde in Austin 12 years before that. Although Houde had been widely despised, Katherine had chosen to look beyond his negative qualities. Lai thought about what Kapono had said about showing love to others: *If we expect people to love others, we need to show love to them.* She smiled as she thought, *You were so right about that, my love.*

"I guess so," Katherine said as if lost in thought. "Anyway, the job's in Baton Rouge, and I start December 3. As soon as we get back from this trip, we need to find a place to live."

"Where are you now?"

"Oh, yeah—we're in downtown Minneapolis for an astroscience conference. Patience came with." Lai heard what sounded like a siren wailing in the background.

"Katherine, what's that noise?"

"Oh, there's thunderstorms headed this way tonight. Must be a severe storm warning." Lai closed her eyes and shivered as she remembered another severe storm in Minnesota, almost 13 years ago.

"Be careful out there!" Lai cautioned her friend.

"Don't worry, we're going to stay in tonight, in the hotel."

"Good! So, how's Patience doing?" Because of Lai's busy schedule, she'd met Patience only once, at the wedding.

"She's doing great." Lai heard a voice in the background say *Hey, Lai!* "Patience says 'Hi'! Her counseling practice is going well, but with my new job she'll have to get established in Louisiana. But, most of her clients are remote, anyway."

"I thought you told me Patience thinks astroscience is 'borrrring'?"

"Oh, she does!" Katherine laughed. "She's not here for the conference. She loves hockey, and her Blues are playing the Wild tomorrow night in Saint Paul, so we're going to the game."

"I thought you *loathed* hockey," Lai kidded.

"I do!" Katherine laughed again. "But, you know what they say: 'happy wife, happy life'!" Lai laughed. She was glad to hear that her friend was doing so well, both professionally and in her personal life. She knew that Prometheus had taken a heavy toll on Katherine in both areas.

"But, enough about Patience and me! How's—" Katherine's voice suddenly stopped. Lai looked at her phone sitting on the side table and saw *Call Disconnected.* She was disappointed, but she was also *very* tired. She pushed the chair back to full recline and closed her eyes.

Must be the lousy 8G service up here. I'll call her back tomorrow, if she doesn't call first... and I gotta go into Blackduck... get some fresh fish, and veggies... Lai fell fast asleep.

With the blinds pulled and her eyes shut, Lai couldn't see the white- and orange-colored reflection on the far side of the lake. The source of the reflection was a glow on the southern horizon, which came from an immense fireball 200 miles away. The fireball had been caused by two 10-megaton thermonuclear warheads that detonated 3.4 miles above Minneapolis and Saint Paul. The blast killed over one million people instantly, destroyed every structure within a 10-mile radius, and created a firestorm that raged almost 20 miles in every direction as it boiled high into the stratosphere.

Who could that be? Anong thought as he heard the knock on the front door, checked his phone, and saw it was 11:47 p.m. He noticed there was still no cell phone service; it had gone out two hours earlier. Then an hour later, the electricity had failed, too. *Not surprising,* he thought. *I'm glad I charged my phone before I went to bed.*

"Can you see who that is?" Minwaadizi called from the kitchen, where she was busy packing food and other provisions into boxes and coolers. Anong had just finished packing some of his clothes.

"Sure, Mom." Anong went from his bedroom to the front door, unlocked it, and opened it. A short, black-haired woman stood on the front steps, illuminated by the headlights of a car that was parked a few feet from the house. *Looks like an old Prius,* he realized.

"Hello, Anong. I'm glad you're here! I'm sorry to bother you and your mother so late, but it's *really* important."

"Dr. Shen! What—what are you doing here? Please, come in!" Anong said, surprised to see Lai Shen at his doorstep. He and Minwaadizi had met Lai several years ago, when she'd come to their home while staying at her cabin one summer. Anong and Lai had talked for hours about how he'd discovered the wormhole named after him and his astrophysics studies at Harvard, and Lai had shared stories about her work at the Harvard Center for Astrophysics, where Anong was working now, and Lawrence Livermore.

"Thanks, but I can't come in. I can only stay for a few minutes."

"Mom, it's Dr. Shen!" Anong called toward the kitchen. The living room and kitchen were softly illuminated by candlelight.

Minwaadizi hurried from the kitchen to the front door. "Dr. Shen! It's good to see you again! But, why have you come tonight, at this late hour?"

Lai looked at Anong and Minwaadizi with what was perhaps the saddest face they'd ever seen. "Have you heard?"

"You mean, the war," Anong replied quietly. "Yes, we know. My uncle told us a couple of hours ago." Anong had flown back home earlier that day from Boston to visit his mother, his uncle, and his friends on the Red Lake Nation reservation. He'd been dead tired from his trip home, and he and Minwaadizi had gone to bed early—only to be awakened by shouts and pounding on their front door. His uncle Bizaan had been able to pick up a few reports about the war on his phone before local cellular services shut down. Anong shook his head; deep sorrow shrouded his face. "World War III... I never thought..."

"I can't believe it, either," Lai said sorrowfully. *And we were making such progress... now it's all gone.*

"Do you need anything, dear? Food, or shelter?" Minwaadizi asked Lai.

"No, thank you, Ms. Wagamese... Minwaadizi. That's not why I've come. The reason I'm here is, I'm going to seek out a safer place, where the aftereffects of the war should be minimal." *South America, maybe... or even Australia, or New Zealand...* "I have room in my car for two or three more people. I was only 30 miles away, at my cabin, and I thought of both of you first."

Minwaadizi reached out to take Lai's hands in hers. "That was so kind of you to think of us. But, I think we'll be fine here." She glanced toward the kitchen. "We're packing up food and other necessities. We're going to join my brother and everyone else at the high school."

"There's a large fallout shelter there, with a generator," Anong explained. "It's been used for storage for many years. I never thought we'd need it for..." he trailed off.

"That's good," Lai said. "That will be okay for the short term, but... are you familiar with the concept of nuclear winter?"

"Yes," Anong replied first. Then he realized *why* Lai had asked them about it. "Oh... of course." He turned to his mother, "Mom, we can't stay here for very long."

Minwaadizi looked quizzically at her son. "Why is that, Anong? What is this *nuclear winter*? I've heard of it, but I don't know much about it."

Anong explained briefly to his mother what nuclear winter was, and how it could endanger the lives of everyone on the reservation within a short time.

"I see," Minwaadizi said as she absorbed what her son had told her. Then she looked at Lai and thought, *She shouldn't be out there alone tonight.* "The Tribal Council will be at the high school. Could you please come there with us and help us ensure they know about the nuclear winter and how it could affect the tribe?"

Lai thought for a few seconds. "Yes... I'll be glad to do that."

"Thank you, Dr. Shen... Lai," Minwaadizi said. "We'll see what the Tribal Council says. But please, stay with us at the high school for the night at least. Then we will think, and pray, about which path to take."

"All right," Lai smiled slightly, and nodded. "Tonight, at least. Thank you, Minwaadizi. Are you leaving soon?"

"We just need to load the car," Anong replied. "If you'd like to go there ahead of us, take Highway 1 west for about one mile and turn right on High School Drive. Just say you're with us." As he spoke, the three of them heard some calm voices from down the street; a neighbor was loading boxes into their pickup truck. Otherwise, the mild November night was quiet and still... an island of peace in a world devastated by nuclear war.

"Thanks, Anong, I'll do that. I'll see you both soon," Lai said as she started back to her car.

"*Giga-waabamin naagaj,*" Minwaadizi called out to Lai. "We'll see you later, dear." Then after Lai had closed the car door, she added, "*Aangwaamaadaadizin.*"

"Why did you wish her a careful journey, Mom? She's only driving a mile."

Minwaadizi looked at Lai's car as it backed up, and then she peered out into the darkness beyond the glow of the candles in the living room. "Lai... all of us... have a much longer and more difficult journey ahead, Son."

| 30 |

October 19, 2054

"Kapono," Aileen's voice announced from the speaker of *Chronos 3*'s primary guidance computer, "you should be able to see the black hole now, although it will be faint."

Kapono sat up in the command couch and peered out the forward windows. Ever since *Chronos 3* had launched at dawn that morning, he'd been waiting eagerly for this moment. He saw a small, pale-yellow dot straight ahead. *Lai was right—it isn't very big for a black hole.* He watched intently as it slowly grew larger. As the black hole that fronted the wormhole loomed closer in the forward windows, it began to look like the images from Hubble that Kapono had first seen five and a half years ago: a swirling white and yellow corona surrounding a dark center, with what resembled a ring across the center and a long jet of plasma gas shooting out from the corona. Kapono was awestruck by the sight. *It's magnificent! But it looks different from Gargantua,* he thought as he recalled the classic movie *Interstellar*, in which a wormhole was involved in an attempt to save humanity from a dying Earth.

"Aileen, ship's status and distance to the wormhole, please."

"All systems are nominal. Distance to the wormhole is, mark, 100,039 kilometers." Kapono switched his microphone to CapCom's channel.

"CapCom, this is *Chronos 3*. I'm just under 100,000 kilometers from the wormhole, and Aileen reports everything looks good. And, you were right, Lai—it's an amazing sight!" Kapono knew there could be no reply to his message for at least three hours due to the one billion miles between the wormhole and Earth, but Katherine had asked him to send regular status reports, nevertheless. He hoped that long before his teammates in Flight Control heard his latest message, he'd be on the other side of the wormhole, about 100 years in the future.

"Kapono, distance to the wormhole is 50,000 kilometers. ETA to the event horizon is 2 minutes 30 seconds. Please prepare for insertion; the G forces will be extreme. I'll reverse Quantum Drive at ETA 2 minutes."

"Thanks, Aileen." Kapono switched back to CapCom. "Just passed 50,000 kilometers to the wormhole—ETA 2 minutes 15 seconds. Aileen will be reversing the Quantum Drive shortly."

"Reversing Quantum Drive now," Aileen reported.

Kapono relayed the status to CapCom: "ETA 2 minutes, Quantum Dr—"

BANG!

Kapono jolted in his command couch from a loud, sharp noise that sounded like a gunshot. The master alarm sounded, and its red warning lights flashed every two seconds. Kapono checked the Alarm Status screen: CABIN INTEGRITY COMPROMISED. He glanced at the Cabin Pressure readout—it was sinking fast: 306 mm... 122 mm... then 0 mm. *"That's* not good!" Kapono exclaimed. Then he noticed a small, elongated hole ahead and to his right—it was near the center of the primary guidance computer. *That's not good, either!* He shut off the master alarm and checked the main command console to confirm that Quantum Drive had been reversed.

"Aileen, ship's status!" Silence. "Aileen, do you hear me?!" Still no response. Kapono looked quickly around the cockpit and got a sinking feeling in the pit of his stomach when he saw another hole, this one larger—*an exit hole?*—in the backup communications console that was behind him and to his left. He quickly realized what must have happened: a micrometeorite had struck the port side of the cockpit, behind him, then exited on the starboard side, in the front of the cockpit. He traced the path of the projectile in his mind and figured it had hit the backup guidance computer first, then the backup communications console, then had passed diagonally through the cabin—*within a few millimeters of my helmet*, he realized as he gulped—and had exited the ship through the primary guidance computer and, finally, the primary communications console. *What're the odds?! Must be at least a million to one.* He decided he'd have to buy some lottery tickets when he got back to Earth.

The black hole fronting the wormhole was looming larger and larger in the forward windows—and it was starting to slide out of view. *Time for Plan H!* Plan H was the solution he and Lai had devised for the problems he'd had during the Manual Override simulation two weeks earlier. He hoped it worked as well in practice as it had in the simulator.

He shut down the Quantum Drive, then pulled his hPhone out of a zippered pocket on the side of his G-suit and turned it on. He stared intently at the small screen, waiting for the phone to connect to the ship's wireless network. *If that's down...* Kapono decided to not finish that unpleasant thought. But his phone *did* connect, and he exhaled a huge sigh of relief. He activated the phone's Aileen app and secured the phone in a charging bracket on the side of the command couch.

"Aileen, please respond!"

"Howya, Kapono?"

Yessss! Kapono grinned, then he remembered something from when he'd helped program Aileen. "Reeling a little, but there's always room for improvement."

Aileen chuckled, "That's grand! How may I help you?"

"It appears both guidance computers are out, so I'll need to navigate manually. We're going to execute Plan H—H for HAL. Can you access radascan telemetry?"

"Aye. Radascan is nominal."

"Great!" *At least THAT wasn't taken out by the micrometeorite.*

"Under Plan H, I'll need to monitor radascan for the size of the wormhole, continually update the wormhole insertion calculation, and display the latest approach vector on the command console's main screen every three seconds. Correct?"

"That's right." Kapono knew that, based on his practice with Plan H in the simulator, he wouldn't be able to react quickly enough to more frequent updates. He hoped that adjusting the ship's course every three seconds would work as well in the real world as it had in the simulator.

"I've connected to radascan, and I'm ready to execute Plan H. Anything else?"

"Yes—please also give me updates on G force. Integer values are fine."

"Grand. Current G force is 1.38. Displaying updated approach vector, starting... *now.*"

Kapono fingered the x-y joystick and z thumbwheel with his gloved hands and shifted his gaze between the command console's main screen and the forward windows. Each time Aileen updated the approach vector, he made tiny course adjustments. Soon the entrance to the wormhole was centered in the forward windows.

"2 Gs," Aileen's voice reported calmly from Kapono's phone. "3 Gs... 4 Gs... 15,000 kilometers to event horizon... 5 Gs..."

Kapono strained to keep his hands on the controls as his cheeks flattened and the rest of his body was pushed harder and harder into the command couch. G force was the one thing in the Manual Override scenario that the simulator couldn't replicate. He knew that, soon, the increasing G force would make it impossible for him to reach the controls. Then, unconsciousness would likely follow.

"7 Gs... 8 Gs... 10 Gs—G force approaching danger level, Kapono!" At that moment, the master alarm started blaring. "Should I abort?"

"Not... on... your... *life!*" Kapono struggled to respond. He could barely reach the controls; it seemed to him as if each of his arms weighed 50 kilos or more.

"Acknowledged. 13 Gs... 16 Gs... 19 Gs—crossing event horizon!"

But Kapono couldn't hear Aileen's report that the ship had entered the wormhole—he had blacked out.

| 31 |

Date: Unknown

K apono's eyelids struggled to open. He felt dizzy, and he had a splitting headache. The master alarm was still blaring. He reached out to cancel it and felt a dull pain in his arm and his back; then he realized most of his body hurt. Yet, he felt tremendous gratitude and relief. *I'm alive! But... where am I? And WHEN?*

"Aileen, are you still with me?"

"Aye, Kapono," Aileen's cheery voice replied from Kapono's phone, still secured to the side of the command couch. "How's the form? I didn't hear you say anything for a few minutes."

"I've felt better, but I'm all right. I must have been unconscious. Can you check communications for me—is it operational?"

"Naw, both primary and backup communications are down."

"I'm not surprised," Kapono replied as he thought of the micrometeorite's path through the ship. "How about radascan—is it still working?"

"Aye, radascan is nominal."

"Good! Does it detect any moving objects?" *Like a ship, maybe?* He hoped that, just as in Lai's dream, Earth of the 22nd century would know exactly when he'd arrive in the future and send a rescue ship. He preferred to not dwell on the alternative—that Earth of the 22nd century wouldn't be in any position to mount a rescue mission.

"Radascan detects no moving objects within range."

What if you travel to the future and no one's home? He was about to ask Aileen for Quantum Drive status, but then he realized it didn't matter. He knew that his G-suit had about 9 hours of oxygen, and he'd already used some of it. The trip to Earth would take at least 8 hours at maximum speed, plus well over an hour for re-entry and landing—which would be extremely difficult if not impossible using only manual controls and no communications with Earth. But he tried to stay positive. *Maybe they're just running a little late. There might be lots of space traffic to navigate through in the 22nd century. I just need to chill for a little while...*

"Aileen, could you sing something for me?"

"Delira and excira to do so, Kapono. What kind of song would you like?"

"Oh, pretty much anything will do… just not *Daisy Bell*."

"Why not *Daisy Bell*?"

Kapono chuckled, "Never mind—that was just a little joke."

"I'm sorry, I didn't get—oh! I get it, now. That was gas!"

Kapono thought for a few seconds. "How about an Irish folk song?"

"Grand. Let me search my music catalog… I think I've found something appropriate; I hope you like it."

As Aileen started singing the old Irish folk song, Kapono was in awe of the AI's developers. *She has a great singing voice!* And there was something about the voice that was familiar; he finally figured out what it was. *She sounds a lot like Sinéad O'Connor!*

Aileen continued singing about two lovers who were seeing each other for the last time: a woman named Grace, and a man who was to be executed at dawn. Kapono couldn't help but think about his last night with Lai and their tearful farewell before he boarded *Chronos 3* early that morning.

I'm gonna start bawling in a minute! "Cancel."

Aileen stopped singing. "Didn't you like that song, Kapono?"

"Oh, no, it was fine, and you sang it well. But I think I need something more upbeat, and happy."

"Upbeat and happy," Aileen repeated. "Let me search my music catalog... I think I've found something appropriate. But I don't think I can do it justice. May I play the original recording for you?"

"Sure, go ahead."

"Here you are."

Kapono heard the buoyant song, which had a recurring theme of "happy days," through his headset. *This isn't familiar. But, it's what I asked for—upbeat and happy!* As he listened, he thought, *This would be fun to dance to!* Then he looked down at his feet. *If I weren't wearing these boots... and if there were a dance floor—and gravity!*

Suddenly the master alarm sounded; Aileen stopped the playback. Kapono canceled the alarm and checked the Alarm Status screen. It displayed: PROXIMITY ALERT.

"Aileen, does radascan show anything close to us?"

"Checking... there's a moving object, distance 908 kilometers, heading x-y 86, z 3, speed 10.2 kilometers per second. It's on a collision course."

Whoa! Kapono figured that the object was approaching from the starboard side at nearly a right angle to the ship. He nudged the x-y joystick forward slightly for five seconds, and the ship's thrusters pushed it ahead. "Aileen, is the object still on a collision course?"

"Checking... naw, Kapono. The object is no longer—correction: the object has changed course, its new heading is x-y 91, z 3. It's still on a collision course."

It's a ship! Kapono realized with excitement and joy. *They DID know I was coming! Let's get a look at it...* He nudged the x-y joystick forward for one second, then turned it slowly to the right to rotate the ship 89 degrees to starboard, so that the approaching ship would be visible in the right front window but *Chronos 3* wouldn't be in the direct path of the other ship. He peered out the window, straining to see the oncoming vessel. He saw a white dot that grew larger and larger; it was slowing down as it approached. Soon, it was close enough that Kapono could make out details. The sleek white cylindrical shape and markings were unmistakable... and familiar.

"*What the...?*" Kapono said with astonishment. He couldn't believe what he saw: the other ship was a Voyageur IV. And he realized that could mean only one thing—*I didn't make it to the future, after all.* He was overcome by a mix of emotions: immense disappointment that his mission had failed, but tremendous gratitude that Captain Otterman had arrived with *Chronos 4* in time to save his life. But that puzzled Kapono. To reach him so quickly, he figured that Otterman would have had to launch less than an hour after he did. *That Katherine! She proactively launched the rescue ship! And if she hadn't, I'd be dead in a few hours.*

Suddenly Kapono realized that Captain Otterman might be trying to contact him to prepare for docking—he may not be aware that *Chronos 3*'s comm systems were out. He grabbed his phone, opened its Morse code app, and pointed the phone's flash out the forward starboard window as he spoke a message: "No comm." The phone flashed the message in Morse code out the window. Kapono hoped that Otterman, a veteran Air Force and NASA pilot, would know Morse code. The answer to that question came shortly, as *Chronos 4*'s beacon lights started flashing a response. Kapono's phone translated it as: I WILL DOCK.

Kapono was glad he'd practiced the docking procedure several times in the simulator. He used the x-y joystick and z-axis thumbwheel to hold *Chronos 3* as stationary as he could. He also opened the hinged nose cone covering the forward docking port and activated the docking clamps. Otterman would have to take it from there. Kapono watched as *Chronos 4* lined up nose-to-nose with his ship, then inched forward until its docking probe slid into the matching receptacle on *Chronos 3* and engaged its docking clamps with a loud *THUD*. Kapono read DOCKING SUCCESSFUL from the Docking Status screen.

Kapono spoke another message into his phone's Morse code app: "No air." Otterman replied via *Chronos 4*'s beacon lights: COME ABOARD. Kapono opened the inner hatch to the docking port, floated into the narrow docking tunnel, closed the inner hatch on his ship, and opened the inner hatch on *Chronos 4*. Otterman grasped Kapono's arms, helped him into the ship, and then closed the inner hatch.

Except... the pilot of the rescue ship *wasn't* Kyle Otterman.

Kapono looked into the clear face mask of the man in front of him in a G-suit and saw, to his surprise, that he had black hair and chocolate-brown skin. The man was watching the Cabin Pressure readout, and when it displayed "750 mm" he gave Kapono a thumbs-up signal and removed his helmet.

"Hello, Dr. Ailana," the man said with a big smile. "I'm Captain Joseph April of the *U.E.S. Chronos 4*. It's my honor to welcome you to the 22nd century!"

Kapono was overwhelmed with joy and gratitude for reaching the future and being rescued by Captain... *April?* But he was also very confused. "Captain, don't get me wrong—I'm really glad to see you! But, how could you possibly be here—with *Chronos 4?*"

"I can understand why you'd be confused, Dr. Ailana. To net it out, I'm here because one of Earth's top quantum physicists figured out almost exactly when you'd arrive here. And based on what we knew about your flight, we thought you might need help getting back to Earth. So, here I am!"

"And *thank you* for being here, Captain! But... why are you flying a 100-year-old spaceship?"

"Well, she's actually not even 90 years old. Oh... today is the 26th of September, 2141. You've traveled 87 years into the future, Doctor. Congratulations on your achievement! But, to answer your question... spaceships are scarce right now. In fact, *Chronos 4* is the *only* ship capable of this type of mission. So we were really lucky that it survived the war. We found it a few years ago in an abandoned Infini-Trek warehouse in West Texas. It had been carefully preserved, as if it had been saved for some reason."

Kapono listened carefully to April's entire response, but his eyes opened wide from shock when he heard the captain say *war*. "Okay, thanks, Captain, but... *what war?*" Suddenly April looked uneasy to Kapono.

"Dr. Ailana, I don't mean to keep you in the dark, but my orders are to bring you back safely to Earth. There you'll get a full briefing by a senior official who will be able to answer all your questions. I was told to ask you to hold off on questions until then. I'm sorry."

Kapono wasn't happy at all about not knowing what had happened to Earth and what war had occurred since he left 87 years ago, but he figured, *I've waited 87 years—I guess I can wait a few more hours.*

April continued, "As you know, it's going to take us a while to get back to Earth, even with some enhancements we've made to the Quantum Drive. If you're tired, feel free to take a nap. I was able to get some sleep on the way here, and I can use the AI Pilot for most of the trip home."

Kapono smiled, "She really did a great job helping me get here in one piece."

April looked puzzled. "She?"

"Aileen—the AI pilot."

"Oh. I just call it the AI Pilot. I didn't know it had a name."

That's odd, Kapono thought. "She does. And did you know she has a beautiful singing voice?"

"Really? I didn't know that. I'll have to check that out on the way home."

"You should. Anyway, I *am* pretty tired—it's been a long day." *But a short 87 years!* "It's going to take about eight hours to get back to Earth, right?"

"More like 14...15 tops," April replied. "It's almost two billion miles back to Earth, you know."

Kapono raised his eyebrows in surprise. "*Two* billion?" Then it hit him... the wormhole in this time wasn't anywhere close to where the wormhole was in his time. He'd known that was a possibility but had hoped the wormhole was in Earth's neighborhood in the future. "I guess I *will* take a nap—maybe a long one!"

Kapono and Captain April buckled into their seats to begin the trip home. As April uncoupled the two ships and turned *Chronos 4* around toward Earth, Kapono took one more look at the black hole at the entrance to the Wagamese Wormhole. *Aloha, my friend—a hui hou. I'll see you again soon... I hope!*

| 32 |

27 September, 2141

Dr. Ailana?

Kapono woke up to a voice coming through his headset. He'd been awake for over 17 hours when *Chronos 4* arrived and had fallen asleep soon after Captain April had activated the Quantum Drive. He'd awakened after a few hours of blissful sleep, had listened with April to some songs courtesy of Aileen, then had dozed off again.

"Uh... yes, I'm here!" Kapono blinked a few times to clear the cobwebs in his head. *I wonder how long I was asleep?*

"We just passed the moon, and we'll be entering Earth orbit soon. I thought you might want to see this—it's really something."

Kapono sat up in the co-pilot's seat, and his back complained. *Not nearly as comfy as that ergonomic command couch.* Then he saw what April was talking about. The beautiful Earth, half in the shadow of night, half in daylight, nearly filled the forward windows. It was nighttime in Europe, the Middle East, Africa, South America, and the eastern half of North America. But as Kapono gazed at the blue, green, brown, and white sphere, he noticed something peculiar—and alarming: there were no large splotches of light from the major cities on the nighttime half of the globe. For London, Paris, Madrid, Amsterdam, Berlin, Istanbul, Moscow, Rome, Cairo, Tel Aviv, Tehran, Cape Town, Rio de Janeiro, Buenos Aires, Washington, New York, Boston, Toronto, Chicago, and many other cities, there were only flickers of light at most. Kapono felt a cold chill course through his body. *Is THAT what Captain April meant by "war"?* He wanted to ask, but April was busy talking with CapCom, preparing for Earth orbit. Plus, he'd been promised that all of his questions would be answered after they landed. So, he waited... and worried about what he'd find out.

They crossed the terminator—the boundary between night and day—over the southeastern tip of the Arabian Peninsula, traveling eastward. It appeared to Kapono that April wasn't busy at that moment, so he decided to attempt a question. "Captain, where are we headed?"

"Auckland." Noticing Kapono's surprised expression, he added, "It's the headquarters."

"Headquarters?"

"Oh, sorry. For United Earth." Suddenly Kapono understood what April had meant by "*U.E.S. Chronos 4.*" As for what *United Earth* meant... he decided to wait for his official briefing.

April guided the ship high above India, Southeast Asia, and New Guinea before heading out across the Pacific Ocean for the final approach to New Zealand. Kapono wondered why Aileen wasn't piloting the spacecraft; he knew she was fully capable of landing an undamaged ship. Then he had a thought that made him a little nervous. "Captain, I was wondering... you've done this before, right?"

April turned his head toward Kapono and smiled. "Sure, lots of times—in simulations. This is the only Voyageur IV on the planet. We didn't want to risk losing her in a test flight. Besides," he added confidently, "it's a piece of cake. But," he cautioned, "please make sure your seat back and tray table are in their full upright position. Make sure your seat belt is securely fastened and all carry-on luggage is stowed underneath the seat in front of you or in the overhead bins." He grinned, "I've always wanted to say that."

As it turned out, the landing *was* a piece of cake. As the ship sailed over New Zealand's North Island coastline and made a sweeping starboard turn over Auckland, Kapono noticed with relief that there weren't any signs of a war—just a beautiful, bustling city. The

Voyageur headed toward a flat peninsula connected to Auckland's airport. Then April tipped the ship so its nose was pointing straight up and fired its boosters and maneuvering thrusters. The sleek white ship descended slowly onto a large concrete pad. There was only a gentle *bump* as the landing struts settled onto the pad. A mobile gantry started creeping toward the spaceship.

"Nice work, Captain! Thanks for the lift."

"My pleasure, Doctor." April looked around the cabin. "The Prometheus Project chose a good ship."

"Yes, indeed," Kapono replied. But he was engrossed in other thoughts as he heard and felt the *thump* of the gantry latching onto the ship.

What's happened on Earth in the past 87 years? What was the war that April mentioned? Will I be able to return to the past through the wormhole? And will I be able to bring good news to Lai, my dad, Katherine, and all the people of Earth in 2054?

Kapono waited impatiently in the small conference room on the 17th floor of United Earth headquarters in central Auckland. Except for some unfamiliar vehicles he'd seen on the roadways while he was being driven from the *Chronos 4* landing site into Auckland, the city didn't seem much different from any large city from the mid-21st century. He made a mental note to ask to see a hospital; he wanted to see if it bore any resemblance to the hospital in Lai's dream.

The conference room wasn't much different from similar rooms from his time. He could see part of Auckland's skyline through the glass wall facing the hallway. The sleek, oblong conference table had what appeared to be a genuine wood top. The gray metal swivel chairs around the table were handsome pieces of modern art, but they weren't very comfortable. The soft green back wall was dominated by a huge flat screen—holographic, Kapono assumed. He wished, wistfully, that his hPhone worked there. *That would be quite the trick. But, who would I call?*

A tall, wiry man dressed in a black short-sleeved polo shirt and gray slacks opened the glass door to the conference room and walked briskly into the room. "Dr. Ailana, my apologies for making you wait. I had to attend to an urgent matter." Kapono stood up as the man approached him and extended his right hand. "I'm Witi Ngata, Council president of United Earth. Please call me Witi." Kapono recognized from Witi's name and physical features that he was of Māori ancestry; the Māori were the indigenous Polynesian people of New Zealand. He had wavy salt-and-pepper hair, brown eyes, and a short black beard tinged with gray. Kapono and Witi shook hands.

"I'm honored to meet you, Witi. Thank you for seeing me. And, please call me Kapono."

"Kapono, believe me when I tell you, the honor is mine. It's not every day one gets to meet a time traveler. Please sit, and let's talk. But first, is there anything you need?"

"I'm okay, thank you, Witi." Although Kapono had suffered bumps and bruises going through the wormhole, he felt much better after his rest and sleep during the trek back to Earth. He'd been served a delicious late lunch when he'd arrived at United Earth headquarters, and there was a water carafe and glasses on the table.

"I've been briefed on the Prometheus Project and on your mission, so I know why you're here. And I know you must have many questions. I will answer them to the best of my ability."

Kapono exhaled a huge sigh of relief. "Thank you, Witi! I do have many questions. But, my biggest question is… my rescuer, Captain April, mentioned a war. The spacecraft he used to rescue me survived that war. And that seemed extraordinary to him. Can you tell me about this war?"

Witi wore an incredibly sad expression. "It was World War III, Kapono," he said quietly.

Oh my God! "What happened, Witi? How did it happen? *WHEN* did it happen?"

Witi leaned forward on the table, his hands clasped in front of him. "The 14th of November, 2057. You know from living in that time there was great tension between the world's major powers, and some smaller nations. By late 2057, those tensions had risen to unprecedented levels. All it would take is one mistake, one miscalculation, to plunge the world into war."

"And that's what happened—a mistake?"

"Yes—*and* a miscalculation." Witi took a deep breath. "A new supreme leader had assumed power in North Korea earlier that year. November 14th was his birthday—the 13th in the United States. He wanted to do something special to celebrate." He paused. "The 'something special' was a demonstration of the country's steadily increasing long-range missile capabilities. North Korea launched four hypersonic ICBMs at once, on trajectories that would take them toward Los Angeles, NORAD headquarters in Colorado, New York City, and Washington."

Kapono gasped, "He must have been out of his mind!"

"Possibly. But, definitely irresponsible in the extreme. The ICBMs carried no warheads, and the plan was to destroy them over the Pacific before they got close to the United States. But there was trouble with the self-destruct mechanism, and the missiles got much closer to the United States than was intended."

"So, the United States reacted?"

"That's right. And that's where the miscalculation comes in. By the mid-2050s, the United States, China, Russia, and a few other nuclear powers had updated their missile defense systems to be AI-based. The objective was to greatly shorten the response time to threats of nuclear attack."

"Did that work in this case?"

"Yes. All too well, I'm afraid. When North Korea realized that they couldn't destroy their missiles in time, they tried to warn the United States through China."

"Why not directly?"

"By 2056, relations between North Korea and the United States had deteriorated to the point that there were no official communication channels between the two countries. But using China as a proxy took precious time. Also, the relationship between the United States and China had been strained by an incident where China almost sank a US aircraft carrier. Meanwhile, the United States' missile defense AI calculated with high probability that the missiles were a preemptive first strike. It recommended a retaliatory strike against North Korea. Given the circumstances, that was a logical analysis. But it performed the analysis and sent its recommendation to the president much more quickly than would have been possible before the AI enhancement. The president and Joint Chiefs decided to accept the recommendation and launched missiles at North Korea."

"They never got the warning from China?"

"They did, but it arrived too late. China's AI missile defense system detected the launches from the United States and determined that they could be targeting North Korea, or China, or both. It recommended a retaliatory strike against the United States and its allies in Asia-Pacific, especially Japan and South Korea." Witi paused. "Do you see where this is going?"

"I'm afraid I do," Kapono replied very quietly.

"Of course, the United States retaliated against China's attack. Meanwhile, China warned its ally Russia, which had already detected the launches from the United States. Russia had a mutual assistance pact with North Korea and China and feared a preemptive strike. Thus Russia launched its own preemptive strike against the United States and the other NATO nations. And of course, they retaliated against Russia."

At this point, Witi had the saddest, most solemn face Kapono had ever seen. "There's more, but... it was over in a few hours. There was almost no warning for civilians—emergency alert systems had been disabled by cyberattacks by the warring nations. Over 500 million people were killed that day. Ultimately, almost seven billion people died from injuries, radiation, and the aftermath of the nuclear winter." Kapono couldn't believe what he'd just heard—*seven billion!* he mouthed silently. "Yes. We estimate that five billion of those deaths were due to starvation during the nuclear winter, which persisted for almost 20 years after the war."

"How… how many survived?"

"Just under three billion. The Northern Hemisphere caught the worst of it. Except for a few pockets there—Iceland, and some remote parts of North America, Scandinavia, China, and Russia—there was near total devastation to cities and military installations. The Southern Hemisphere fared relatively better. Some of the major cities in Africa, South America, and Australia suffered bomb damage, and many millions of people on those continents died from radiation or the nuclear winter. As for the smaller island nations, including New Zealand… we were very fortunate."

Kapono feared to ask this question—but he had to ask. "How about Hawai'i?"

"Hawai'i was one of China's primary targets. I'm sorry, Kapono."

Kapono digested that news, and his sorrow turned to anger. "So… AI *did* end up nearly destroying the human race, just as many people feared would happen."

Witi shook his head. "Oh, no, not at all! No, the AI-based defense systems did *exactly* what they were designed, *by people*, to do. We have no one to blame but ourselves. We failed to realize that faster isn't always better. In this case, faster was disastrous. Without that, the war could likely have been avoided, as it had been before."

"What do you mean?"

"At least four times—in 1962, *twice* in 1983, and in 2027—World War III was averted because *one person* chose to not do what they were supposed to have done, given the circumstances. Each time, that person acted from his conscience, and his heart, rather than going by the book. That took courage. And, it required *time* to follow a different course than what seemed to be the obvious one. In 2057, the speed of AI eliminated those extra few crucial minutes. And," Witi added, "it all but removed conscience, and heart, from the equation."

Kapono considered everything he'd heard from Witi. "How is the world doing now?"

Witi's expression brightened a bit. "We're through the worst of it. Most large cities were decimated, and we have yet to start any significant rebuilding there. But in rural areas, in cities that weren't completely destroyed by bombing, and in much of the Southern Hemisphere, life for the survivors and their descendants has returned to almost as it was before the war... except for one thing, that is."

"What's that?"

"Since you're a physicist, you know Newton's Third Law of Motion, yes?"

"Of course: for every action there is an equal and opposite reaction." *What could Newton's Third Law possibly have to do with World War III?*

"And you're probably aware that law can be applied to *human* behavior?" Kapono nodded. "We believe that's what happened after the war. World War III was such an immense act of violence, on a global scale, that it caused an opposite reaction of equal magnitude by people all over the world."

"And the opposite reaction to violence and hate is..."

"Peace, and love," Witi finished Kapono's thought. "The survivors realized that the only way they'd make it was if they embraced love for one another, instead of the distrust and hatred that had caused World War III. It's similar to the behavior seen after a natural disaster, such as an earthquake or cyclone." *Or a fire*, Kapono thought. "After such disasters, there are no considerations of race, religion, nationality, politics... everyone just helps each other, is kind to each other, loves each other. Well, that's what happened after the war—except on a global level, and much longer lasting."

"That makes perfect sense, Witi." Kapono remembered how a Muslim family they didn't even know took him and his father into their home after the Maui fire of 2023 and let them live there at no charge for many months afterward, until their home was rebuilt.

"It's been such an incredible change. Kapono. Would you believe, there's almost no crime."

"In Auckland?"

"*Anywhere in the world.* Violent crime is almost unheard of. Also, there's almost no homelessness and hunger now, worldwide. If someone doesn't have a place to live or enough to eat, someone will take them in, or help them find shelter and food."

"That's amazing, Witi!"

"Yes. And there were a few other benefits—if you could call them that—from the war. The nuclear winter reversed most of the effects of climate change, albeit to the extreme. Earth's climate cooled, glaciers reformed, the Atlantic Meridional Overturning Circulation restarted, ocean levels receded." Witi looked sorrowfully at Kapono. "But the cost of those so-called benefits was far too great to bear." Kapono nodded in agreement, and the two men sat in silence for a few moments.

"Witi, could you tell me more about United Earth?"

"Oh, yes, of course. After the war, the survivors realized that they needed to work together to recover, and to prevent wars and other crises in the future. But they realized that the old United Nations wasn't always effective. So, they created a new organization, United Earth, through which nations could collaborate on matters affecting multiple countries. Auckland was chosen as the headquarters because New Zealand was relatively unscathed by the war."

Kapono was puzzled. "How is that different from the United Nations?"

"Good question," Witi replied. "There are a few differences. First, there's only one governing body, the Council, in which all nations participate as equals. There are no vetoes. When a decision is made by the Council, it's binding on all nations."

"Okay... so how are the Council's decisions *enforced?*"

Witi smiled. "Ah! United Earth has a militia and a small navy, even a few spacecraft, but we haven't had to use them except for humanitarian missions. The reason for that is, there's another major difference compared to the UN, and it's related to our earlier discussion. United Earth's charter includes in its preamble a Guiding Principle, to be applied whenever there's disagreement over what course of action the Council should take. The Guiding Principle is: *Love one another.*" Kapono's head jerked up to full attention.

"Did you say, *love one another?*"

Witi's smile broadened. "That's right. It originated from the LOA movement—that's Love One Another—that began shortly before the war."

I wonder... could it be...? "What was the LOA movement all about?"

"It was an attempt to embed the theme of love for others into the law. It had gained quite a following before the war. Hawai'i was adopting it, several other states were considering it, and several nations besides the United States showed strong interest. After the war, the LOA movement continued to grow, and it reinforced and greatly amplified the effect of Newton's Third Law. That movement was the impetus for making Love One Another the Guiding Principle of United Earth. Nearly every nation has adopted the same guiding principle. In fact," Witi continued, with sadness returning to his voice, "sociologists believe that, had the LOA movement started 30, or even 20 years earlier, there would have been no Third World War."

"How did the LOA movement start?"

"It began in late 2054, I believe, and initially was led by two people: former United States President Daniel Bennett..." Witi's smile broadened to a grin, "... and Dr. Lai Shen."

Kapono's face lit up with joy, blended with surprise. "I *know* Lai! Well, I knew her. That was a *dream* she'd had! I encouraged her to consider making it more than a dream, but I wasn't sure she'd actually *do* it. This is just so incredible—and wonderful!"

Witi hadn't lost his grin. If anything, it was getting bigger. "Yes, Kapono, I'm familiar with the story of how LOA began. It's become folklore, actually. And I know about Lai Shen. In fact, I had the great pleasure of working with her many years ago. She was a driving force behind the genesis of United Earth. Much of what the world is today, we owe in large part to her." He paused and looked through the room's glass wall toward the headquarters' plaza outside. "Did you notice the statue in the plaza when you entered this building?"

"No, I didn't. I was talking with the gentleman who drove me from the landing site. Why?"

"That's Lai's statue. She protested our erecting it—and used some rather colorful language in doing so. But, you know, she was like that."

"Oh yes, I know… I know," Kapono replied, tears welling in his eyes. "What happened to Lai? She's not…?"

"Lai lived a long, full life. She passed away about 30 years ago." Witi looked at his watch, and his smile returned. "But her daughter, Yinuo, is still alive." *Lai had a daughter!* Kapono was overjoyed to learn that Lai had had a child. Witi added as his smile widened, "*Your* daughter." Hearing that, Kapono was about to burst from joy. "And Yinuo has a son—your grandson—An. They live in Sydney but dashed here as soon as they heard you were on your way to Auckland. They should be here by now. Would you like to see them?"

Kapono nearly jumped out of his chair, "Oh yes, I would—very much!"

"Charlotte, have Dr. Shen-Martin and her son arrived yet?" Witi said into his watch.

"Yes, Mr. President. They're waiting in the Pacific conference room," Charlotte replied.

"Would you please show them to the Coral Sea conference room?"

"No worries, I'll do that straight away. Cheers."

Witi noticed that Kapono wore the type of silly smile that new fathers tend to have. "I take it you didn't know you have a daughter?"

"Uh, no, I didn't. I expected some surprises when I arrived here, but not *that*. And what a wonderful surprise! A daughter—and a grandson!"

Kapono saw three people round a corner in the hallway and head toward the conference room door: a 40-something woman with curly purple hair—Charlotte, Kapono supposed; a short, elderly woman, who must be Yinuo; and a middle-aged man—his grandson, An—who was carrying a pad. As soon as Yinuo and An saw Kapono through the glass wall of the conference room, they smiled excitedly and hurried past Charlotte and into the conference room.

"Makuakāne!" Yinuo cried, tears streaming down her face.

An, also in tears, said "Kupunakāne!"

Kapono, beaming and crying himself, opened his arms wide and embraced both of them, feeling honored by their use of the Hawaiian terms for *father* and *grandfather*. "It's so wonderful to meet you—the family I didn't know I had!" Kapono cried. "I am truly blessed." After more hugs and greetings, the three of them sat down at the conference table.

Kapono figured that Yinuo was 86; An appeared to be in his late forties or early fifties. Only Yinuo's gray hair and finely wrinkled skin betrayed her age. She had a youthful face for her age, with Kapono's brown eyes and broad nose, but otherwise she could pass for an older version of Lai. An had black hair with graying temples, his grandmother's green eyes, and a smile that reminded Kapono of his father's.

"I should let you talk and catch up," Witi said as he stood up from the table.

But Yinuo spoke up, "Witi, we'd be honored if you'd remain with us, if you have time. We may discuss some topics for which your perspective would be helpful." Kapono added his agreement, but he thought, *I wonder what topics she's thinking of?*

"All right, I'll be glad to stay until my next meeting," Witi replied as he sat back down at the table.

"Kupunakāne, your voyage to the future must have been incredible!" An said. "I'd love to hear all about it—every last detail. But, I think there's some things you'd like to discuss with my mum, right?"

"Yes, you're right, An. But I promise to share with you and your mother *everything* about how I came to the future." He looked at Witi, "Assuming the Prometheus Project is no longer classified Top Secret?"

Witi laughed, "Oh, no—share away! As I mentioned, it's the stuff of legend, now."

Kapono, Yinuo, and An talked for over 90 minutes about how Lai and Yinuo, then only a toddler, had survived the war through Lai's resolve, and some luck; how they'd eventually managed to get themselves and several others to relative safety in Sydney, and how Lai had used it as a base to continue her efforts on LOA, with Yinuo's help as she grew into her teens; how Lai had become United Earth's chief physicist while Yinuo followed in her mother's footsteps and received a PhD in quantum physics at the Australian National University in Canberra; how she'd met a wonderful young man there, Liam Martin, who became her husband and the father of their son, An; how An had married his childhood sweetheart, Linda, had become a civil engineer, and was helping rebuild cities ravaged by the war; and how Lai, Yinuo and An never lost hope that Kapono would one day appear at the other end of the wormhole. Yinuo explained how she and her mother had worked for years to determine when Kapono would arrive from the past, but the date and time couldn't be pinpointed by Yinuo until the wormhole appeared almost six years ago.

"Yinuo, is Liam here with you?" Kapono asked. Yinuo's expression told Kapono the answer before she replied.

"No. He suffered long-term effects of radiation poisoning from the war. He died 24 years ago."

Kapono reached across the table with both arms to clasp his daughter's and grandson's hands. "I'm so sorry. I wish I could have met him."

Yinuo smiled. "I wish you could have, too. He was a kind, generous man. He loved the ocean… he served in the United Earth Navy, and he loved going surfing at Crescent Head. I think you two would have really hit it off."

Kapono turned to An, "How is Linda? Is she here?"

An's face brightened, "Linda's doing great! She sends her regrets. She would love to have been with us today, but she's out of the country, with the Peace Corps."

"Peace Corps? It survived the war?"

"Not exactly," Witi explained. "The *idea* survived. United Earth borrowed the concept from the United States. Its Peace Corps, unfortunately, did not survive the war. But we thought it was a splendid way for the more fortunate in the post-war world to share their skills and knowledge with those in need of help—and to put our Guiding Principle of Love One Another into action."

"It's... that's so perfect," Kapono said as he turned back to An. "Where is Linda deployed?"

"She's in Northern California, helping rebuild communities in the Sacramento Valley," An replied, his face beaming with pride and love. "And before she went to California, she was in West Texas. It was Linda and one of her teammates who found *Chronos 4* in an abandoned warehouse there four years ago. She was so excited when she gave me the news."

"Really? I owe them a big *thank you*... and a huge debt of gratitude!" Kapono exclaimed. *How ironic that my grandson's wife would find the ship that saved my life... like some sort of weird, reverse Grandfather Paradox—but a happy one!*

"We're just beginning to recover in the areas decimated in the war," Witi elaborated. "It's a long, slow process. We believe it will take at least another 100 years to recover from the devastation of a single day."

Kapono nodded solemnly. Then he suddenly remembered *why* he'd come to the future. *But, will it work?* "Yinuo, you said you and your mother worked for years on the time travel calculations, is that right?"

"Yes, makuakāne. My mum taught me everything she knew about quantum mechanics in general, and the Wagamese Wormhole specifically. One thing I was glad to discover was that you'd be traveling only 87 years into the future, instead of nearly 100 as was originally thought." She smiled, "If we had to wait 100 years, I might not have been here to meet you!"

"I'm glad for that, too," Kapono said happily. "But, why the difference?" Before Yinuo could respond, the answer popped into his head. "The wormhole contraction! That affected the temporal variance also, didn't it?"

Yinuo nodded, "That's right. And it also complicated the work my mum and I did on confirming that it was possible to return to the past." Witi shot a glance at Yinuo. But Kapono didn't see the reaction from Witi—he'd zeroed in on what Yinuo had just said.

"So, it *IS* possible to return? You're *certain?*" Yinuo looked uncomfortable; she started to respond, but Witi interjected.

"It's *theoretically* possible, yes." Witi's expression became stern as he looked at Yinuo, then Kapono. "But neither you, nor anyone else, will be traveling back in time through the wormhole."

Kapono was mystified. "Witi, if it's possible to travel back to my time, I'll gladly take that risk! Don't you *understand* what that could mean for the world? I could warn Earth of 2054 about the war! They'd have time to correct the mistakes, and the miscalculations, that caused it. Most of the world wouldn't be destroyed in a nuclear holocaust. And, most of all, s*even billion lives* would be spared!"

Witi looked at Kapono, his expression a mixture of empathy and sadness. "Kapono, believe me when I tell you, I *do* understand." He paused, as if struggling to think of how to convey his thoughts. "But this isn't some science-fiction novel or movie, where the hero travels back in time, changes the past to prevent a tragic future, and everyone lives Happily Ever After. No... this is the *real* world, where the laws of physics apply."

Kapono understood what Witi was saying—he'd just forgotten about it for a few moments while he was caught up in his desire to save the world from World War III. "You're talking about the Novikov self-consistency principle, aren't you?" Kapono asked quietly. "The principle that the present can't be changed by making some change in the past, because if we try to do that, the universe will just rearrange events so the present remains the same."

"Yes, makuakāne," Yinuo said sadly. "But even if Novikov's principle doesn't apply—and my mum wasn't convinced it would—there's another possibility, which has potentially catastrophic consequences: if someone were to go back in time and make even a small change, it could cause a ripple effect of unintended changes."

"The Butterfly Effect," Kapono recalled, and Yinuo nodded. "But, unless quantum mechanics has evolved since my time, it was decided long ago that the Butterfly Effect doesn't apply to quantum mechanics, only to classical mechanics." Kapono remembered the lengthy discussions he'd had with Lai and the other Prometheus physicists about Novikov's seminal work and the Butterfly Effect. Lai had believed that Novikov's principle was flawed, and there had been consensus among the scientists that the Butterfly Effect wouldn't apply when returning from the future through the Wagamese Wormhole. Lai had been working on confirming that with certainty at the time of Kapono's mission to the wormhole.

"That's still true today," Yinuo confirmed. "The question is, does time travel through the wormhole follow the laws of quantum mechanics, or classical mechanics?"

Kapono thought for a few seconds. "Well, I've always believed that quantum mechanics would apply."

Witi leaned forward, and his eyes bored into Kapono's. "*Are you 100 percent certain of that?* Because if you *were* to go back in time and change the past, the future of the human race depends on it."

Kapono's lips compressed to a thin line, and he shook his head. "No. I can't say that with absolute certainty," he admitted.

"Exactly," Witi replied. "And thus my predecessor—President Patel—and the Council decided, unanimously, that there will be no traveling to the past in an attempt to prevent World War III, or for any other reason."

"All right, I understand your position... although I can't say I'm crazy about it. But, what if someone managed to take a ship through the wormhole without permission?" Kapono posed.

Witi raised his eyebrows. "Oh, it's not a matter of *permission*."

"What do you mean?"

Witi looked down at the table for a few seconds, then returned his gaze to Kapono. "Bringing you back safely to Earth wasn't Captain April's only responsibility. *Chronos 4* launched with a probe in its cargo bay. The probe carried a five-megaton thermonuclear warhead." Kapono's expression of curiosity became one of shock. "A few of those survived the war. We keep them around for planetary defense—asteroids getting too close to Earth, and so forth. Captain April deposited the probe near the black hole fronting the wormhole before he picked you up. The probe had thrusters for station-keeping. He waited until the ship was safely out of range, then he detonated the warhead. The wormhole is gone." *I must have been sleeping when he did that,* Kapono realized. "We had to act quickly," Witi continued. "We knew that the Prometheus team was preparing a rescue mission—they didn't know if you'd crossed the event horizon, or not."

"My mum told us that some of the blast did traverse the wormhole," Yinuo interjected. "We didn't want the rescue ship from your time to be anywhere close to it when the warhead exploded."

"And we wanted to prevent anyone else from going through the wormhole, in either direction," Witi continued. "We left it open only as long as necessary to rescue you." He paused, looked at Yinuo, and smiled. "Yinuo was quite insistent about that. She has, and Lai had, many friends on the Council. You could say, we owed them one."

Yinuo's expression was sympathetic—even apologetic. "I'm the chief physicist for United Earth, makuakāne. I advised President Patel and the Council that the wormhole should be destroyed after you arrived here. I'm sorry."

Kapono nodded, his expression one of resignation, and then he looked at Witi. "Thanks again for the rescue." He turned to Yinuo and An, "And thank *you* for your faith that I'd make it to the future."

Yinuo replied with a smile, "My mum was certain you'd find some way to get through the wormhole. I was, too."

"I was thinking, kupunakāne... the name of your project was quite fitting," An said.

"Do you mean because Prometheus could see the future?"

"Yes, that. But for a couple of other reasons, too. When Prometheus foretold humanity's future, he saw that they would live in misery and pain because his brother Epimetheus, who in Greek mythology created the animals, gave them all the gifts of the gods and left nothing for people. So Prometheus took it upon himself to help humans by giving them the gift of fire."

"I didn't know that. But it's been a long time since I studied Greek mythology," Kapono said. "What was the other thing you were thinking of?"

"Although Prometheus could see the future, those insights were known only to him. He couldn't share them with anyone else."

Kapono smiled slightly, "Ah! As it turned out, it really was an appropriate name, wasn't it?"

Witi's watch buzzed, and he checked it. "I'm sorry, but I must go to a meeting. Please excuse me." He stood up from the table and looked at Kapono. "If there's anything you need, please let me know."

"I don't suppose you know where I could find a five-dimensional tesseract?" Witi stared blankly at Kapono, but Yinuo smiled at the reference to the classic sci-fi movie her mother had saved on her holopad. "Never mind." *I don't know Morse code, anyway, and I doubt my phone's apps would work inside the tesseract.*

"I'd like to continue our conversation later, if that's all right with you?" Witi asked Kapono. "Also, members of the media are, quite understandably, very interested in talking with you. But, that can wait for a while—when you're feeling up to it."

"That'll be fine, Witi. Thanks again for everything." Witi said goodbye to Yinuo and An, then he opened the glass door of the conference room and walked down the hallway.

Kapono thought about what Yinuo and An had told him about Lai, and he realized they'd not mentioned if she'd had a partner during all those years. He hoped she did. "Yinuo, did your mother ever get married, or have someone special in her life?"

"No, she didn't. For quite a while after the war, she was focused on survival, and getting both of us and some other people to safety. Once we arrived in Sydney, she restarted the worldwide LOA movement and helped found United Earth while trying to give me as normal a childhood as was possible in the post-war world." She smiled at Kapono, "After that... she told me she never met anyone who quite measured up to *qīn'ài de*—'my love'... of course, that was you, makuakāne."

Yinuo's smile disappeared, and her face became shrouded in sorrow. "And then, she got sick." Kapono asked *What happened?* with his eyes. "After the war, many people who'd been exposed to radiation became ill—my Liam among them. My mum was diagnosed with pancreatic cancer when she was 78." Yinuo saw the look of shock and grief on Kapono's face. "Treatment of radiation sickness and its downstream effects such as cancer advanced greatly after the war, due to the hundreds of millions of cases that doctors had to treat. So my mum was able to live a fairly normal life with the cancer, until near the end." *There's no need for him to know what "fairly normal" really meant for my mum.* "I say that, so you'll be prepared."

Prepared? "How do you mean?" Kapono asked.

"Shortly before she died, my mum recorded a video for you. She was at the end of Stage IV then."

Kapono nodded solemnly, "I understand."

"Would you like to see the video now, kupunakāne?" An asked.

Kapono's eyes filled with tears. "Oh, yes... I would like that very much."

An handed the pad he'd brought to Kapono. "My mum and I can leave and give you privacy, if you'd like."

Kapono looked at both of them. "I'd appreciate it if you would stay with me. Have you seen the video before?"

Yinuo nodded, "An and I were with her when it was made at my home."

"Oh, that's good." Kapono placed the pad directly in front of himself on the conference table and saw an object called "For Kapono" on the screen. "Open 'For Kapono'," he said, and then after the video player appeared, "Play."

The date stamp on the video read "23 December, 2111." Lai was reclined in what looked like a hospital bed, in a sunny room with soft blue walls and a large window with bright-colored curtains. There was a tall container—oxygen, Kapono presumed—and a medical monitor to Lai's left.

Although Kapono had steeled himself for how Lai might appear, he was shocked, nevertheless. Much of the shock was due to the fact that when Kapono had last seen Lai less than two days earlier, from his perspective, she was a vibrant young woman in the prime of her life. But the woman on the video was 92 years old, with wispy white hair. She also looked very thin and frail—*probably due to both age and the cancer*. Her skin had a yellowish tone. But, Kapono noticed happily, Lai's green eyes were still bright.

"Kapono, my love," Lai began in a weak but clear voice. "You made it—as I always knew you would. And you're with our daughter or our grandson—or both of them, I hope. They've so looked forward to meeting you. Yinuo has been such a gift—a gift of your love... of our love. I'm so grateful for her, and for An." She paused and licked her lips. "There's so much I want to tell you, but... I get tired so quickly now. It really sucks getting old, Kapono. I don't think I could even *pick up* a damn bowling ball now." Kapono smiled at the memory from the bowling alley from a few days ago, it seemed to him—because it was.

Lai looked ahead, to the side of the camera—*probably at Yinuo and An*, Kapono thought. "Yinuo is a lot like you—a kind, loving heart, and smart as a whip. She likes to have a beer now and then, too." Kapono and Yinuo exchanged smiles. "An is a lot like his father, Liam. And I'm glad to say An actually *builds* things—he's not just a damn theorist, like us." An chuckled as Yinuo and Kapono grinned. "Liam is the best son-in-law anyone could ask for. And An's sweetheart, Linda—she's such a joy." She looked off camera again. "You need to get going and *propose* to her, An!"

An smiled and looked at Kapono. "I proposed a few days later, on New Year's Eve."

"I met your father, Kapono... and Akela," Lai continued. Kapono smiled as he thought about his father and the old lab. "Keone told me how much you loved me." Kapono noticed Lai's eyes were glistening. "I wish I hadn't waited so damn long to tell you how I feel about you. Honestly, I don't know how I kept my hands off you for as long as I did, with those brown eyes of yours." Kapono, Yinuo and An all smiled at that remark.

"Life is short. And... we never know what's going to happen." Lai paused again, as if catching her breath. *This must be hard for her,* Kapono thought with admiration, and love. A younger Yinuo approached from behind the camera and gave her mother some water from a cup and straw. "Thanks, sweetie," Lai said as Yinuo stepped back out of view.

"As you probably know by now, I got your message—that video you left for me. I thought a lot about what we talked about right before you left on your mission. And about something you said when I was in the hospital after my trip to the wormhole. My memory isn't what it used to be, but I think it was, 'Deep within, there is something profoundly known, not consciously, but subconsciously.' I knew, subconsciously, that the only way to save humanity was for people to love each other more. But consciously, I didn't think there was any way in hell that could work. You gave me the faith and hope to try. But I knew I needed lots of help. And you pointed me in the right direction—to Daniel Bennett.

"There wouldn't have been an LOA movement without Daniel. It was his idea to start in Hawai'i. And they went for it. They passed a referendum on adopting it, right before the war. I bet that makes you feel good." *It does,* Kapono thought. *But I'm not surprised the people of Hawai'i would be in the forefront on LOA.* "And Daniel was so kind and helpful—for LOA, but also to me personally. Like you, he had faith in me. That helped me keep going after... after he was killed while saving my life."

Kapono started. "Pause!" He turned toward Yinuo, in shock.

"During a rally in Honolulu, a man tried to shoot my mum. President Bennett stepped in front of the bullets," Yinuo said sorrowfully. "He saved both of us—she was three months pregnant at the time."

And he probably saved my life, too! Kapono thought. *Who knows what the world would be like now if he hadn't made that ultimate act of love?* After a few seconds, Kapono said, "Resume."

"But none of this would've happened without your faith, and love. Those meant everything to me. It was your faith that gave me the courage to seek out Daniel to help with LOA. And it was your love that kept me going through the, uh, tough times after the war." Kapono shook his head. *I can't imagine what that must have been like for Lai and Yinuo—and all the survivors.*

"There's... uh... something you said once... something that Jesus said, about how loving one another is the greatest commandment," Lai said, her voice quieter, as if she were growing tired. "I looked that up, and... that's not *all* that He said. Jesus said, and I might not get this completely right, 'Love the Lord your God with all your heart and with all your soul and with all your mind'... *that* is the greatest commandment. And the second is, 'Love your neighbor as yourself'." She closed her eyes for a few seconds, then opened them again. "I met many non-believers in my travels who loved their neighbors as themselves. And I met many people of faith... at least, who *said* they were people of faith. I noticed that many of those people weren't hella good at loving their neighbors. I think maybe that's because they didn't follow that greatest commandment... they didn't love God... they loved something or someone else more. Or maybe that something or someone had *become* their god." She stopped again and took a few breaths. "But I met many people who really did seem to love God with their whole heart, and their whole soul, and their whole mind... and they always loved each another, too."

Lai paused for a few seconds and lowered her head, and Yinuo said from off camera, "Are you okay, Mum?"

Lai's head popped up, her face set in determination as she snapped, "I'm fine! I'm talking to your father, now!"

Kapono grinned, *That's the Lai I know!* He noticed Yinuo and An were chuckling.

"But, back to the LOA movement... sorry, I'm kind of wandering here. About your idea of putting love for others into the law... I'm sorry, my love, but Daniel was right—you can't legislate love. Oh, I know Hawai'i was going down that path, and maybe they would've been able to pull it off, given the chance. They needed more time... we all needed more time. But what I learned from Daniel, and Klement—do you remember him, from the bowling alley?—and all the people I met, all over the world, while working on the LOA movement, was something Katherine told me once: *'It's what's inside that counts.'* If each person would strive to have empathy for others and try to love them as they are, there'd be no need for love to be embedded in law. People would be guided by the love in their hearts. And, people *do* have the ability within themselves to love one another. We know that because of what happened after the war... love for others became commonplace, like—like *breathing*. It's just... it's so sad that it took a world war and seven billion people dying for that to happen."

"Pause," Kapono said. "Yinuo, did your mother ever say what happened to Katherine—Katherine Etter? We both worked with her."

Yinuo's face grew somber as she recalled a vague memory of the kind, red-haired woman she'd briefly known as Auntie Katie. "Yes. I'm sorry to say, she didn't survive the war. But my mum told me that Katherine got married, and she seemed happy and at peace the last time they talked."

Kapono smiled, "I'm glad to hear she found that happiness and peace. Resume."

"But it doesn't hurt to be reminded to love others, once in a while. That was behind my idea of making Love One Another the Guiding Principle for United Earth. And it seems to help, whenever the Council gets into what the Aussies call a 'sticky wicket.' I think Daniel, and some of my other good friends like Kaleo Peleke, Jim Kassenbaum, and Francis, would've approved." *I know Peleke is—was—the governor of Hawai'i,* Kapono recalled, *and I think Kassenbaum was a US senator at one time. And Francis... Pope Francis II? Lai really did get around!*

"I know you want so much to return to the past and prevent that awful war. But I have to tell you, my love, from the research that Yinuo and I've done over the last 30 years or so, we think it would be a terrible idea. There's just too much uncertainty about what your returning to the past could do to Earth's future. There's no way to know if it would prevent World War III from happening in 2057. And if it did, the alternate future could be worse—maybe *far* worse... maybe more like what that RAND study, and the others, predicted. By the time you hear this, I expect the president and the Council will have decided what to do about it. And, if it's not the answer you hoped for, please try to understand and respect their decision. I know it'll be a difficult one.

"But if you do return to the past, be sure to tell me, and everyone you can, about what I just said... about *every person* having the ability to set aside their anger, and hatred, and fear, and love one another. I learned how to do that—others can, too. It doesn't have to take a world war. Doing that, more than anything else, would have prevented World War III... and I hope, all wars."

Lai paused to take a few breaths; she was speaking more slowly with each passing minute, and her voice was growing weaker. "You asked me a long time ago... well, not long for you... if I believe there's something beyond the physical. And all I did was quote a line from *Hamlet*. I've had a while to think about it. And what I think... I hope that there is. Because I'd really like to see my parents again. And Daniel, and Katherine... and Hannah and Ben, and Kaleo, and all my other dear friends. And more than anything, I'd like to see you again, my love." Kapono had been trying to hold back his tears, but he lost that battle. "I'm still not certain about what God is, or means. But I guess I'm going to find out pretty damn soon. And if there is a God, and he—or she?—is a loving God, as most people say... I'm hoping for forgiveness, and that we'll be together again.

"The last time I saw my friend Kaleo, a few days before the war, he hugged me as I was leaving, and he said, 'Aloha.' But then he added, 'a hui hou.' I asked him what that meant, and he said, 'Until we meet again.'" Lai looked into the camera, her eyes glistening. "Aloha, Kapono, my love... a hui hou."

The video faded to black. Kapono wiped his face with his hands and noticed that Yinuo and An were fighting back tears also. "She passed away two days later," Yinuo said. "Liam, An, Linda and I were with her."

"I'm glad you were all there," Kapono said, and he turned to An. "Thank you for saving this for me. May I get a copy later?"

"Of course, kupunakāne," An replied. "A few videos of nanna's speeches and interviews from before the war survived. Also, there's quite a few photos and videos of her from after the war—family pictures, her addresses to the Council, and so forth. I'll make sure you get those, too."

Kapono smiled gratefully. "Thank you, An. I'd love to see those, and other family photos and videos." He gazed out through the glass wall of the conference room, toward the outdoors plaza. "But now... I want to take a walk down to the plaza—there's something there I'd like to see. Would you both come with me?" Yinuo and An smiled and nodded.

"We'd love to do that, kupunakāne." They got up from the table and headed for the door. "And when you're feeling up to it, we'd like to show you around Auckland, and then have you come visit us in Sydney—you can stay as long as you'd like," An said as they started walking down the hall, toward the elevators.

"I'd like that. Thank you—both of you." They reached the elevators, and An pushed the *Down* button. "I guess I'd better think about getting a job."

"I was hoping you might consider replacing me as chief physicist," Yinuo said as they stepped into the empty elevator and the doors closed. "I've been doing that job for over 35 years, and I'd like to retire soon. I'm not getting any younger!"

Kapono smiled as An said, "Ground floor," and the elevator started descending.

"I appreciate your asking, but... I don't know. My physics knowledge is a little dated."

Yinuo laughed, "Don't worry about that—physics hasn't changed all that much. And quantum physicists are in short supply. That field wasn't a priority after the war. I was lucky to get into the PhD program in Canberra. We could use your help on multiple programs, especially antimatter research." The elevator stopped, the doors slid open, and they stepped into the bright, soaring atrium for the main entrance.

Antimatter? That sounds interesting! "I'm happy to help, however I can," Kapono said. "Besides—I do need a job!"

As they walked toward the doors leading to the plaza, An saw Kapono pinch his arm. "Why did you do that, kupunakāne?"

Kapono stopped, looked at his grandson with love, and smiled. "I just wanted to be sure this isn't a dream."

So faith, hope, love remain, these three; but the greatest of these is love.

The Apostle Paul, *1 Corinthians 13:13*

REFERENCES

Prologue

1. (…Large Ultraviolet Optical Infrared Surveyor…) Wikipedia. "Large Ultraviolet Optical Infrared Surveyor." Accessed June 19, 2024, https://en.wikipedia.org/wiki/Large_Ultraviolet_Optical_Infrared_Surveyor.

2. (I have fought…) 2 Timothy 4:7 (New International Version).

3. (…Quantum Drive update) Orf, Darren. "The 'Impossible' Quantum Drive Supposedly Defies Newton's Laws of Motion." *Popular Mechanics*, November 16, 2023. https://www.popularmechanics.com/space/satellites/a45850635/quantum-drive-space-test/.

4. (They're running short of water…) City of Phoenix. "Drought Information." Accessed June 19, 2024, https://www.phoenix.gov/waterservices/resourcesconservation/drought-information.

5. (Boozhoo Manidō…) Turtle Lodge International Centre for Indigenous Education and Wellness. "Anishinaabemowin Prayer." Accessed June 17, 2024, https://www.turtlelodge.org/anishinaabemowin-prayer/.

Chapter 1

6. (By most measures, Proxima Centauri…) Wikipedia. "Proxima Centauri." Accessed June 19, 2024, https://en.wikipedia.org/wiki/Proxima_Centauri.

Chapter 3

7. (...Quantum Drive was supposed to...) Orf.

8. (...send someone through the wormhole) Leman, Jennifer. "Human-Safe Wormholes Could Exist in the Real World, Studies Find." *Popular Mechanics*, August 31, 2022. https://www.popularmechanics.com/space/deep-space/a35795047/traversable-wormholes-could-exist-in-real-world/.

Chapter 6

9. (How's the burger?) Bernabucci, Umberto. "Climate change: impact on livestock and how can we adapt." *Animal Frontiers* 9, no. 1 (January 2019): 3-5. https://doi.org/10.1093/af/vfy039.

Chapter 7

10. (Second star to the right...) Barrie, J.M. *Peter and Wendy*. New York: Charles Scribner's Sons, 1911.

Chapter 9

11. (All I ask...) Masefield, John. "Sea-Fever." In *The Collected Poems Of John Masefield*. London: William Heinemann, 1928.

Chapter 11

12. (...Randall-Sundrum II model wormholes...) Maldacena, Juan and Alexey Milekhin. "Humanly traversable wormholes."

Physical Review D 103, no. 6 (March 2021). https://journals.aps.org/prd/abstract/10.1103/PhysRevD.103.066007.

13. (…the human body could withstand…) Rawes, S. "What are maximum G forces humans can survive?" Aviation StackExchange, March 9, 2017-May 10, 2022. https://aviation.stackexchange.com/questions/36168/what-are-maximum-g-forces-humans-can-survive.

Chapter 13

14. (Deep within…) Hodge, T.F. *From Within I Rise: Spiritual Triumph over Death and Conscious Encounters With the Divine Presence*. Frederick: America Star Books, 2009.

Chapter 18

15. (…the long-predicted collapse…) Ditlevsen, Peter and Susanne Ditlevsen. "Warning of a forthcoming collapse of the Atlantic meridional overturning circulation." *Nature Communications* 14, no. 4254 (July 2023). https://www.nature.com/articles/s41467-023-39810-w.

16. (Have you heard of ho'oponopono?) Sword, Rosemary K.M. and Philip Zimbardo Ph.D. "Ho'oponopono: 'To Make Things Right'." *Psychology Today*, November 21, 2021. https://www.psychologytoday.com/us/blog/the-time-cure/202111/hooponopono-to-make-things-right.

17. (…there was a clinical psychologist…) Vitale, Joe and Ihaleakala Hew Len. *Zero Limits: The Secret Hawaiian System for Wealth, Health, Peace, and More*. Hoboken: Wiley, 2008.

18. (There are more things...) Shakespeare, William. "Hamlet (Folio 1, 1623)." In *Internet Shakespeare Editions*, edited by David Bevington, 863-864. Accessed June 19, 2024. https://internet-shakespeare.uvic.ca/doc/Ham_F1/page/7/index.html#about.

19. (Whoever loves others...) Romans 13:8 (New International Version).

20. (...Buddhists believe love is...) "Love According to Buddhism: Everything You Need to know." *East Asian Cultures*, February 17, 2021. https://east-asian-cultures.com/love-according-buddhism/.

21. (...God is so loving...) "Love for Allah." *The Ismaili Portugal*, April 26, 2022. https://the.ismaili/portugal/love-allah.

Chapter 20

22. (...she realized the video was...) Roddenberry, Gene and Robert Bloch, writers. *Star Trek*. Season 2, episode 14, "Wolf in the Fold." Directed by Joseph Pevney. Aired December 22, 1967, on NBC. *Paramount Global*, 1967, streaming.

23. (...lightning in the collied night) Shakespeare, William. "A Midsummer Night's Dream (Quarto 1, 1600)." In *Internet Shakespeare Editions*, edited by Suzanne Westfall, 155. Accessed June 19, 2024. https://internetshakespeare.uvic.ca/doc/MND_Q1/scene/1.1/index.html.

Chapter 21

24. (…all of God's children…) King, Martin Luther, Jr. "I Have a Dream." Speech, Washington, DC, August 28, 1963. American Rhetoric. http://www.americanrhetoric.com/speeches/mlkihaveadream.htm.

25. (Dr. King believed…) Lee, Alicia. "Martin Luther King Jr. explains the meaning of love in rare handwritten note." *CNN*, February 9, 2020. https://www.cnn.com/2020/02/09/us/martin-luther-king-jr-handwritten-note-for-sale-trnd/index.html.

Chapter 22

26. (Since the huge reductions worldwide…) Bilen, Christine, Daniel El Chami, Valentina Mereu, Antonio Trabucco, Serena Marras, and Donatella Spano. "A Systematic Review on the Impacts of Climate Change on Coffee Agrosystems." *MDPI* 12, no. 1 (December 2022). https://www.mdpi.com/2223-7747/12/1/102.

27. (We'll fight the good fight…) 2 Timothy.

Chapter 23

28. (… I have promises to keep…) Frost, Robert. "Stopping by the Woods on a Snowy Evening." In *The Poetry of Robert Frost*, edited by Edward Connery Lathem. New York: Henry Holt and Company, Inc., 1969.

Chapter 26

29. (…when someone's been angry…) Taylor, Jeri, writer. *Star Trek: The Next Generation.* Season 4, episode 12, "The Wounded." Directed by Chip Chalmers. Aired January 28, 1991, in broadcast syndication. *Paramount Global*, 1991, streaming.

30. (…put on love…) Colossians 3:14 (New International Version).

31. (Love is patient) 1 Corinthians 13:4 (New International Version).

Chapter 28

32. (People must learn to hate…) Mandela, Nelson. *Long Walk to Freedom.* Boston: Little, Brown & Company, 1994.

33. (Love never fails) 1 Corinthians 13:8 (New International Version).

34. (O God, I could be…) Shakespeare, "Hamlet," 1300-1302. Accessed June 20, 2024. https://internetshakespeare.uvic.ca/doc/Ham_F1/scene/2.2/index.html.

Chapter 29

35. (The fireball had been caused…) Wikipedia. "Effects of Nuclear Explosions." Accessed December 22, 2023, https://en.wikipedia.org/wiki/Effects_of_nuclear_explosions.

Chapter 32

36. (…five billion of those deaths…) Savitsky, Zack. "Nuclear war would cause yearslong global famine." *Science*, August 15, 2022. https://www.science.org/content/article/nuclear-war-would-cause-yearslong-global-famine.

37. (… in 1962…) Walsh, Bryan. "60 years ago today, this man stopped the Cuban missile crisis from going nuclear." *Vox*, October 27, 2022. https://www.vox.com/future-perfect/2022/10/27/23426482/cuban-missile-crisis-basilica-arkhipov-nuclear-war.

38. (…twice in 1983…) Aksenov, Pavel. "Stanislav Petrov: The man who may have saved the world." *BBC News*, September 26, 2013. https://www.bbc.com/news/world-europe-24280831.

39. (…twice in 1983…) Morra, Brian J. "The Near Nuclear War of 1983." *Air & Space Forces Magazine*, December 2, 2022. https://www.airandspaceforces.com/article/the-near-nuclear-war-of-1983/.

40. (…the Novikov self-consistency principle…) Novikov, I. D. "Time machine and self-consistent evolution in problems with self-interaction." *Physical Review D* 45, no. 6 (March 1992). https://journals.aps.org/prd/abstract/10.1103/PhysRevD.45.1989.

41. (…the Butterfly Effect doesn't apply…) Tyler, Craig. "The Quantum Butterfly Effect." *Los Alamos National Laboratory*, August 1, 2021. https://discover.lanl.gov/publications/1663/2021-august/the-quantum-butterfly-effect/.

42. (… deep within…) Hodge.

43. (Love the Lord your God…) Matthew 22:37-39 (New International Version).

TIMELINE OF EVENTS

Spoiler Alert: There are spoilers for the book in the timeline below!

1969

June 28 - Daniel Bennett is born in Boston, Massachusetts

1970

July 26 - Arnaud Houde is born in Paris, France

1991

April 7 - José de la Cruz is born in Monterrey, Mexico

2003

September 10 - Arnaud Houde emigrates to the United States

2006

May 5 - Ben Abwao is born in Nakuru, Kenya

2008

February 18 - The de la Cruz family emigrates to the United States

March 30 - Katherine Rose Etter is born in Ankeny, Iowa

2017

August 21 - Ru and Jun emigrate from China to the United States

2018

March 12 - The Abwao family emigrates to the United States

August 25 - Kapono Ailana is born in Maui, Hawai'i

2019

April 25 - Lai Shen is born in San Jose, California

2023

August 8 - Kapono's mother dies in the Maui Fire

2028

March 8 - Hannah Ochrankyne is born in Gainesville, Florida

November 7 - Aida Pendamai & Daniel Bennett are elected president and vice president of the United States

2030

January 7 - Ben joins the Secret Service

2032

November 2 - Aida & Daniel are re-elected

2034

October 2 - Ben joins Daniel's Secret Service detail

2035

February 12 - Tyson space telescope enters Final Design and Fabrication phase

December 21 - Camp David Covenant is signed

2036

January 7 - Aida resigns as president; Daniel takes the Oath of Office

January 31 - Aida dies

February 13 - American Security Act (ASA) becomes law

February 14 - Toronto Climate Agreement is ratified by Congress

September 2 - Kapono starts at the University of California, Berkeley

2037

February 23 - FBI investigation of Ru and Jun begins

May 9 - Lai attends the senior prom with Tony

September 8 - Lai starts at Stanford University

2038

March 12 - Dr. Shen is dismissed from his professorship at Berkeley

2039

February 13 - ASA protest at Stanford

August 1 - Lai begins serving her sentence at FCI Dublin

September 29 - Lai is released from prison

October 8 - Lai drives along the Pacific Coast on California 1

October 31 - Lai is accepted into the physics program at the University of Minnesota

December 6 - Jared is sentenced to 18 years in prison (FCI Mendota)

2040

January 17 - Lai starts at the University of Minnesota

May 12 - Kapono graduates from Cal Berkeley

June 4 - Kapono starts PhD program at MIT

2041

August 30 - Kapono earns his PhD in quantum physics at MIT

2042

May 9 - Lai graduates from the University of Minnesota

August 18 - Katherine attends an astroscience conference in Austin, Texas

June 21 - Lai starts PhD program at Cambridge University

2043

August 28 - Lai earns her PhD in quantum physics at Cambridge

October 5 - Lai starts working at the Harvard Center for Astrophysics

2045

January 13 - Lai's parents are killed in an accident

2048

July 11 - Tyson space telescope is deployed, three years late

November 12 - Anong Wagamese discovers the wormhole to be named after him

2049

February 10 - Anong confirms the wormhole is stable and reports his discovery to NASA

February 11 - Hubble space telescope ceases operation

March 22 - RAND Corporation's Top Secret study *The Future of Humanity* is released

May 3 - The USA starts a Top Secret research project on the Wagamese Wormhole

October 14 - First successful test of Quantum Drive by NASA and DARPA

November 1 - Lai starts working on fusion research at Lawrence Livermore National Laboratory

2050

June 12 - Hannah earns her undergraduate degree at Stanford

November 15 - NASA sends a probe to the Wagamese Wormhole

2051

July 19 - Katherine is confirmed as director of the Prometheus Project

2052

June 16 - Hannah earns her master's degree in Public Policy at Stanford

July 15-24 - Hannah swims in the Olympics

August 1 - Hannah joins the Secret Service

August 5 - Kapono joins the Prometheus Project as chief scientist

October 22 - Lai meets Katherine and accepts job as chief scientist on Prometheus

October 30 - Lai's Top Secret clearance is approved

November 4 - Lai joins the Prometheus team

November 6 - Prep work for *Chronos 1* test begins

2053

December 9 - Prep work for *Chronos 1* test is completed

December 10 - *Chronos 1* test flight is unsuccessful

December 12 - José tells Katherine about the delay in replacing *Chronos 1*

December 15 - José reluctantly agrees to Lai's piloting *Chronos 2* without a backup ship

2054

March 6 - Lai's flight on *Chronos 2*

May 21 - Lai has a dream and tells Kapono about it

June 8 - Lai offers to go with Katherine to see the Prometheus Oversight Committee (POC)

June 17 - POC hearing in Washington

June 21 - Katherine asks for help getting replacement ships

October 5 - Lai and Kapono prep for his flight and go bowling

October 17 - Lai and Kapono talk over pizza in Lai's quarters

October 19 - Kapono's flight on *Chronos 3*, launched at dawn

October 21 - Lai finds a video Kapono made for her

October 29 - Lai meets Daniel at his home in Boston

November 3 - Kaleo Peleke is re-elected governor of Hawai'i

November 10 - First meeting with Governor Peleke, at Washington Place in Honolulu

November 11 - Lai meets Keone in Maui

November 23 - Second meeting in Honolulu, with Governor Peleke and other officials

December 2 - Daniel, Lai, and Ben visit the University of Kansas in Lawrence

December 4 - Lai meets with Tony and Jared in California

December 7 - Lai and Daniel attend Governor Peleke's inauguration in Honolulu

2055

January 20 - Lai speaks at a rally in Honolulu

July 15 - Yinuo is born in San Francisco, California

2057

May 19 - Katherine gets married in Kansas City; Lai and other Prometheus team members attend

November 6 - Hawai'i passes a referendum

November 13 - Lai visits her cabin in northern Minnesota

2059

October 27 - Lai et. al. arrive in Sydney, Australia

TIMELINE OF EVENTS

2065

October 24 - United Earth is founded

2088

November 10 - Yinuo marries Liam Martin in Sydney

2090

April 9 - Yinuo's and Liam's son An is born in Sydney

October 24 - A statue is erected outside United Earth headquarters

2111

December 23 - Lai records a video

December 25 - Lai dies

December 31 - An proposes to Linda

2112

October 19 - An marries Linda in Sydney

2117

September 8 - Liam Martin dies

2135

October 18 - Wagamese Wormhole appears in the future

2137

August 15 - Linda makes a discovery in West Texas

2141

September 26 - Kapono arrives in the future

September 27 - Kapono is briefed at United Earth headquarters

ACKNOWLEDGEMENTS

About two years ago, an idea for a science-fiction story popped into my head. That was remarkable for two reasons. First, I don't think of many ideas for stories. Second, I thought the idea was pretty good... and if it wasn't unique, I wasn't aware of any published story quite like it. I ran the idea by a few friends and family members. They said it sounded like a good story... although I did consider that they might be humoring me. Then I pushed my story idea off to a far corner of my brain and got back to the real world, which included a more-than-full-time job.

But the story kept resurfacing from synaptic limbo. And each time it did, I tweaked it. I added twists and turns—including a couple of big twists. I added characters and scenes. After a while, the story in my head had grown in size to the point that I thought it might be long enough for a novella, or perhaps even a novel. But I hadn't written any fiction—intentionally, anyway—since high school, and I had no clue how to go about writing a novel. (My wife and daughter are the writers in the family.) Plus I had no *time* to write a novel or novella, or even a short story.

Then in July 2023, I retired. *Hey*, I thought, *now I have time to write that novel!* But I still had no clue how to do it, or even start doing it. Fortunately, I was not alone in my desire to write fiction with no idea how to go about it. I found out that many books are available to guide aspiring fiction writers like me. At my local library, I selected three books that each had a different take on that subject: *Never Say You Can't Survive* by Charlie Jane Anders, *Just Write* by James Scott Bell, and the classic *Bird by Bird* by Anne

Lamott. The expert advice from those authors was invaluable to me. Without it, I never would have been sitting here at my laptop writing the *Acknowledgments* section for my first novel.

Armed with that advice, I started transcribing my story into pixels. I soon realized I needed to do a lot of research. For although my novel is (mostly) science fiction, much of it takes place only about 30 years from now. I wanted the world I was creating for my novel to seem familiar to readers, given its near-future setting. But I also wanted my book to be realistic in terms of what scientists believe the Earth could be like about 30 years from now. Here again, I was fortunate in that there's a vast number of articles and scholarly papers that predict what the world might be like in our near future. Those resources (see *References* in the back of the book) were indispensable for supporting my story's plot with hard science, or at least fact-based scientific opinion.

I chose to use excerpts from several literary works (see *References*) in my book. A couple of those quotes are just for fun, but most are important to the story. An example of the latter is the title, which is from Shakespeare's *A Midsummer Night's Dream*. Additionally, I borrowed from a famous speech (see *References*—but I recommend you wait until *after* you finish the book). Because I'm a big science-fiction fan, I thought it would be fun to pay homage in my book to some of my favorite sci-fi books, movies and TV shows. Most of those references are obvious, but some are more subtle. (I hope you're in the mood for an "Easter egg" hunt!) Not all of those sci-fi references are for fun; a few are crucial to the story. In fact, there's one sci-fi TV show episode that plays a starring role.

One of the bits of advice I read about writing fiction is to write about what you know. I tried to do that as much as possible. Many situations depicted in my book are based on my real-life experiences, or those of people I know. But if I had to depend on only what I know for my book, it would be a short—and most likely quite boring—novel. I also wanted my book to reflect the rich diversity of our world; it isn't populated only by WASCs (White Anglo-Saxon Christians) like me. Thus I incorporated many characters with cultures, practices, and faith traditions different from my own. I supplemented my own limited understanding of these cultures, practices and faith traditions with research. I strove to be as accurate and respectful as I could, using publicly available information. I apologize and ask forgiveness if I've unintentionally offended anyone from one of the cultures or faith traditions portrayed in my book.

 Another piece of advice I read about writing fiction is that shitty first drafts are okay. I am happy to report that I followed that advice! Perhaps "shitty" is too harsh. Let's just say my first draft needed a *lot* of work—not just many iterations of editing, but also significant changes and additions. Fortunately, I had help from several reviewers with a high tolerance for pain. Those with the highest tolerance reviewed multiple versions of the manuscript: my sisters, Linda Lockman and Martyne Backman; my daughter, Hannah Backman; and my friends and former business colleagues, Jeff Evans and Bob Lewis. Also, Barbara Kohl and Ed Ungemach provided valuable point-in-time input on my book.

 When I retired last year, my wonderful wife Joanna thought she was finally getting her husband back, full time. *Plot twist!* That didn't happen. Instead, she supported my efforts as a fledgling novelist, just as she'd supported me for nearly 40 years as I worked long hours and traveled during my IT career. For all the people who've told me they were surprised I was able to write a first novel so quickly (even though it didn't *seem* that fast, to me): the only way I was able to do that was because of Joanna's support and encouragement—including the lunches she brought to my desk when I thought I was "on a roll" and didn't want to stop to eat.

In *Never Say You Can't Survive*, Charlie Jane Anders wrote that you can tell when a story was written with love, versus when someone did their duty. I hope you'll be able to tell this book was written with love, as a labor of love. And I hope you're glad you devoted a few hours from your life to read it. Thank you for sharing those precious hours with me. I love you.

Dave Backman
Apple Valley, Minnesota USA
July 2024

David Backman was born and raised in Minneapolis and has lived most of his life in the Twin Cities. However, he is also officially (by order of the Governor of Texas) a naturalized Texas citizen, y'all. *The Lightning in the Collied Night* is his debut novel.

Dave retired in 2023 from a 44-year career in Information Technology that focused on enterprise software architecture, design, and development. He wrote a lot during his career, including co-authoring a couple of books, but he didn't write fiction . . . at least he didn't *intentionally* write fiction. In addition to writing, Dave enjoys volunteering and spending time with his wife Joanna and their three children. His main hobby is searching for a parallel universe in which the Minnesota Vikings have won a Super Bowl, or even been in a Super Bowl in the past 45 years.

Dave is a life-long sci-fi fan. He earned a bachelor's degree in mathematics (most of which he forgot a long time ago) and an MBA in Information Management. He holds certifications in several IT-related subjects including all the major cloud providers, which helps him keep his head in the clouds while writing.

https://thecolliednight.com